a Dear Daphne novel

Dating,
Dining,
and
Desperation

MELODY CARLSON

a Dear Daphne novel

Dating, Dining, and Desperation

B&H
PUBLISHING GROUP

Nashville, Tennessee

978-1-4336-7931-5

Published by B&H Publishing Group,
Nashville, Tennessee

Dewey Decimal Classification: F
Subject Heading: CHRISTIAN LIFE—FICTION \ DATING (SOCIAL
CUSTOMS)—FICTION \ FOSTER CHILDREN—FICTION

1 2 3 4 5 6 7 8 • 18 17 16 15 14

Chapter 1

Daphne Ballinger never imagined that life would turn out like this. As she sat on the front porch of the restored Victorian house, peacefully enjoying her coffee and morning sun, she felt pleasantly amazed. After so many years in New York, she'd nearly forgotten how lovely summertime in Appleton could be. And since it was nearly August, she wanted to make the most of this glorious season before it all frittered away.

But like the fly in the ointment, she was also reminded that she now had less than ten months to find Mr. Right, plan a wedding, and seal the deal . . . that is, if she wanted to continue living here in Aunt Dee's lovely old home. And she did!

Oh, she tried not to pay too much heed to the calendar, and she wanted to trust God to send her the perfect man, but as days slipped into weeks, a quiet niggling tickled the back of her brain. What if it didn't happen?

"Que sera, sera." She leaned back into the wicker rocker. "What will be *will be*." Then she took in a deep breath. No sense fretting over situations she had almost no control over. And no sense getting bummed about it either. Admittedly she'd been feeling a little blue the past few days. As a result she'd spent those days sequestered in Aunt Dee's office—rather *Daphne's* office, although that seemed more uncertain lately depending on the day or her mood.

Still she was getting a lot of writing done. She was caught up on the advice column and had even managed to draft several more chapters for her novel. Whether it was good or not still remained to be seen, but at least she'd been productive. And productivity seemed a good antidote to hopelessness.

Daphne sighed, remembering how hopeful she'd been several weeks ago. The future seemed exceedingly bright—almost as if the stars were aligning, as if God was about to shed his favor upon her. She truly believed that her aunt's attorney, Jake McPheeters, was genuinely interested in her. Hadn't he insinuated as much? And she knew without a doubt that she was interested in him. Although true to her nature, she had not said as much. But that was only because she wanted to take it slowly, wanted to savor each moment, wanted to be absolutely positively certain before she threw caution to the wind and jumped in with both feet.

And for the better part of July, it seemed like she was getting closer to the jumping-in place. Her confidence had been growing daily and she felt herself getting ready to become very vulnerable. She saw Jake almost daily. And every time they were together, conversation flowed freely, and they both seemed to be enjoying themselves immensely. It had been perfectly lovely!

Then just a week ago, everything seemed to change. Just like that glass of soda that's been left in the sun too long, it all seemed to fizzle and go flat. It started with a little disagreement over the column. Jake had wanted Daphne to start sending her pieces directly to the manager of the syndicate—just like Aunt Dee used to do. But Daphne put her foot down, telling him she wasn't ready for that yet.

"Sure, you're ready," he told her.

"But I like having another set of eyes on it."

"You already have plenty of eyes on it." Then he listed off the various editors who went over each column with care and expertise.

"But I don't *know* them personally," she said.

"Maybe . . . but they know you." He held up the local newspaper as if to make his point. "You see their work after they finish their editing and proofing. You don't have any complaints, do you?"

"No, of course not." She frowned. What she'd wanted to say was that having Jake read her work wasn't just about not trusting the editors. The truth was, it was simply reassuring. Plus it made her feel closer to him. It was intimate. And she wasn't ready to let go of it yet.

"Besides," he said lightly. "What will you do when I'm gone?"

"Gone?" A wave of panic rushed through her.

He had simply shrugged, then looked away. "On vacation for instance."

This had led to some more disagreeing. Nothing terribly toxic or concerning. But it was the first time they'd been at odds like this. Finally recognizing that she was not going to win this argument, she had reluctantly given in. Perhaps he was right. Maybe it was time for her to take the next step as a writer. Maybe she needed to grow up . . . stand on her own two feet.

But as soon as she'd agreed to send the columns directly to the syndicate, she felt a distinct sense of *snipping*. Just like a pair of sharp, invisible sheers had cut some vital thread that had been joining them together. Oh, she knew it was silly and she was probably just imagining things. But when most of a week passed without a word from Jake, she felt fairly certain that something was wrong between them.

It was only her pride that kept her from calling him and demanding "what gives?" However, when her teenaged cousin Mattie Stone stopped by to pick some zucchini on Thursday, Daphne was not above making a subtle inquiry. After all, Mattie was best friends with Jake's daughter, Jenna. She'd probably know what was up.

"They went on vacation," Mattie said as she cut the stem of a long dark green zucchini. "They left a couple days ago. They'll be gone two weeks."

"Oh . . ." Daphne nodded like this was no surprise to her. "Now that you mention it, Jake did say something about vacation. Kind of slipped my mind."

"Yeah. They have this awesome cabin on Lake Tamalik. With a dock and a ski boat and Jet Skis and canoes and everything. I've been up there a lot. I would've gone this time too, but marching band practice begins on Monday. I can't believe football season starts in just a few weeks."

"This summer is flying by."

"Tell me about it."

Daphne handed her another zucchini. "So what's your mom going to do with all these?"

"She makes zucchini bread."

Daphne looked at the nearly full grocery bag. "That's a lot of zucchini bread."

"She doesn't make it all at once. She grates and freezes the zucchini to use later on."

"Oh." Daphne stood up straight. "Good idea."

"I think this is enough," Mattie told her. "Especially since I'm on my bike. But at least I have a big basket."

"Well, be careful," Daphne warned as she walked Mattie around to the front yard. "I've noticed that a heavy load in my bike basket makes steering tricky."

"Yeah, I know." Mattie glanced at Daphne with a slightly concerned expression. "I hope you're not feeling too bad about Mr. McPheeters being gone and all that."

Daphne forced a smile. "No, of course not."

"'Cause according to Jenna, her dad was pretty surprised that her mom wanted to go too. It's not like he planned *that* or anything."

Daphne tried not to look shocked. "Mrs. McPheeters is at the lake too?"

Mattie nodded as she put the bag of zucchini into her metal bike basket. "Yeah, it's always been a big deal for their whole family. A bunch of Jenna's relatives have cabins up there too. It's like they have this big, old family reunion every summer. It's always the first two weeks of August. But Mrs. McPheeters doesn't usually go. Not since the divorce anyway."

Daphne's smile stiffened. "Guess you can't blame her. A family reunion like that sounds pretty fun."

"Yeah." Mattie frowned. "I wish I was there too."

Daphne just nodded. "Well, being in marching band sounds like fun."

"Marching in the hot sun?" Mattie shrugged as she swung her leg over the bike frame. "Anyway, thanks for the zucchini."

"Tell your mom hi." Feeling slightly blindsided, Daphne watched her young cousin riding down the tree-lined street, slowly disappearing into the leafy shadows. She hadn't wanted to admit it to anyone, but in that moment, she felt like crying. Jake was off taking a two-week vacation—*with his ex.* It felt as if someone jerked the ground right out from under her.

Today Daphne was tired of moping. She was determined to put her confusion and hurt behind her. During the weekend she had rationalized the whole thing into a tidy explainable package. She had convinced herself that Jake had only meant to offer her his professional advice as well as a platonic level of friendship—right from the beginning. She had simply misread his signals, making it into something he had never intended. And it wasn't the first time she'd been mistaken about a man. In all likelihood it would not be the last. Chock it up to hopefulness and just plain desperation. It was her mistake and she needed to own up to it. The next time she saw Jake, probably not until mid-August, she would act perfectly natural—she might be slightly cool, but she would be kind.

Today she just wanted to get on with her life. It was time to pick herself up, dust herself off, and get back onto that proverbial horse. And maybe, if she stayed motivated, she might already be dating someone else by the time Jake returned from his cozy reunion vacation. At least that was her goal. As she sat on her porch, looking out over the sunny neighborhood, she was determined not to be discouraged or disheartened by her flattened expectations over Jake.

The only problem with her recovery plan was that she still needed to explain it all to her good friend Olivia. And Olivia would probably pick it to pieces. She had been banking on Jake being the perfect guy for Daphne. And even though Olivia was keeping quiet about it, Daphne was certain she was already planning the wedding. Olivia would see right through Daphne's game face, and to make matters worse, she'd probably be all sympathetic. The last thing Daphne wanted right now was sympathy. That would be her undoing.

"Yoo-hoo! *Hello?*"

Daphne peered across the street to see a blonde woman waving eagerly from the other side. Wearing only a short pink kimono robe, she had a little dog in her arms and a frustrated expression on her face.

"Hello there, neighbor," the woman called out. Daphne stood and waved, hurrying down the porch steps to see what was going on.

"Hello," Daphne called as she crossed the street. As she got closer, she could see this petite, albeit scantily, clad woman was exceptionally pretty. But when she was a couple feet away, the brown ratlike dog in her arms began to bark wildly. Daphne had never been fond of Chihuahuas, but when this one started baring its teeth and fiercely growling, she was ready to hurry back across the street.

"Don't you mind little Tootsie here." The woman spoke with what sounded like a Southern accent. "His bark's way worse than his bite." She giggled. "Although I'll warn you he does bite occasionally. He's very protective of little ol' me."

Daphne cautiously folded her arms across her front, keeping a safe distance. "You must be the new neighbor. Didn't I see you moving into the Tremonts' house over the weekend?"

"That's right. I didn't arrive until late Saturday night. I followed the moving vans all the way up here from Atlanta—what a gruelingly long day." She paused to quiet the still-barking dog, then finally gave up. "I think it's taken a toll on poor Tootsie."

"Welcome to the neighborhood," Daphne said loudly to be heard over the nonstop yipping. "I'm Daphne Ballinger."

"And I'm Sabrina Fontaine. I feel just terrible to interrupt your quiet morning. It looked like you were enjoying yourself on your porch. But I find myself in need of a good neighbor at the moment."

Wanting to cover her ears to block the sharp barking, Daphne made an uncomfortable smile. "Well, you're surrounded by good neighbors, Sabrina. This is one of the sweetest neighborhoods on the planet."

"It's certainly pretty enough." Sabrina shook her finger in front of the dog's nose now. "*Tootsie Roll Fontaine!* You knock it off, *you hear?*" Now she clamped her hand around the dog's muzzle. To Daphne's relief, the obnoxious Chihuahua was silenced. "I was completely blown away when I got up on Sunday morning," Sabrina continued, "just to see how charming and pleasant it is here. All the big green trees and flowers and neatly mowed lawns."

"You moved here sight unseen?"

"I discovered this house on the Internet. The photos were marvelous. My mama told me I was a complete fool, but I loved the house and immediately made an offer."

"Really?" Daphne considered this. "That was brave."

"I suppose it seems brave, but the truth is, I just wanted a place to start all over and I'd already picked Appleton. But there wasn't a lot of real estate listed." Sabrina smiled. "Isn't Appleton just the sweetest name for a town?"

Daphne nodded. "I like it too. Now what can I do to be a good neighbor?"

"Well, I'm embarrassed to ask, but I just don't think I can stand myself for one more day if I don't."

"Ask what?"

"May I *please* take a shower at your house?"

Daphne tried not to look overly surprised. "You don't have water?"

"Oh, I've got water. The problem is *hot* water. I didn't realize when I bought the house that the hot water tank requires propane. Apparently I've run all out of propane. Or else the hot water heater is broken, but I hope not. The water turned ice cold on me Sunday evening right in the middle of a shower. I called the Realtor and she gave me the number of the propane company. Of course, they were closed. So I called them today, but they couldn't schedule me until tomorrow. Anyway, I've been trying to get by with using my teakettle to heat water. You know, like our ancestors used to do. But I am just sick to death of myself now. Living amid a maze of boxes and feeling like a slob." She ran her fingers through her mussed blonde hair. "And seriously, I'm sick of being housebound. But I refuse to go out in public looking like a hot mess."

"Of course, you can shower at my house."

"Oh, bless your precious heart," Sabrina said happily. "I'll run and get my things and be right over if you don't mind."

Daphne pointed at Tootsie. "You might want to leave him home. I—uh—I have a couple of cats."

Sabrina laughed. "Oh, don't you worry. Tootsie likes cats just fine."

Daphne started to respond in defense of her cats, but Sabrina had already turned around and was happily hurrying back toward her house. Daphne had difficulty believing that devilish dog would *like* anything—particularly a couple of docile elderly cats. But one thing she knew, Ethel and Lucy would *not* like Tootsie one bit. Suspecting her new neighbor might bring that obnoxious little dog with her,

Daphne hurried back across the street. She would make certain the kitties were safely cloistered in the spare room. Only when they were secured, did she place some fresh towels in the downstairs bathroom.

Chapter 2

When Sabrina arrived to borrow the bathroom a few minutes later, she was toting both a zebra-striped rolling bag and her brown little dog. "This is so kind of you," Sabrina said as Daphne showed her the full bath in what used to be Aunt Dee's bedroom suite. "I will be forever in your debt."

"No problem." Daphne watched as her new neighbor set her bag on Aunt Dee's bed and unzipped it. Daphne wanted to ask Sabrina how long she planned to stay but instead told her to make herself comfortable and left. Still, a suitcase to take a shower?

Daphne sat in the living room, thinking she'd wait for Sabrina to finish up and offer her a cup of coffee. But after thirty minutes passed with no sign of her neighbor, Daphne went to her office. She hadn't really planned to work today, but there was no harm in getting ahead with the column.

However, as she waited for her computer to warm up, she was tempted to write the letter that she'd been noodling on inside her head for the past few days. Not to use in the column, of course. That would be humiliating. But perhaps she could write it simply for thera-peutic purposes. And since her neighbor seemed bent on remaining in the bathroom all morning, Daphne decided to give it a shot. Just for fun.

Dear Daphne,

I was involved with a divorced man and truly felt he might be the one. Because I'd been wounded in a relationship before, I was being very careful this time. But just when I was about to reveal my true feelings, he pulled the rug out from under me by heading off for a two-week vacation with his ex-wife. Now I feel confused and hurt and somewhat lost. Was I a complete fool to fall for him in the first place?

Brokenhearted in Appleton

Dear Brokenhearted,

All relationships are risky. And relationships with previously married people sometimes carry even more risks. You say you were being very careful this time. Perhaps that was your inner voice warning you that this man really wasn't the right one. Is it possible you were wrong about him from the start? It seems obvious that if he's chosen to take a vacation with his ex-wife, he does not care for you as much as you care for him. I suggest you get on with your life. Start dating other men. And always remember to listen to your inner voice.

Daphne

Daphne sighed as she read the response one more time. Once again, it seemed that *Dear Daphne* had hit the nail on the head. Now Daphne was fully aware that she was actually *Dear Daphne,* but often when answering letters for the column, it could feel as if she were putting on a different persona. Almost as if she was trying to be inside Aunt Dee's head. She tried to see things how Aunt Dee might see them, answer questions with Aunt Dee's wisdom and wit and honesty. Daphne still had much to learn in doling out advice, but so far she hadn't received any complaints.

"*Hello?* Yoo-hoo, Daphne?"

"In here," she called out, glancing at the clock to see that it'd been more than ninety minutes since Sabrina and Tootsie took occupancy of Aunt Dee's master suite. What could she have been doing in there for that long?

"Oh, there you are." Sabrina entered the office with a smile. Dressed in a bright floral sun top, white capri pants, and heeled sandals, she had on full makeup and every blonde hair was in place.

"You look nice," Daphne told her as she hit Save and stood. "What happened to Tootsie?"

"I let him out in your lovely fenced backyard. I hope you don't mind. I'm sure he needed to go potty."

Daphne tried not to grimace at the thought of Tootsie leaving little brown "Tootsie Rolls" in her backyard. "How did Tootsie get his name anyway? From the candy?"

Sabrina grinned. "Not exactly. You see I wanted a girl dog, but my ex, well, he got me a boy dog instead. So I bought girl dog clothes." She giggled. "I would dress him up in this little pink tutu and all sorts of cute girlie getups. My friends started calling him Tootsie—you know like the movie? Anyway, since he was brown like a Tootsie Roll, I thought the name fit him better than Sherman. That was his name—Sherman, if you can imagine. But he's my little brown Tootsie Roll now."

Daphne picked up her empty coffee cup. "Would you like some coffee before you go home?"

"Oh, that would be just divine. I haven't been able to find the packing box with my espresso maker yet. I've been drinking nothing but oolong tea, and I'm just dying for some real coffee."

"I'll make us a fresh pot." Daphne led the way to the kitchen.

"Your home is just lovely," Sabrina gushed as they went through the living room. "Is there a Mr. Ballinger around?"

"No," Daphne said as they passed through the dining room. "I'm single."

"Well, your house is exquisite. I can tell someone has put a lot of effort into it. Very stylish."

Daphne explained about Olivia's help. "She's got a great eye for color and all that. I never could've done it without her."

"I'll have to get your friend's number." Sabrina sat on a kitchen chair. "Although I was curious about that master suite. It seems to be stuck in some kind of time warp. I mean, compared to the rest of the house."

As she measured coffee, Daphne explained about her aunt's recent death. "It was hard to change her room. And I'm perfectly comfortable upstairs."

"Oh, honey, I'm sorry for your loss."

"Well, Aunt Dee was rather old . . . and she had a very interesting life." Daphne waved a hand. "And I can't complain for her leaving this to me. I always loved this house growing up."

"You are a lucky girl, to have inherited such a big, beautiful home."

"Yes . . . but it's not quite as simple as all that." Daphne poured the water into the maker and turned it on. How much did she want to say?

"What do you mean?"

"It's just that there were some stipulations to my inheritance. If I don't keep my end of the deal, I'll lose the house next May."

"Oh my!" Sabrina's hand came over her mouth. "That is dreadful. Surely you're willing to do whatever it is your aunt specified—aren't you?" Her brow creased. "Unless it's something horrible. It's not, is it? I read a creepy novel about a man who left his son a fabulous inheritance, but only if the son murdered his mother. Very gruesome."

"No, no, it's nothing like that."

"What is it?" Sabrina asked.

"It's not something I'm at liberty to talk about."

"Oh." Sabrina frowned. "Well, now you've gone and made me real curious. I'll probably stay awake at night until I figure it all out."

Daphne chuckled and set the sugar and creamer on the table. "Sorry about that."

Sabrina continued to chatter, trying to guess what Aunt Dee had stipulated in her will as Daphne got out a package of lemon-drop cookies and placed them on a plate. Some of her ideas were so crazy that Daphne couldn't help but laugh.

By the time Daphne set the coffee on the table, Sabrina was getting too close for comfort. "I'll bet your aunt said you *have* to get married." She stirred cream and sugar into her cup. "I'm sure that's what my mama would do if she could exercise some control over me. She'd have me married off again in a heartbeat."

"So you're not currently married?" Daphne asked, hoping to change the focus of the conversation.

"Thank the good Lord, no." Sabrina took a slow sip of coffee and sighed. "I am divorced. Happily divorced."

"Oh." Daphne nodded as she slid the plate of cookies to Sabrina.

"Now, I'm not trying to sound as if I think divorce is a good thing. At least not under normal circumstances. But my ex-husband, Edward, was not normal."

Daphne reached for a cookie.

"Edward is wealthy—I will give him that—but he is also a mean, cheating, lowdown scoundrel. And fortunately the courts agreed with me." She nodded toward the window that faced the street. "That is why I could afford to cash out that house. And why I will most likely never need to work another day in my life."

"Is that why you chose Appleton—I mean for your fresh start?"

"Precisely. I wanted to be far away from Atlanta. That's where my ex lives. I did not want to chance running into him. To be honest, I don't completely trust the old polecat. He was so angry about my divorce settlement, I wouldn't be surprised if he hired someone to torch my house or murder me in my sleep."

"Really?" Daphne looked at Sabrina in alarm. "You think he'd do something like that?"

Sabrina smiled. "Well, probably not. But take it from me, the man was severely vexed. I prefer to keep some distance between us."

Daphne heard the shrill sounds of a dog barking outside and remembered Sabrina's Chihuahua. "Is that Tootsie?"

"Oh?" She tipped her head to one side. "That silly dog, he hears a noise or sees someone and he goes off like a fire alarm. Some people don't much care for him. My father, bless his heart, can't stand poor little Tootsie Roll. Threatened to step on him once, if you can believe that."

Daphne could believe it. "Maybe we should let him into the house before he disturbs the neighbors."

"You're probably right." Sabrina went to the back door and called him. She had to yell a few times, but eventually the little brown dog was trotting around the kitchen. Nervously smelling and exploring everything, it was as if he couldn't stop moving. He reminded Daphne of a windup toy. Too bad there wasn't a way to wind him down.

"But back to you," Sabrina said as she reached for a cookie. "Your aunt said you have to get married, didn't she, honey?"

Daphne looked down at her coffee and shrugged. She didn't like to lie, but she wasn't sure she wanted Sabrina to be in on this. Why had she said anything about Aunt Dee's will in the first place?

"I knew it!" Sabrina declared triumphantly.

Daphne looked up, locking gazes with her. "I've really been trying to keep this quiet. I would be extremely grateful if you didn't mention it to anyone."

"Well, I don't know a single soul in this town. Well, aside from Robin Wright, the Realtor, who helped me get the house. But even if I did know someone, your secret would be safe with me, Daphne. Remember I owe you for letting me use your lovely shower."

"I appreciate that a lot." Daphne sighed. "It's not easy dealing with it in the first place. A lot of pressure, if you can imagine."

"Have you ever been married?"

"No." She shook her head.

"Oh my. And you only have until May to tie the knot?" Sabrina's brow creased. "That won't be easy."

"Tell me about it."

Sabrina pointed at Daphne. "Is that how you usually dress?"

Daphne looked down at her oversized chambray shirt and baggy cargo shorts. "Well, I planned to work in the garden a bit today."

Sabrina shook her head with a slightly disgusted look. "You mean you'd actually go outside wearing those clothes—where people can see you?"

"It's not like a lot of people see me working in the garden," Daphne replied. "Well, except for The Garden Guy."

"Is that a kid?"

"No." Daphne smiled to think of Mick. Whenever he popped over unexpectedly, he usually brought some extra sunshine into her day. But what would he think if he found her dressed like this? Maybe Sabrina was on to something.

"Do you want to know what I believe, Daphne?"

"What?"

"Ever hear the old Dress for Success motto? That you should dress for the job you want, not the job you have?"

Daphne nodded. "But I'm a freelance writer and I'm not looking for a job."

Sabrina smiled. "That's nice, honey. I mean that you're a writer. But you missed my point. In the same way you dress for the job you want, you should dress for the husband you'd like to snag."

Daphne frowned. "Is that how you got Edward?"

Sabrina's nose wrinkled. "Unfortunately, yes. But I didn't know he was such a lowlife back then. All I saw was his good looks and his seemingly unlimited bank account." She held up her hands. "But my tactics worked. I landed the loser."

"Well, that's all very interesting. But I can't see myself dressing up to work in the yard."

"But you only have—" Sabrina stopped herself, counting on her fingers. "Less than ten months. And, believe me, Daphne, summer is the best time to put your best foot forward." She stuck out a sleek-looking tanned foot. Her sandals were feminine and pretty and her toenails were a peachy pink. "Now let's see yours."

Daphne stuck out her much larger foot, clad in a paint-speckled pair of Old Navy flip-flops. Her toenails, which needed trimming, were also dirty. Not a pretty picture. But that was from working in the garden.

"See? What kind of man is attracted to *that*?"

"I—uh—I don't usually wear open-toed shoes when my feet look like this," Daphne said.

"I can understand that." Sabrina laughed. "I'm sorry. I didn't mean to sound cruel. But I do have an idea. To express my gratitude to my good neighbor, I'm going to make an appointment at the spa my Realtor recommended."

"What spa?"

"You don't mean to tell me you don't know about Appleton's renowned spa?"

"I guess not."

"Before I agreed to purchase my house, I made sure that Appleton had my list of necessity businesses. A good spa was near the top of my list."

"Really?"

"That's right. I wanted a spa as well as a good health-food store and a coffee shop where they roast their own beans, a first-rate hair salon and . . . well, a lot of simple pleasures that make life nicer."

"Wow. I'm glad our little town measured up."

"So am I." Sabrina set down her empty cup. "And I'm going to book us some spa time."

"Well, I don't—"

"No, no. Don't refuse. I sense we're going to become fast friends, Daphne. Especially considering how you shared your secret with me. I want to do this. Please, I'm begging you, let me do this."

"Oh . . . okay."

"Good. You won't regret it. I promise." Sabrina stood. "And I have another good idea. Let's do lunch together too. I haven't had a chance to get groceries yet, and I'm sick and tired of canned soup." She patted her midsection. "Although I must admit I've probably taken off a pound or two."

"Sure, we could do lunch sometime."

"Let's do it today," Sabrina insisted. "Please, say you'll do lunch with me, Daphne. I'm so lonely I could scream bloody murder."

"Well, I—"

"You have to eat, don't you?" Her big blue eyes got sad. "Or maybe you don't want to go out with little ol' me. Is that the problem, honey? I know I can come on awfully strong sometimes. Edward used to say I talked way too much. But that's just how the good Lord made me. Since I was knee high to a grasshopper, I just say whatever comes into my head." She sighed. "And sometimes regret it later. Some people don't like being with a chatterbox. I suppose that's what you're thinking now too."

Daphne felt sorry for her. "Lunch sounds like fun. In fact, I told myself this morning that I need to get out more. I've been a hermit these past few days."

Sabrina's whole face lit up. "Then we need to get you out. And it's my treat, honey. I insist. What time do you want to go?" She glanced at her watch. "Is one thirty okay? Too soon? Too late?"

"No, that's perfect." Daphne made an awkward smile.

Sabrina called out to Tootsie, who came bounding around the corner and back into the kitchen. "Time to go home, pup." She scooped the dog up into her arms, holding him out to Daphne like a toy. "See, Tootsie likes you just fine now. No more growling or barking. He just needed to get to know you better."

"I guess you're right." Daphne walked them through the living room.

Collecting her zebra bag, which she'd parked by the front door, Sabrina grinned at Daphne. "Do you want me to drive us to town?"

"I thought it'd be nice to walk."

"*Walk?*" Sabrina looked down at her high-heeled sandals. "I don't know about that. I think I'd rather drive." She pointed to the driveway where, thanks to the lovely weather, Daphne had left her copper-colored Corvette parked. "And if you don't mind, I'd love to take a spin in *that*. What a little sweetheart of a convertible!"

Daphne agreed, but as she watched Sabrina trotting back across the street, she couldn't help but feel she'd just been run over by a train. Sure, it was a pretty little Southern train, but a train nonetheless.

Chapter 3

Although Daphne changed from her gardening clothes, she knew that her denim capri pants, white canvas sneakers, and blue gingham sleeveless blouse would look rather mundane next to her stylish little friend. But she felt comfortable. And what was wrong with that? Besides Appleton wasn't anything like Atlanta. Really, it was a fairly laid-back town—and Daphne appreciated that. Perhaps she could help Sabrina to see that life was different in the slow lane.

"Here I am, honey," Sabrina chirped as Daphne opened the door. "Are you ready?"

"Sure." Daphne nodded as she came out to the porch, looping her purse strap over a shoulder and jingling her car keys.

"That's what you're wearing?" Sabrina sounded disappointed.

Sabrina had changed into a pink-and-white striped sundress, which not only showed off some skin, but her figure as well. "Don't you look pretty," Daphne said uneasily.

"Yes, well, it's my first time to go to town. I wanted to put my best foot forward." She stuck out a dainty pink sandal. "Is it too much, do you think?"

The truth was, Daphne did feel it was too much but didn't want to hurt Sabrina's feelings. And even more than that, she didn't want to have to wait for Sabrina to change. "You look lovely. And your handbag matches too."

Sabrina giggled as she held up the boxy purse, showing Daphne that there was some kind of netting on one end. "This isn't a handbag, Daphne, it's Tootsie's doggy carrier."

"Oh?" Daphne blinked. "Tootsie is going to lunch with us?"

"I couldn't bear to leave him home. He'd get so lonely. This move has been terribly stressful for him. You know he's twelve years old? And even in little dog years, that's fairly elderly."

"Oh, really, I thought he was more of a puppy."

"Well, he is *my* wittle puppy," Sabrina said in a babyish voice. "Mama's wittle boy wants to go bye-bye too."

As she got into the car, Daphne tried not to look as unsettled as she felt. It wasn't that she didn't like Sabrina, but she'd never had a friend quite like this. And she wasn't quite sure how to handle it . . . or if she even wanted it.

"Your Vette is just fabulous," Sabrina gushed as Daphne drove the short distance to town. "Edward would be drooling with envy over it. He collects cars. But he only has one Vette. And it's a seventy-five, which in my opinion wasn't a great year. Too spacey looking. What year is this one?"

"It's a fifty-five." Daphne explained how her aunt had bought it new. "Straight off the assembly line. And since my aunt worked at home, it has really low miles. My aunt named her Bonnie."

"And Bonnie comes with the house?"

"That's right."

"So you don't get to keep her," Sabrina lowered her voice, "I mean if you don't get married in time?"

Daphne grimaced. "Pretty much."

"Oh no! We have to do everything we can to find you a man, Daphne. We just have to! Think about Bonnie."

She took in a slow breath. "So . . . where do you want to eat?"

"I haven't the slightest idea. I glanced at the restaurant list the Realtor gave me, but I couldn't believe how short it is. Atlanta must have a thousand eating establishments. Maybe even more."

"Well, you're not in Atlanta anymore."

"And I haven't had a chance to try any of the eateries here yet. What do you recommend?"

"A friend of mine owns Midge's Diner."

"A diner?" Sabrina sounded unimpressed.

"It's called that because it's always been called that. But it's actually a nice little restaurant. Ricardo, that's the owner, is a really good chef. And they have outdoor seating. I thought it'd be nice to sit outside to eat. And since you brought Tootsie, that might be the best plan anyway."

"All right then. Midge's Diner it is."

Before long, they were seated out in front of the restaurant. And after Sabrina soothed Tootsie, quieting his whining with a doggy biscuit, he seemed to settle in beneath the table.

"I didn't see Ricardo around." Daphne perused the menu. "But he's a nice guy. I'm sure you'll like him."

"Hello, Daphne," the waitress said in a slightly curt tone. "Can I get you gals something to drink?"

"This is Kellie." Daphne took a moment to introduce them and explain to Kellie that Sabrina had just moved into her neighborhood.

"You live in the same neighborhood as Ricardo's mom, right?" Kellie asked with a creased brow.

"Yes, she's just a couple houses down," Daphne said.

"I thought I'd heard that." Kellie turned to study Sabrina. "Welcome to Appleton. Now do you want something to drink or not?"

"I'll have sweet tea," Sabrina told her.

"Our iced tea is unsweetened," Kellie informed her. "But I'll bring some sugar."

Sabrina looked surprised. "Oh . . . all right."

"I'll have iced tea too," Daphne said.

After Kellie left, Sabrina frowned. "Is it just my imagination or does that waitress seem a bit rude?"

Daphne made a half smile. "Yeah, she's not terribly fond of me."

"Why's that?"

"Probably because I'm too friendly with Ricardo."

Sabrina's fine eyebrows arched. "Is Ricardo married?"

"No. And I think Kellie's keeping her eye on him."

"How about Ricardo? Is he keeping an eye on her?"

"Well, you saw the girl," Daphne said. "She's gorgeous."

"Gorgeous is only skin deep, Daphne. And sometimes I get a sense about people. And take it from me, that waitress is *not* a nice person. If this Ricardo is really your friend, you should be concerned if he's interested in someone like that."

Daphne shrugged. "I think Ricardo is mostly focused on making this restaurant a success. And Kellie is a dependable waitress."

"With an attitude."

Daphne couldn't disagree, but instead she pointed out what she felt were good choices on the menu. "Although I've never had a meal I didn't like here." She closed her menu.

Eventually they figured out what they wanted to eat and eventually Kellie returned to take their order. "Is she always this slow?" Sabrina asked after Kellie went back inside. "I mean it doesn't seem that busy here right now."

"I know." Daphne frowned. She'd been thinking the same thing. "I think she's giving us a message, like take your business elsewhere."

"Someone should tell Ricardo."

Daphne nodded. "I wonder where he is." Then as if by magic, she spotted Ricardo strolling down the sidewalk toward them. "Well, speak of the devil. Here comes Ricardo now."

Carrying a pair of shopping bags that seemed to be bulging with produce, Ricardo paused by their table. "Daphne," he said warmly. "I haven't seen much of you lately. I was about to ask my mom if you were on vacation or something."

"I've been here. Just holed up. Working on my novel."

"Ah, the writer's quiet life." His dark eyes twinkled as he held up his bags. "Been to the Apple Basket. Truman's been getting some great produce this summer. I may start getting all of it from him year round." He paused to peer down at Sabrina with curiosity.

"I'm sorry." Daphne quickly introduced them. "Sabrina just moved in across the street."

"Welcome to Appleton," Ricardo told her.

"Thank you. I've heard such wonderful things about your diner here," Sabrina said cheerfully. "I'm really looking forward to my gazpacho soup and spinach salad. Daphne recommended it." She glanced at her watch. "It is coming, isn't it?"

Ricardo got a concerned look. "Have you been waiting long?" He glanced from Sabrina to Daphne.

"It's been about twenty minutes," Daphne admitted uneasily.

"Twenty minutes?" He looked aggravated.

"Maybe it's busy," Daphne offered.

"On a Monday? At two?" He firmly shook his head. "Let me go see what's wrong."

After he was gone, Sabrina made a slight smirk. "It's not that I wanted to get that waitress in trouble, but Ricardo seems like such a nice guy. He should know if his workers are slacking."

Daphne nodded. "You're probably right. But this is a small town. And I'm not comfortable having Kellie know we ratted on her."

"We did not rat on anyone." Sabrina shook her head. "I simply made an innocent comment about the service. If I stepped on any toes, I'm sure I'll be forgiven. After all, I am new in town." She leaned down to check on Tootsie and rewarded his patience with another doggy bone, then sitting up, she smiled innocently. "You're writing a novel?"

"I'm trying."

"What kind of novel? Romance, by any chance?"

"Not really. Although there is a romantic thread. But really, it's suspense."

Sabrina's eyebrows arched. "Suspense . . . hmmm. Sounds interesting."

Ricardo emerged with a tray of food. "Here you go, ladies. My apologies for the delay. Seems there was a misunderstanding in the kitchen." He carefully arranged their soups and salads on the table. "Anything else I can get you?"

"This looks yummy," Sabrina said.

"Bon appétit!" He bowed.

"Um, this is really delicious," Sabrina proclaimed after a few bites. "And that Ricardo . . . well, he's rather delicious too, don't you think?"

"He is good looking. But more than that, he's a really good guy."

"And a really good cook too." Sabrina glanced into the restaurant. "A girl could do far worse."

Uneasy with the direction this was going, Daphne decided it was time to take control of the conversation—what better topic than what seemed nearest and dearest to Sabrina's heart? "You mentioned Tootsie was twelve years old. Have you had him for that long, or did you adopt him later in his life?"

That seemed to be the magic question because suddenly Sabrina was telling Daphne her whole life story. Or so it seemed. Starting with working for a legal firm, hoping to marry one of the younger partners, but instead Edward Fontaine III swept her away with his attention and his pocketbook. Never mind that he was old enough to be her father.

"I grew up watching *Sabrina* a lot."

"The teenage witch?"

Sabrina laughed. "No, silly. *Sabrina* the movie. At first I really liked the remake with Julia Ormond, probably because I was a teen when it released. But then I saw the original *Sabrina* and was totally swept away by Audrey Hepburn."

"Oh yes, I like that version better too." Daphne still felt confused.

"So I watched it a lot. You know, because of the name and all. And I suppose it was because of Linus's age difference. Remember Humphrey Bogart played him? Well, anyway, thanks to Linus I wasn't that concerned about Edward." She frowned. "Unfortunately, what I failed to realize was that Linus hadn't been married three times. And Linus wasn't selfish. And he wasn't a philanderer either. That would've been David, I suspect, if Sabrina had married him."

Daphne was still confused. "So you're saying Edward was nothing like Linus? Except for the age difference?"

"Exactamundo!"

Ricardo was coming out again. "Looks like you ladies enjoyed your meal."

"It was lovely, Ricardo." Daphne smiled. "Well worth the wait."

He looked uncertain as he cleared the table. "Just the same, it's on the house."

"Oh, Ricardo," Daphne said. "You can't always do that."

"I don't always do that. I'm only doing it now because I'm sorry you had to wait so long."

"But you don't—"

"No arguing, Daphne." He winked at Sabrina. "Besides, I want to set a good example for your friend. I'm hoping she'll want to be a regular here."

"You can count on that," Sabrina assured him.

"But, Ricardo—"

"Shh." He told Daphne. "If it makes you feel any better, I'll make you pay for your dessert." He grinned at Sabrina. "You are going to have dessert, aren't you? After such a light lunch, I think you should consider it."

"Absolutely." Sabrina nodded. "Daphne already told me about your apple pie ice cream. It sounds delightful."

"It is," Daphne said. "It tastes just like apple pie and ice cream . . . but there's no apple pie."

"I'll have mine with coffee," Sabrina ordered.

"Make that two," Daphne added.

Something funny happened as the two of them sat outside enjoying their ice cream and coffee—Daphne realized she was actually having fun. Despite their differences, she really liked Sabrina. And when people passing by stopped to say hello, Daphne took the time to introduce them to Sabrina. And Daphne didn't even feel uneasy calling Sabrina her *friend*. Especially since it seemed clear that everyone was happy to meet the Southern belle. And she caught a lot of second glances from the fellows too. But why wouldn't they be drawn to her? Not only was Sabrina adorable in her pink-and-white sundress, she was cheerful and attentive and sweet. What guy didn't like that sort of thing?

"I just remembered you asked me about Tootsie." Sabrina licked the last bit of ice cream from her spoon and set it neatly on the dish. "I've had him for twelve years. Ever since he was a puppy. I used to call him my payoff dog."

"Payoff?"

"Yes, from Edward. And it was surprising because Edward despises dogs."

Daphne frowned to remember her first impression of the ill-mannered Chihuahua. "If Edward despises dogs, it seems he might not be too fond of Tootsie."

"Edward hates Tootsie."

"I don't understand."

Sabrina nodded sadly. "Of course not. A normal person couldn't possibly understand. You see, Edward didn't want children. Well, to be fair he already had children. Grown children. He just didn't want any more. I was only twenty-three when we got married and I really wanted children. But Edward was adamantly opposed. So much so that he insisted I take permanent measures to ensure we didn't have any."

"He *made* you—"

"That's right." She nodded. "I suggested he get himself fixed instead, but he claimed he couldn't afford to miss work. And after all, he was the breadwinner and I was totally dependent on him. So I agreed. But after it was all said and done, I was so upset over what I'd done that I fell completely apart. I was a mess. That's when Edward got me Tootsie. My payoff." She smiled sadly. "That's probably why I spoil Tootsie, why I call him my wittle baby." She leaned down to check on her dog. "My mama still hasn't gotten over it. I mean, me not able to have children."

"Oh my." Daphne shook her head. "Edward doesn't sound like a very nice person."

"You wouldn't know that if you met him. His people skills are very polished. But believe me, he's not nice. Not to me anyway." She set her coffee cup down. "But I suppose I should be thankful for his meanness toward me . . . now."

"Why's that?"

"Because he had me sign a prenup."

Daphne felt confused again. How was a prenuptial agreement a good thing if you were married to a louse? "But didn't you get a good settlement?"

"I certainly did."

"What about the prenup?"

"Thanks to Edward's despicable nature as well as his less-than-sterling reputation, the judge was merciful with me. I owe thanks to my divorce lawyer too—now that's the guy I should've gone for, but he's happily married with four kids now. Anyway he fought for me and got me a fair settlement."

Daphne sighed. "Wow . . . you've been through a lot."

"But now it's time for a new beginning." She picked up her coffee cup, holding it like a toast. "Here's to *fresh starts*—for both of us."

"To fresh starts." As Daphne clicked her cup against Sabrina's, she couldn't help but think of Jake. She'd already begun a new fresh start. It was time to accept he was not going to be anything more than her friend and attorney. And it was high time she got used to being without him. Maybe the distraction of her new neighbor would help.

Chapter 4

With the garden coming on so well, Daphne found herself elbow deep in produce. And while she was eating better than ever with delightful salads and freshly steamed veggies, it was impossible to consume them all. As a result Mrs. Terwilliger insisted on teaching Daphne how to "can." On Tuesday morning, she showed up at Daphne's back door with a boxful of jars, a gigantic stainless-steel pot, and a big smile.

"Ready to go to work?" Mrs. Terwilliger asked.

"I guess so." Daphne took the load from the older woman.

"Good. I'll go back for another box of jars."

"Are you sure we need that many?"

Mrs. Terwilliger pointed to the rows of tomatoes and cucumbers lining all the flat surfaces of the laundry room area. "It looks like it to me."

Daphne nodded. "And more are ripening up in the garden right now."

Because of Mrs. Terwilliger's age, Daphne insisted she sit at the kitchen table to do the prep work. And from there she directed

Daphne through all the steamy steps of home canning tomatoes and pickles. They broke for lunch but continued the arduous process of peeling, packing, seasoning, boiling, and so on clear into late afternoon.

"This is a lot of work." Daphne put the last batch of pickles into the hot bath.

"But isn't it worthwhile when you look at all those lovely jars of preserves?" Mrs. Terwilliger pointed to the counter filling up with jars that were still cooling. The rest had been safely stowed in the pantry already.

"It is rather amazing. Aunt Dee never did anything like this."

"That's because she was busy writing those textbooks." Mrs. Terwilliger shook her head. "I was always so impressed with her mind . . . being able to write such academia."

Daphne chuckled to herself as she replaced the lid on the canner and set the timer for twenty minutes. What would Mrs. Terwilliger think to find out that Aunt Dee's "textbooks" were really Penelope Poindexter's romance novels? Not that Daphne had any intention of letting Aunt Dee's true identity out. Some secrets were best left secret.

"Thank you so much for your help," Daphne told Mrs. Terwilliger, "but I can tell you're tired."

"Nonsense, this has been fun."

"But it's time for the fun to end." Daphne picked up the box of canned goods she was giving to her neighbor in payment for her help. "I'm going to carry these for you and walk you home."

"But you haven't finished the last of those yet." Mrs. Terwilliger pointed at the tomatoes still in the laundry room.

"I know how to do it now," Daphne said as they went outside into the much-cooler air. "I'll finish them tonight." Although even as she said this, Daphne was tempted to finish them right into the compost pile.

"Oh, good for you. It's a sin to waste good produce."

Daphne nixed the compost idea as she waited for Mrs. Terwilliger to open her back door and let them into her pint-sized kitchen. Daphne thanked her again as she set the box on the table. "I never could have done all this without you."

"And just wait until the green beans and beets and all those other goodies start coming in good. We'll have even more canning to do." Mrs. Terwilliger smiled with flushed cheeks.

Daphne nodded uneasily, trying to think of an escape from spending the rest of August in a sweltering kitchen, packing glass jars with vegetables. "Yes, but I'm also considering sharing some of the produce with the others too. Do you think anyone would be interested?"

"Of course they would. I used to keep a big garden, back when I was young enough to tend it properly. If it produced more than I could use or can, I would set a wooden box in the front yard and neighbors would just take what they wanted from it."

"That's a great idea."

"It was much appreciated and a nice way to get folks together. I'll bet I still have that old apple crate out in the shed."

"Well, I think I'll give that a try." Feeling relieved to have an option that might nip this canning madness in the bud, Daphne thanked her again. "But I better get back home to remove the next batch of jars from the canner."

Back in the still-steamy kitchen, Daphne decided to be true to her word—she would persevere with the preserves by canning the remainder of the produce. It was like running a tomato marathon and she didn't finish until after ten o'clock. But at least she was done with it. And as far as she was concerned, she was done with canning too. At least for this summer.

As she was wearily brushing her teeth before bed, she couldn't believe what all that steamy heat had done to her naturally curly auburn hair. She looked like Little Orphan Annie's much older sister. But too tired to do anything about it, she tumbled into bed where all she could see in her mind's eye were tomatoes and cucumbers . . . cucumbers and tomatoes. She would probably be dreaming about them too!

In the morning, after sleeping in a bit, Daphne still felt like she was recovering from her day at the "cannery." But seeing as it was starting out to be another lovely day, she took her coffee outside and enjoyed the cool morning air in the beautiful garden. Besides all the vegetables that Mick the garden guy had planted, there was a big bed of cutting flowers as well. And near that was a small table and chairs Mick had set up in order to experience the garden in a leisurely way. She'd had many a morning cup of coffee out here.

Of course, as often happened after her coffee was gone, she would notice a new weed that had popped up or a plant that needed some attention, and soon she was down on her knees with her hands in the dirt.

"Yoo-hoo?" called a cheery voice that sounded an awful lot like her new neighbor.

"I'm back here," Daphne called out. "In the garden—go through the little green gate."

"What're ya'll doing?" Sabrina asked as she found Daphne getting back to her feet with a trowel in hand.

"A little weeding." Daphne pushed a curly strand of hair from her eyes, wiping her dirty hands on the front of her baggy khaki shorts.

"Oh, my goodness!" Sabrina's eyes lit up as she looked around. "What a beautiful garden. Did you plant all this yourself?"

"No way. But I try to help with the upkeep." Daphne dropped the trowel into a bucket. "Only I have to admit, it's getting a little overwhelming."

Sabrina pointed to Daphne's hands. "And just look what it's done to your nails."

Daphne looked at her short, dirt-filled fingernails.

"Which is exactly why I came over." Sabrina beamed at her. "I made you an appointment for both a pedicure and manicure. Today at two. Does that work?"

"Uh, sure . . . I guess so." Daphne frowned at her hands. "That is, if you really think they can do anything with these. Might be a lost cause."

"I'm sure they can improve them, but my mama would scold you for going into the garden without your gardening gloves. A lady doesn't do that."

"You're probably right, but this whole gardening thing is pretty new to me."

"Hello in the garden," called a masculine voice.

"That sounds like Mick," Daphne told Sabrina. "He's The Garden Guy."

"Good day, Daph." Mick smiled at her, then glanced curiously at Sabrina. "Thought I heard voices back here. What's up?"

She introduced him to Sabrina and couldn't help but notice the nod of appreciation he gave as he shook her hand. "Pleasure to meet you. And welcome to Appleton."

"Thank you," Sabrina said eagerly. "I was just admiring your fine handiwork, Mick. I don't think I've ever seen such a beautiful garden in my life. It's like a living work of art. Did you really do the whole thing yourself?"

"I set most of it up, but I send my workers 'round to help with it sometimes." He nodded to Daphne. "And Daph here tries to do her part."

"I was just confessing to Sabrina that it can get a bit overwhelming."

"That's because it's the first year and all the beds were in great shape. As a result they're producing bumper crops. Plus we've had the perfect weather. Hard to complain about that sort of success. Even so, we might want to cut back a bit next year." Mick gave Daphne a slightly quizzical look, almost as if he was seeing her from a different perspective. But without saying anything more, he turned back to Sabrina. "So tell me where did you get your accent? You don't sound like the rest of the Yanks."

She told him about being from Georgia and then inquired about his accent.

"I'm an Aussie. From Down Under."

She told him about a trip she'd taken to Sydney a few years ago. "My ex had been just dying to go down there. But after one day on the beach, he was stuck inside the hotel with a horrible sunburn. So I spent most of my time exploring on my own. I even learned how to drive on the wrong side of the street."

"You mean the *right* side. It's you Yanks that drive on the wrong side," he teased. But now they started comparing notes about beaches and weather differences, and eventually Sabrina was making plans with him to create a garden for her next year.

"Not as big and fancy as this one. But something sweet and

intimate might be nice." Was Sabrina actually batting her eyes at him?

Mick started shooting ideas to Sabrina, and suddenly Daphne realized her presence in this conversation was completely unnecessary. In fact, she doubted they would miss her if she vanished into thin air. "Excuse me," she said quietly. "I need to check on something inside."

As she scampered away, she could still hear them cheerfully chattering. Probably relieved she was gone. As she went into the kitchen, she felt slightly put off but wasn't even sure why. What was wrong with Sabrina making plans for a garden with Mick for next spring? Mick would get a new client and Sabrina would get a great garden. Daphne should be pleased for both of them. Except she wasn't. Certainly she wasn't jealous. That was ridiculous. Mick was just a friend. Wasn't he?

As she washed her hands in the kitchen sink, she could see how bad her fingernails actually looked. Cracked and dry and dirty, she could already hear the manicurist gasping in horror. For some reason this reminded Daphne of her wild hair from yesterday's canning. She reached up to touch it. It probably looked even worse now.

Feeling slightly horrified to imagine her disheveled and unkempt appearance, she hurried to the downstairs powder room to take a quick inventory. She gaped at herself in the well-lit mirror. It was no wonder Mick seemed to look right past her. He was either being polite or just couldn't bear to see her looking such a mess. Or more than likely, he'd simply found that Sabrina was much easier on the eyes.

Determined that she could do better than this, Daphne took a long shower and spent nearly an hour relaxing the curl in her hair.

Feeling much improved, she dressed casually, then went back downstairs. After the all-day canning session yesterday, the kitchen was in need of a thorough scrub-down, and she was determined to set it right before the appointment at two.

Daphne had never been to *Restorations,* Appleton's renowned day spa, but she'd heard Olivia raving about it before. The truth was, Daphne had never been to any kind of day spa. And she hadn't had a manicure or pedicure since her early days in New York. It was partly due to financial reasons, but she also convinced herself that she was a relatively low-maintenance girl. Obviously that would not describe her new friend.

"While you're getting your nails done, I'll be having a complete facial," Sabrina explained as they waited in the foyer. "It's been more than a month since my last exfoliation, and I'm starting to feel like a wrinkled old prune."

"You gotta be kidding?" Daphne frowned. "I can't see a wrinkle anywhere."

"Well, thank you ever so much, honey. Flattery will get you anywhere."

"I'm serious. Your skin is absolutely beautiful."

"Thank you once again." Sabrina giggled as she bent down to check on Tootsie. Today he was being toted around in a pale blue carrier-handbag that matched Sabrina's polka-dotted sundress. Apparently the spa people were not opposed to canines. "I would like to say I owe my complexion to my fabulous genes, but the truth is . . ." Sabrina lowered her voice, "I believe in Botox." She frowned slightly at Daphne. "Why don't you give it a try too?"

"Botox?" Daphne felt a bit alarmed at the thought of hypodermic needles containing toxins poking into her face.

"Sure. My girlfriends and I used to have Botox parties all the time back in Atlanta. Saved us a lot of money and at the same time it was a hoot."

"But I'm only thirty-four and I . . . I mean I realize you're probably even younger, but I just don't feel ready for Botox yet."

"I happen to be thirty-six," Sabrina said proudly. "But I'm happy to look like I'm still thirty. And I plan to do everything possible to continue looking this good twenty years from now."

"Wow." Daphne nodded, trying to imagine Sabrina in twenty years. "I just want to grow old gracefully, you know?"

Sabrina grinned. "Absolutely. Gracefully and with no wrinkles, sags, or bags."

Fortunately they were both called in for their appointments because Daphne wasn't even sure how to respond. She didn't want to hurt Sabrina's feelings, but looking like she was thirty at fifty-six seemed unrealistic, to say the least.

Daphne barely had her feet in the soaking tub before she apologized to the pedicurist. "I've been working in the garden," she said sheepishly. "Not taking very good care of my nails."

"No problem. That's why I'm here. Now why don't you just lean back and relax. Let me pamper you a little."

"Oh . . . okay." Daphne sighed as she leaned back into the soft leather chair. Maybe Sabrina was onto something. Getting pampered was rather nice.

By the time her appointment was over, Daphne not only felt prettier, she felt relaxed. "Thank you so much." She looked at her fingernails, which looked clean and new thanks to the French manicure.

Then she admired her toes, which looked perky and fresh with their shining coat of pale coral. "You're a miracle worker."

"Thank you for encouraging me to do this," Daphne said as she and Sabrina walked out to Sabrina's car. "It was really nice."

"How about if we get a coffee or something?" Sabrina suggested as they got into her car. Like Daphne's car, this one was a convertible too. A late-model BMW, and Sabrina had put the roof down today.

"Sure. Sounds good. Have you been to the Red River Coffee Company yet?"

"No, but I'd love to go there."

Before long, they were seated out on the coffee company's patio sipping iced mochas. "Two girls on the town," Sabrina said happily. "Isn't it fun?"

Daphne smiled. "Yeah, it is." Now she remembered the few times she'd been able to do something like this with Olivia. But unfortunately, for Daphne anyway, Olivia worked full-time running the florist shop during the week, and her weekends were often spent with her husband, Jeff.

"Now there's a pair of good-looking guys." Sabrina smiled at a couple of men carrying their coffee to a nearby table. "You can have the tall, cool drink of water and I'll take the blond." She laughed.

"They don't look very old to me," Daphne said uncomfortably. Hopefully Sabrina didn't want to try to pick up some total strangers.

"Age is just a number." Sabrina smiled directly toward the table, slightly nodding her head as if to draw their attention. Both of the men returned her gaze—and her smile. It was obvious they found her attractive.

"Sorry to bother you boys," Sabrina said innocently. "But ya'll caught my attention. You see, I'm new to town and I'm just so pleased to find that little ol' Appleton has such a nice selection of good-looking guys."

They laughed. "Thanks," the blond guy called back to her. "Welcome to Appleton."

"I like your accent," the other guy said.

Once again, Sabrina explained she was from the South, exchanging some cheerful chitchat with the attentive guys. But during their short visit, Daphne felt similar to how she'd felt this morning with Mick. It was like she was left out again, pushed to the side, ignored even. The men seemed intently focused on Sabrina. And why wouldn't they be? She was captivating, engaging, and cute as can be in her polka-dot sundress with matching dog carrier. Sabrina was sweet and adorable and everyone within twenty yards seemed to know it.

Meanwhile, Daphne felt invisible. On one hand, she didn't care since these fellows didn't even look like they were thirty. But on the other hand, it was disconcerting to be overshadowed by her petite and pretty companion.

Chapter 5

When Daphne got home, an apple crate with a little hand-painted sign wired onto it sat on her front porch. "Free Produce" the sign enticed. And yet the box was empty, which was actually a good thing since the last thing Daphne needed was more produce. Still, she was curious as to how the box got there. Then as she went inside the house, she remembered Mrs. Terwilliger. Of course. It had to be from her.

Daphne wondered about her neighbor's theory—if she set the crate out there, would the neighbors come? She'd test it by filling the crate with a variety of veggies. Then she set the heavy box in her front yard just a few feet from the sidewalk. As she walked back into the house, she imagined some bored juvenile delinquents utilizing the tomatoes to pelt at her recently painted house. Or her neighbor's. And if that happened would she be responsible? Or was she just still in a New York state of mind?

Deciding things like that didn't happen in Appleton—at least not in this neighborhood—she went into her office and sat in front of her computer. It was late in the day to start working on her novel, but something inside was begging her to write an answer for the column. Now if only she could find the letter she'd read last week—a letter she skipped over because she had no good answer. But maybe she'd given up too easily. First she looked in the Later file. Then the Much Later one. Finally she found it in her Much, Much Later file. And the first line hit her smack between the eyes.

> *Dear Daphne,*
> *I feel like I've become invisible when it comes to guys. It wasn't always like that, but the past couple of years, it seems like whenever I go out with my girlfriend, the guys are drawn to her like bees to honey. Meanwhile I feel like a bad-smelling wallflower. My friend and I are about the same height and weight, and I've even been told that I'm better looking than she is. The only obvious difference is she takes more care with her appearance and dresses with more flash than me. But I find it hard to believe that's really the problem. I'm afraid it's more due to my own insecurities. Or maybe I'm sending out bad vibes. Or maybe I just need a complete makeover. Please, can you help me?*
> *The Invisible Woman*

> *Dear Invisible Woman,*
> *It does sound as if you're suffering from some insecurity. And that in and of itself can send out "bad vibes," as you call them. Meanwhile, it's not helping that your friend is on top of her game, but*

I'm glad you're not faulting her for this. First of all,
I'd encourage you to remember all your good inner
qualities and strengths. Maybe even list them on an
index card that you keep handy. After that, you might
want to consider doing a little makeover. Sometimes a
small thing like a manicure or a new outfit can work
wonders for your confidence. Keep in mind that most
good guys are looking for the complete package. Not
just the wrappings, but what's inside too. However,
some good guys might not discover what's on the inside
if the wrappings look too uninviting.
    Daphne

As Daphne hit Save and stored these letters in the Keep file, she felt like she'd hit the nail on the head. It was time for her to take more care with the wrappings of her package. She'd gotten some Appleton-friendly clothes while shopping with Olivia a couple of months ago. But that was simply to replace her stiff-looking business clothes from New York. The items she'd purchased hadn't exactly been geared toward getting male attention. And it wasn't as if she was ready to start running around in strapless gowns or miniskirts, but perhaps she could do something to spice things up.

Daphne picked up her phone and called Sabrina. "Hey, neighbor. Are you busy?"

"Not too busy for you, honey."

Daphne explained her makeover idea. "It's not that I want to completely reinvent myself. But I think I could make some improvements."

"You most certainly could." Sabrina laughed. "Sorry, I don't mean to insinuate that you're a big ol' mess. Honestly, my first impression of you was that you have good bones. Your eyes are lovely and your hair color is fabulous. I suspect it's natural, right?"

"Yeah . . ."

"I know a lot about hair. I went to beauty school and actually worked in a salon for a spell. But it was hard work. Standing on my feet all day—and my shoulders got so sore. That's when I decided to become a legal secretary instead."

"Oh." Daphne was having second thoughts now. Maybe she would be wise just to leave well enough alone.

"Anyway, you've got great hair, but some highlights might take it to the next level. And you're very pretty too. Well, once we get the garden grime off of you and put you into some attractive clothes, that is. I honestly think you could be a real head-turner, Daphne."

She held up her hands. "The problem is, I really don't know where to begin. I've never been that much into my appearance. I think of myself as fairly low maintenance and no-nonsense and—"

"*And* you've come to the right place, honey. I would love to be involved in your little ol' makeover. And considering you've got to catch yourself a man, I say we've got no time to waste."

Suddenly Daphne felt worried. This was crazy. Handing herself over to Sabrina like this? What was she thinking?

"Let me do some research, okay? I'm still not quite acclimated to our little town and according to the Realtor, the best clothing stores are in a town called Fairview. Are you familiar with it?"

"Yes. There's a nice outdoor mall there."

"Does it have some big stores? Like Nordstrom or Macy's?"

"I . . . uh . . . I'm not sure."

"Never mind. Leave it all to me, honey. When it comes to

shopping, no one does it better than Sabrina Fontaine. I am a force to be reckoned with. Trust me. We can do this."

"Okay." Daphne nodded with uncertainty. "I will."

"Oh, I'm so excited. This is going to be a real hoot." Sabrina promised to get back to her tomorrow with a detailed plan.

"You don't have to be in that big a hurry." Daphne was backpedaling. "Just take your time and we can—"

"Are you kidding? My mama taught me to strike while the iron's hot. If we're going to snag you a man in time to plan your big ol' wedding before May. If I'm helping you with this, you gotta be ready to jump when I say jump."

Daphne imagined herself jumping—leaping through a flaming hoop being held by her diminutive neighbor as she cracked a whip on Daphne's backside. Of course, that was ridiculous. And so despite her concerns, Daphne agreed. Really, how bad could it be? It's not like Daphne couldn't say no if she thought Sabrina was pushing her too far.

On Thursday morning, Daphne was driving the Corvette toward Fairview with Sabrina and Tootsie happily seated next to her. Sabrina had the whole day planned for the three of them, starting with a hair appointment.

"One thing is for sure," Daphne declared. "I am not cutting my hair."

"No, of course you're not." Sabrina flipped her own blond locks over her shoulder. She had insisted on having the top up in order not to muss her hair. "Most guys secretly love long hair, honey. And yours is barely on your shoulders. Although it might need a little trim to clean it up some. Hey, maybe we should get you some extensions."

"No." Daphne firmly shook her head. "No extensions."

"This salon sounds like a good one. I looked it up online and it had mostly five-star reviews. I'm very picky about where I get my hair done, but it will be helpful to see how they do with you."

"Meaning I'm your guinea pig?"

Sabrina laughed. "Well now, I wouldn't put it quite like that."

When they arrived, Daphne had to admit the salon seemed clean and stylish and inviting. And Karla the stylist was both professional and considerate. She seemed to genuinely listen to Daphne's concerns about looking unnatural.

"The last time I got highlights was more than a decade ago," she admitted to Karla. "And it turned out horrible. I actually went to another salon and got the streaks covered up with my own hair color."

"I'll use a very light touch. Your natural hair color is so gorgeous, I wouldn't want to do anything to ruin it."

"I just don't want it to look brassy," Daphne said nervously as Karla was applying the lightener and wrapping the strands in aluminum foil.

"It won't." She gave her a reassuring smile. "Just relax. Why don't you read the magazine your friend brought you?"

Daphne looked down at the thick, slick fashion magazine in her lap. Sabrina had told Daphne to peruse it for clothing ideas. But as Daphne flipped through the pages, she felt like everything in it was aimed at a much younger woman. Not Daphne.

It took more than an hour, but when Karla finally proclaimed her done, Daphne was truly impressed. Not only did the layered cut

soften her angular face, but because Karla had smoothed her naturally curly hair out, it now felt sleek and shiny. And the golden highlights against the copper were fun and fresh looking. "I *really* like it."

"Oh, honey," Sabrina said as she joined them. "It is stunning. I
swear it takes at least five years off you."

"Like I'm twenty-nine?" Daphne held up the hand mirror to
examine the back.

Sabrina chuckled. "Well, that's assuming you looked like thirty-
four *before*."

"Oh." Daphne grimaced at the not-so-subtle hint. Of course
Sabrina would feel that Daphne looked older than her real age. After
all she hadn't been spending the past several years going to Botox
parties. Daphne frowned at her image in the mirror. Besides her hair,
which did look great, she really did look a bit dowdy and frumpy and
faded. She could probably pass for someone in her forties. Was that
really the image she'd wanted to put out there?

Their next stop was the makeup section of the salon. Sabrina had
made another appointment for Daphne with a cosmetologist named
Brianna. Still feeling pleased with her hair results, Daphne decided
to be more trusting. She tried not to be too negative as Brianna tried
various samples and colors on her. And eventually, with a little input
from Sabrina, they finally decided on a look that was both somewhat natural, but flattering. "You'd been wearing the wrong colors,"
Brianna informed Daphne as she removed the makeup bib and tossed
it into the trash.

"Now you look *ten* years younger," Sabrina proclaimed.

As Daphne studied her image in the mirror, she had to agree she
did look younger. Not twenty-four, thankfully, since Daphne had
no desire to look that young. But the improvement was remarkable.

Daphne settled the bill and, after waiting for Tootsie to have a potty break, they went to the Fairview Shoppes where they got some lunch to fortify themselves for an afternoon of shopping.

"Now if I work you too hard, you just let me know," Sabrina said as they went into another clothing store. "Some of my Atlanta friends can't keep up."

As they looked and gathered items for Daphne to try on, Sabrina continued to insist that Daphne was buying clothing that was one size too large.

"But I'm more comfortable." Daphne turned around to show Sabrina the black capri pants.

"Come here," Sabrina said to a stylish-looking salesclerk. "We would like your honest opinion." She pointed at Daphne. "Do you think those pants are a little too big?"

The salesclerk looked closely at Daphne and slowly nodded. "Yes. They're not meant to be baggy. They're meant to be slimming. Can I get you a different size?"

Sabrina pointed to the pair she'd hung on the dressing room door. "No, I got a smaller pair already, but I couldn't get her to try them on."

"Oh, you should try them," the woman said. "You have a lovely figure, and those great long legs. It's a shame to hide all that under clothes that are too big."

Sabrina laughed. "See, Daphne. What did I tell you?"

"Did you pay her to say that?"

The salesclerk laughed too. "No, she didn't. But your friend seems to know what she's talking about. How about if I get you a smaller top too? It will definitely be more flattering."

Daphne agreed with reluctance. Once she tried the slightly

smaller garments on, she had to admit they really did look better. "But what if they shrink?"

"Don't put them in the dryer," Sabrina warned. "You'll be fine."

By midafternoon, Daphne was exhausted but Sabrina seemed unstoppable. "You remind me of the Energizer Bunny," Daphne told her as they stood outside, waiting for Tootsie to take care of his business again. Shopping with a little dog came with its own challenges. "But I really feel like I'm done."

Sabrina looked disappointed. "Well, I'm guessing we did do some significant damage to your pocketbook. I suppose we can call it a day. If you're really that worn out."

Daphne nodded eagerly. "I am. I'm not used to this."

"I'll agree to quit now if you promise to go to dinner with me tomorrow."

Daphne glanced at Tootsie. "I'll promise to go to dinner with you if you promise to leave Tootsie at home."

Sabrina frowned. "Well, I guess it won't hurt to let him be on his own for a couple of hours."

"Really?" Daphne was surprised.

"Sure, it'll be good for him." Sabrina pointed at Daphne. "And when we go to dinner, I want you to wear the green sundress and those killer sandals we got to go with it."

"Why?"

"Because I want to show you off." Sabrina laughed as she tugged on Tootsie's leash. "Come on, wittle boy. Auntie Daphne wants to go home."

As Daphne drove them home, she had to wonder about this new extended family she'd recently picked up. Being an aunt to a spoiled Chihuahua wasn't exactly her dream relationship. Although she couldn't deny that the temperamental brown dog was growing on her. At least he didn't bark when he saw her coming anymore. And who knew, if this catching-a-man thing didn't work out, perhaps she would get herself a dog. Not a Chihuahua of course! But a Labradoodle might be fun.

Chapter 6

Daphne couldn't believe how many bags she had to carry into the house. Had she really bought all that? Perhaps she'd return some of it later . . . without mentioning it to Sabrina. But as she laid it out on her bed, she had to admit that everything they'd picked out did have a fun, youthful vibe to it. And compared to most of her other clothes, these pieces really were more flattering. The question still remained, would she feel comfortable in them?

As she hung things up, she reminded herself of the old *I Love Lucy* shows she used to watch with Aunt Dee. Lucy had always dressed with such splash and style. And since Daphne was occasionally compared to a young Lucille Ball, perhaps it was time for her to start emulating Lucy's love of fashion as well.

Starting tomorrow, she would try out some of these new clothes. Not the dressier ones, but some of the casual pieces Sabrina had convinced her were a huge improvement over Daphne's other clothes. Maybe she'd pay Olivia a visit and get her response. It might even be fun.

As Daphne was feeding the cats, she noticed a slightly built man walking into her yard. Curious as to what he was doing, she peered out the window to watch. He was an older gentleman with thinning gray hair and a narrow mustache. Upon a closer look, she realized she knew him. Mr. Renwald from Appleton High. He'd been her favorite English teacher and part of the reason she'd become so interested in writing. Thinking he was coming to her front door, she dropped the cat food can into the sink and hurried to meet him. But from the big front window, she saw him stooping down in front of the free-produce box. However, the box must've been empty because he stood up straight and then, looking over his shoulders as if embarrassed, he backed off.

She went out to the porch, thinking she'd call out to him, but seeing him scurrying away, she suspected he did not want to be seen foraging through an empty produce box. He crossed the street and went directly into the house next door to Sabrina's. So Mr. Renwald lived in her neighborhood.

Feeling badly that he'd discovered the box empty and eager to speak to him again, she grabbed a basket and went out to her garden, quickly picking a nice selection of ripe produce. After the basket was nearly full she paused to admire the pretty selection of veggies. Hooking it over her arm, she marched over to his house and rang the doorbell.

He answered with a quizzical expression. "Can I help you?"

"Mr. Renwald."

"Do I know you?"

She grinned, holding out the basket. "Probably not, but I went to Appleton High and you were my favorite English teacher."

He brightened slightly. "You do seem familiar, but I've been retired for ten years and I'm afraid my memory is fading fast."

She told him who she was and that she lived across the street. "I noticed you stopped by for some produce. My garden is producing out more vegetables than I can ever use. So I brought this for you."

He stared down at the basket. "Why thank you, Daphne. That's very kind. Are you sure you can't use them?"

She told him about her canning experience with Mrs. Terwilliger. "I don't want to do that again anytime soon. So I'm very glad to share with the neighbors."

"I noticed the neighbors helping themselves to your box," he confessed. "I kept thinking I'd go over, but I didn't . . . and by the time I got there it was picked clean."

"Well, I'm glad I saw you and glad you were home. It's very nice to see you again, Mr. Renwald."

"Since I'm no longer your teacher, why don't you call me by my first name. Wally."

She smiled. "Okay, Wally. I'm glad to know you're my neighbor."

He frowned as he took the basket from her. "I'm afraid our neighborhood is going to the dogs."

"What?" She tipped her head to one side. "How so?"

He nodded his head toward Sabrina's house. "That horrible woman and her yappy little dog have been testing my patience."

"Oh? What's going on?"

"She lets her dog out and he immediately runs directly into my yard to relieve himself. If I go out and tell the little rat-dog to vacate the premises, he makes a terrible scene, barking and growling as if *I* am the trespasser." He scowled.

"Oh, dear. Have you mentioned this to Sabrina?"

"Sabrina?" He looked suspicious. "You *know* that woman?"

"Yes. I mean, I only met her this week. Her dog barked at me at first too. But now he doesn't."

"I can't even go out into my yard without concern that the little beast will bark at me. He's stolen my peace and quiet."

"I'm sorry. That must be miserable. Hopefully Sabrina will put up a fence."

"I doubt that will help. He'll still bark."

"Maybe he just needs to get used to the place."

Wally grimly shook his head. "No, I doubt it. I've seen little dogs like that. Nothing stops them from barking. I'm halfway tempted to sell my home. I've been considering downsizing anyway. This old house is really too big for one person."

"Oh, I hope you're not leaving too soon. I'm so pleased to discover you're my neighbor."

He gave her a weary half smile. "Well, I'm sure I'll be around for a while anyway. Thanks for the produce. Do you want me to empty it right now so you can have your basket back?"

"No, just leave it on my front porch if you like."

"I'd invite you in, but it's rather messy in here. It's never been quite the same since Molly died."

"Was that your wife?"

He nodded. "She passed on six years ago."

"I'm sorry."

He jerked his thumb over his shoulder. "We'd just moved in here before she got sick. She'd inherited this house from her parents. I never really wanted to live here, but she was thrilled." He sighed. "And now I'm stuck with it." He glanced over to Sabrina's again. "And stuck with that horrid little dog too."

"If you don't mind, I'd like to tell Sabrina that Tootsie is bothering you."

"*Tootsie?*" He shook his head. "It figures that such a foolish dog would have an equally foolish name. I suppose she named him for the Tootsie Rolls he leaves in my yard."

Daphne couldn't help but laugh. "I'm sorry, Wally. I promise to do all I can to see that you get your peace back."

He looked unconvinced but thanked her anyway. As Daphne went home, she couldn't help but feel sorry for the old guy. It really wasn't fair that Tootsie was invading his yard and stealing his peace. The poor old guy did not deserve that.

After a fairly long phone call where Daphne had to interrupt Sabrina numerous times to finally get her point across regarding Tootsie, Sabrina eventually agreed that it was time to put in a fence. "I was hoping to get completely unpacked first." Sabrina sighed. "I'm still living in a maze of boxes."

"I just assumed that you were all settled in," Daphne said. "You shouldn't have sacrificed a whole day's worth of your time just for me today."

"Oh, that's all right. That was fun. And I was ready for a break."

"Well, I appreciate it. Let me know if I can help you with the unpacking as a repayment. I could come over tomorrow if you like."

"I'll think about it, but I'm so unorganized, you might get frustrated."

"Not if I was helping you. I tend to be fairly organized."

"Really? Maybe I'll take you up on the offer."

Daphne looked out the window to see Tootsie in Sabrina's front yard now, wandering over the sidewalk and into the street. "And you will do something about getting a fence up too? Not just for Wally's sake, Sabrina. Tootsie could get hit by a car roaming out there in the street like he's doing right now."

"What?" Daphne could hear the sound of Sabrina's footsteps running through the house, and then she was out in the yard yelling at Tootsie to "Come!"

"Even though there aren't many cars in this neighborhood, you never know."

"That's true," Sabrina said breathlessly. "Poor Tootsie is used to having five wooded acres to roam freely upon."

"Even more reason you need that fence."

"I'm afraid you're right, honey. I'll see what I can do. Say, do you think Mick the garden guy might be able to help me with it?" Sabrina sounded hopeful.

"Mick is a good place to start. If he doesn't have guys already working for him who can do it, I'm sure he'll have good contacts."

"Okay then. That's just what I'll do."

"And I'll come by tomorrow to lend a hand," Daphne promised. "Around ten okay?"

"Perfect. See ya'll then."

The next morning, Daphne was tempted to put on one of her new outfits, but the thought of scrounging around and unpacking boxes did not seem conducive to sprucing up. So she just put on her old khaki shorts and a T-shirt and went over. However, when Sabrina answered her door, trying to muzzle Tootsie's crazed barking,

Daphne was surprised to see that, as usual, Sabrina was immaculately dressed with every hair in place.

"Are you going somewhere? Because I thought you wanted me to help you unpack today."

"That's right, I do." Sabrina opened the door wider. "Come on in."

"Wow." Daphne looked through the rows of boxes in the front room. "You weren't kidding about the maze."

"I know, and it's overwhelming. The problem is, I'll open a box and then instead of putting things away like I ought to, I wind up studying each piece . . . going down memory lane, you know?"

Daphne nodded. "What you need is some objectivity." She pointed to a box marked *kitchen*. "Can I assume that the boxes are labeled correctly?"

"Why, of course."

Daphne picked up the kitchen box. "Then I will take this to the kitchen and we'll start putting it away." Daphne smiled to remember how Olivia had helped her in this very same way. Maybe it was karma that she was helping Sabrina now.

"But what if it won't all fit?"

"We'll put away what you need and want—as long as it fits— then we'll put the rest of it back in the box and store it in the garage until you decide what you want to do with it."

"What a fabulous plan." Sabrina beamed at her. "I'll get another kitchen box too."

"No. Let's do one at a time to start with, see how that goes."

They managed to unload four boxes and were just getting a momentum going when Tootsie started wildly barking. "That must be the door," Sabrina said. "Excuse me."

Daphne continued unpacking, eager to keep them moving forward. Sabrina had been right about having too much stuff, but it was interesting to see what was in each box. It was clear that Sabrina and Edward must've been extremely well off. However, it was just as clear that most of the items winding up in the garage were not essential.

"I'm back. That was the fence boys at the door. Mick sent them over. He suggested we put a temporary wire fence in place until he works up a landscaping plan for my whole backyard."

"As long as it keeps Tootsie out of Wally's yard and off the streets, it will be a great improvement." Daphne held up what had to be the fifth wine decanter set. "How many of these do you have anyway?"

"Oh my, I don't know. But that one came from Italy. I'd like to keep it."

"You must've had a large kitchen." Daphne set the decanter on the counter.

"I suppose this kitchen as well as the living room would all fit into my kitchen back in Atlanta. Our house was more than twelve thousand square feet."

"You're kidding? Who needs that much space?"

"Edward did." She sighed. "To be perfectly honest, I didn't mind it too much either. It gave me plenty of places to get away from him." She looked around the average-sized kitchen. "Goodness knows what I'd do if I had to live with that man in a house this small."

They took a lunch break at one, sharing a can of soup, crackers, and cheese out in the backyard where a couple of young men were running wire around some temporary metal fence posts. Daphne didn't want to complain, but this transparent fence would do little to reassure Wally. But perhaps she could communicate the grander plan to him.

"Good day, ladies!" Mick entered the backyard, tipping his straw cowboy hat to them. "Didn't mean to interrupt. But I thought I'd drop by to check on the progress as well as take some measurements for your garden, Sabrina."

Hopping to her feet, Sabrina went over to greet him, effusively thanking him for coming to her rescue by sending his team over. "I just hate making enemies of my neighbors before I've even finished my unpacking." She nodded over to where Daphne was still sitting in the shade. "And look who came over to help me out."

"Oh, hi, Daph. Didn't mean to ignore you. How ya doing?"

"I'm fine, thanks." Again she felt slightly dismissed. However, since this was Sabrina's house and her fence project, it seemed expected.

"Will you excuse me?" Sabrina told Daphne. "I'd like to walk through the yard with Mick . . . to see what he's got in mind for me."

"Not at all." Daphne stood. "I can keep unpacking the last of those kitchen boxes if you like."

"That'd be wonderful. You seem to know what I want and need in there almost better than I do anyway. Thank you so much!"

As Daphne continued unwrapping items and placing them in cabinets, she caught glimpses of Sabrina and Mick walking around the yard. Sabrina was chatting and laughing as usual, but Mick was giving her what seemed like his undivided attention. In fact, unless Daphne was mistaken, he was almost mesmerized by the petite Southern belle.

As Daphne carried the last of the kitchen boxes to the garage, she realized that to a man, Sabrina probably was truly mesmerizing. Pretty and old-fashioned and sometimes painfully polite—she could be many a man's dream for the perfect woman.

Daphne set the box down on the stack of others with a dull thud. She supposed there were a few things she could learn from Sabrina, but she had to draw the line too. There was no way Daphne was going to start cooing and catering to any man the way Sabrina seemed to be doing to Mick right now. That might work for a sweet Southern belle, but it would not work for Daphne, primarily because she refused to do it.

Still, she told herself as she walked back to her house later in the day, it wouldn't kill her to soften up a little. After all it was possible that her years of working for a hard-nosed newspaper editor and living in New York had toughened her up a little too much. She remembered some of the arguments she'd had with Jake. To be fair, she had argued with him right from the get-go.

To start with, she had questioned Aunt Dee's will. Then she had actually questioned Jake's legal expertise. Even their last conversation had turned into a test of wills. Although, in her own way, she was trying to show him that she needed him. However, it was possible he was fed up with her. Besides that, he was getting ready to go on vacation with his ex. And why was she even thinking about this?

She slammed the door to her house, then marched upstairs to take a shower. It was a waste of time to pine for Jake. Clearly he didn't have that kind of interest in her. And really it wasn't as if she was in love with him. She had simply grown attracted to what had suddenly gone out of reach. Like forbidden fruit. It was perfectly understandable that she'd fallen for it. And thanks to Sabrina, she'd been doing a pretty good job of distracting herself from thinking about him for most of this week. So why was she giving in now? Appleton might be a small pond, but Jake McPheeters was not the only fish in it.

Chapter 7

"Okay, this isn't exactly a blind date," Sabrina said as she got into Daphne's car.

"What?" Daphne turned to stare at her.

"You see, Mick was being so helpful today, dropping everything to come and help with my yard, well, I just couldn't help but invite him to dinner too. And if my house was in order, I would have invited you both to dine at my house, which really wouldn't seem like a date, but, well, you know how that is at the moment."

"I still don't understand the bit about the blind date," Daphne slowly put the key into the ignition. "I already know Mick. How could he be a blind date?"

"Because he's bringing a friend. An Aussie fellow. His name is Collin and he and Mick have been best *mates*—that's what Mick calls him—their whole lives. Apparently Collin went through a bad breakup last year, and he came out to visit Mick to sort of clear his head."

"Oh, I hadn't heard about Collin."

"Anyway, so we're clear, just because Mick is bringing Collin does not make this a blind date. Or even a double date. It's just four people going out for dinner together." Sabrina giggled nervously. *"Okay?"*

Daphne started the engine. "Sure, if you say so."

Sabrina let out a sigh. "Oh, good."

They met the guys at The Zeppelin, and just like Sabrina had described, it did not feel like a date. It was just four people dining together and sharing a few laughs. Daphne had chosen to wear one of the new outfits—a lime green off-the-shoulder shirt paired with a flounced print skirt that showed off her legs. She'd even put on the beaded earrings and necklace Sabrina had insisted were perfection. This bright ensemble, combined with some sassy-looking Nine West sandals, made Daphne feel happy and carefree and young. She was surprised that mere clothing could make her feel this good. Or maybe it was just the company she was keeping.

Collin, not unlike Mick, was easy on the eyes. His dark curly hair and earnest-looking hazel eyes, combined with his easy smile, drew her right in. Add to that his Aussie accent and goofy sense of humor and Daphne was enjoying his company. Both Mick and Collin seemed to be on top of their game this evening, sharing some hilarious stories from their youth Down Under. Other diners glanced their way when laughter erupted. Their table was clearly one of the happiest in the restaurant.

"You Aussies are such fun," Sabrina said happily. "I can't remember when I've had a better time at dinner."

"I agree." Daphne nodded. "Hopefully, we're not disturbing the other diners." Some of the faces were familiar and judging by their expressions, she suspected they might be writing their own scripts for the merry foursome. But Appleton was a small town. It was only normal that people would be interested. Sometimes to a fault.

However, when Daphne noticed Olivia coming over to their table with her husband in tow, she felt a bit uneasy. That was because of Olivia's expression. Olivia's brow creased as if she was confused, but she and Jeff simply said a curious hello. Hoping she was imagining things with Olivia, Daphne introduced the couple to Collin and Sabrina. But before they left the table, Olivia gave Daphne one last questioning look, almost as if she didn't approve. And for some reason Daphne knew that the next time she saw Olivia, just like Ricky used to tell Lucy, Daphne would have some "'splaining to do."

"Collin's return flight is booked for Monday," Mick told them as they were finishing up their desserts and coffee. "But I'm not ready to see him go yet."

"I've been in the States a whole fortnight. Time to get back to the old grindstone."

"That's too bad," Sabrina said. "I feel like I've just barely gotten to know you too. I hate to see you leave."

"Mick's been encouraging me to stick around awhile longer," Collin told her.

"That's right," Mick said. "I'm lobbying for him to stay put awhile. Hoping he'll find out it's not such a bad place to hang your hat."

"I reckon I could get my flight to Sydney changed." Collin seemed to study Daphne as he rubbed his chin. "There's a lot of the States I haven't seen yet, and I've been considering taking a full year sabbatical for ages. You know, see the world. And I doubt the investment brokerage would miss me much—some of my work mates are probably thrilled I'm gone now." He chuckled. "Less competition."

"Right-o, mate." Mick slapped his shoulder. "Stick around awhile. And who knows? You might decide you like it here." He winked at Daphne. "You sure can't complain about the sheilas."

"No complaints from me." Collin grinned at Daphne. "I don't know why Mick was keeping you girls from me."

"Because I knew you'd try to steal them away?" Mick teased.

"This bloke still hasn't gotten over our time at uni," Collin confided to Daphne. "He's still certain I stole his sheila."

"Aw, that's not true. Even if you had stolen her, you would've been doing me a favor, mate." Mick told another funny story about their college days.

Finally, the check came and Sabrina, who had already told them she was treating, insisted on taking it. "Don't think of this as being on me," she said as she filled in a generous tip. "Think of it as being on my ex!"

They all laughed, making some additional "ex" jokes as well. Sabrina had told them enough about Edward to garner their sympathy as well as provide a few chuckles.

They prepared to part ways as they waited for the parking valet. "If I end up going back Down Under next week, do not take it personally," Collin told Sabrina and Daphne. "I would've enjoyed getting better acquainted with both of you." But as he said this, Daphne could feel his gaze fixed on her, sending a pleasant rush through her.

"Well, I hope you figure out what's best for you," Daphne told him.

"I'll see what I can do to persuade him," Mick promised as his Jeep rolled up. "See you ladies later."

They waved. Then while waiting for Daphne's car to show up, Olivia and Jeff came out of the restaurant. "Daphne," Olivia said a bit anxiously. "I'm curious as to what's become of Jake. I haven't seen him around town lately."

"Oh, he's on vacation. On Lake Tamalik. With the family."

Olivia frowned. "The *family*? You mean with Jenna?"

"Jenna and Gwen and—"

"Jake took his ex-wife on vacation?" Olivia's eyes were wide. "Seriously?"

"Some of their other relatives are at the lake too. I hear it's an annual get-together." Daphne pointed to where her car was coming around the corner. "I'll fill you in on all the details later."

"Oh, yeah." Olivia nodded. "You bet you will."

As Daphne drove them home, Sabrina asked about Olivia. "Why was she acting so curious about this Jake guy? It almost seemed as if she was insinuating something."

"Well, Olivia is my good friend and I haven't spoken to her all week."

"Is that because of me. I know I've been taking up an awful lot of your time. But I don't want to come between you and your friends."

"No, it's okay. Olivia works full-time at the florist shop. She owns and manages it."

"So what's the deal with Jake? Who is he?"

Realizing that Sabrina already knew about some of Aunt Dee's inheritance conditions, it hardly seemed worth keeping information about Jake from her. "Jake McPheeters is my attorney. Actually he was my aunt's attorney. The past few months we'd been spending a lot of time together. So much so that I suppose I got the wrong idea about the whole thing."

"Did you fall in love with Jake?"

Daphne shook her head. "Oh no, it hadn't gotten that far along. But I did feel like we were very close to becoming a couple."

"And then he went on vacation with his ex-wife?"

Daphne sighed. "Yes. And I only found out about it after he left. I was in a bit of a funk for a while." She smiled at Sabrina. "But you've actually helped to pull me out of it. Thanks!"

"You are more than welcome, honey. You've been like a breath of fresh air and sunshine to me since I got here. And wasn't tonight a hoot?"

Daphne laughed. "Yes, I think it was a real hoot."

Sabrina laughed even louder. "Hearing you say *hoot* is hilarious. But you give me some time and I'll get you talking proper Southern yet."

"I felt like the foreigner at the table." Daphne pulled into her driveway. "The Aussies and the Southern belle. I was the only one talking without an accent."

"Without an accent?" Sabrina cocked her head to one side. "Don't kid yourself, honey. You got an accent all right. It's just that it's a Yankee one."

They both laughed as they got out of the car. Daphne thanked Sabrina for dinner. "Hopefully Collin will extend his vacation and we can do it again sometime."

"Oh yes. And if I can get my house in order, I could have all of you over for a nice homemade dinner. I just love to cook."

As Daphne went inside the house, she could hear the phone ringing in the kitchen, and thinking it might be her dad since he usually called on the landline, she hurried to get it.

"So you're home," Olivia said triumphantly. "I texted you and even left a message on your cell phone. I figured you might've gone out dancing or for *more* drinks."

"More drinks?" Taking her time to fully react, Daphne kicked off the high-heeled sandals that had started to pinch her toes about an hour ago. "What is that supposed to mean?"

"Well, I'm not passing judgment, Daphne. But I just never thought of you as a party girl."

"A *party girl?*"

"Sorry, I didn't mean it to sound like that. But I couldn't help but notice the beer was flowing freely at your table."

"Mick and Collin had a couple of beers," she admitted with irritation. "Does that make me a party girl?"

"I'm sorry, Daph, but as your friend I felt—"

"So . . . Olivia, *how are you?*" Daphne would give Olivia one last chance to redeem herself.

"Never mind about me. What was going on with you and those guys tonight?"

"We were having dinner, Olivia. Just like you and Jeff."

"But it just seemed all wrong."

"All wrong?" Daphne went to the living room.

"Sorry, but that group just didn't look like your kind of people."

"My kind of people?" Daphne flopped down onto the sectional.

"Oh, I don't mean to sound snooty. That's not it at all. I mean I like Mick just fine. And his friend seems okay. And your new neighbor, well, she's sure a chatterbox, but she's probably nice."

"Uh-huh, then what's your problem with them?"

"It's just that you seemed out of place with them. That's all."

"I was actually having a really great time. They're all such fun. And Collin is a really nice guy."

"But what about Jake, Daphne?"

"What about him?" She watched the cats stealthily approaching her, and before long Lucy settled into her lap and Ethel snuggled up next to her.

"I thought he was the one."

"Well, you were obviously wrong." Daphne felt herself relaxing as she petted the cats.

"But I thought you had feelings for him."

"Yes, that's true . . . I did." Daphne slowly admitted. "But I've always been a little concerned. That he might not have finished with his marriage yet."

"But he said he was finished. And Gwen was dating Frank Danson. In fact, as far as I know they're still a couple. Or they were."

"Maybe Frank hasn't heard about Lake Tamalik yet." Daphne forced a smile.

"Oh, Daphne, I'm so sorry. I know you really liked Jake."

Daphne sighed. "Yeah . . . I did."

"Why didn't you call me and let me know what was going on?"

"I had intended to. But Sabrina moved in and she's so, well, sort of needy right now. She's taken up a lot of my time this week. To be honest, it's been kind of a relief. She's a good distraction. I haven't had much of a chance to feel too bad about Jake."

"But I know you must be brokenhearted."

"Que sera, sera," Daphne said lightly. "If it's not meant to be, there's no use crying over it. Right? You're the one who's always saying there are lots of available bachelors in town—more fish in the sea."

"Obviously you're not suffering any shortage of them," Olivia teased. "I must admit that Mick's friend is just as good looking as

Mick. Maybe even more so. Do you think you're interested in him, Daph? He sure seemed to have his eye on you."

"Oh . . . I don't know."

"Is he really a good guy? I mean I hear that some Aussie men can be pretty chauvinistic. Hopefully he's not one of those. Mick doesn't seem to be. And what about all that beer swilling?"

"Beer *swilling?*"

Olivia laughed. "Well, I've heard that Aussie men are really into their beer."

"I haven't noticed that about Mick. And I don't really know Collin well enough to say. But he seemed nice and polite. If he doesn't go back to Australia next week, maybe I'll get to know him better."

"He's leaving?"

"Possibly."

"Well, we won't give up, Daphne. The right man for you is out there. A part of me is still holding out for Ricardo." She let out a sigh. "That would be almost like having you as part of our family."

"And Ricardo is definitely a great guy. I really do like him—a lot. But that server of his—Kellie—she seems to be marking her territory. I'm not sure I'd want to cross her." Daphne told Olivia about how Kellie treated Sabrina and her earlier this week. "It's like she took our order and just disappeared. She never even brought our drinks. It was weird."

"Someone should tell Ricardo."

"We gently let him know. He did what he could to amend things."

"He should just fire her. That girl is nothing but trouble."

They talked awhile longer and it felt good to catch up, but Daphne didn't appreciate Olivia's subtle putdowns in regards to

Sabrina. Daphne wasn't sure if Olivia was jealous of the friendship or just plain didn't like Sabrina. And to be fair, Sabrina was an acquired taste. But Olivia should at least give her a chance.

"I hope you can get to know her better," Daphne finally said. "There's a lot more to her than meets the eye."

"Well, I am glad she's helped you in getting over Jake. I still can't believe he's gotten back together with Gwen. That just seems nuts. Are you absolutely sure about this?"

"Mattie Stone told me the whole story."

"Oh . . . well, Mattie should know. She and Jenna are practically joined at the hip. How come Mattie didn't go on vacation with them?"

Daphne told her about marching band.

"Yes, summer is fading fast. And that just makes me feel even more anxious for you, Daphne. You really need at least six months to plan for a proper wedding. That means you need to be engaged by early December—no later." She paused. "And that only gives you less than four months to reel in a guy."

"Reel in a guy?" Daphne teased. "Such a lovely image."

"You know what I mean."

"I know. But when I said que sera, sera, I meant it. What will be *will be*."

"Meaning you don't want to stay here in Appleton? Or live in that house? Or drive that car?"

Daphne forced a laugh. "Seriously, Olivia, I think you're more worried about all this than I am."

"Sorry." Olivia released a loud exhale. "I think I must've had too much caffeine today. For some reason I feel really worked up about this. I worry about you."

"Well, that's sweet. But for your sake, take some deep breaths . . . step back. And instead of worrying, shoot up a quick prayer. That would be more helpful to both of us."

"You're probably right. Just tell me the truth before I let you go. You're really not brokenhearted over Jake, are you?"

"The truth is, I *was* a little broken . . . *okay?*"

"Okay. At least that's believable. It's encouraging that you're not in complete denial. And I suppose it makes sense that you'd be gallivanting around town acting all happy and silly in order to get over him. Jake's a pretty cool guy, Daphne. I could've imagined you guys together for the long haul."

Daphne let out a slow sigh. "Yeah. But really, I've put him behind me now. I want you to do the same. Time to move on. Okay?"

They talked some more, but Daphne was relieved when they finally said good-bye. Olivia meant well, but as Daphne hung up the receiver, a wave of sadness washed over her. Okay, so maybe she wasn't quite over Jake yet. But she would get there. With God's help—and perhaps with Sabrina's distractions too—she would get past this.

Chapter 8

I got to thinking about you and your lawyer friend last night," Sabrina said the next morning as she and Daphne sipped coffee on Daphne's front porch.

"Oh?" Daphne frowned. Why was everyone so obsessed with Jake McPheeters right now? Furthermore, how was Daphne supposed to get over him if her friends kept bringing him up?

"Didn't you mention that he was your aunt's attorney?"

"Uh-huh." Daphne focused on her coffee, swirling it around in the mug.

"Then he obviously knows the conditions of her will, doesn't he?"

"He drafted it for her."

"So perhaps he realizes it's unethical to be involved with you."

"Unethical?" Daphne said slowly.

"Because he knows you'll inherit if you get married. And as far as I understand, no one else knows this, right?"

"Well, Olivia knows. She figured it out too." Daphne took a sip of coffee, wishing for a different conversation topic.

"Right. But I can understand why you want to keep quiet about it. You wouldn't want to get a bunch of lowlife loser-types hoping to marry into money. Right?"

She nodded. "But what does this have to do with Jake?"

"Perhaps he felt guilty for having the inside track. Maybe he felt he was taking unfair advantage of your situation. Marrying you for money."

"Oh no." Daphne waved her hand. "We even talked about that. We were both very clear on it. That isn't the problem, Sabrina. I'm sure of it."

"So you really think he's getting back together with his ex?"

"That's what it looks like to me." Daphne forced a smile.

"Well, since Jake sounds like a good guy, I think that's nice." She leaned back in the chair. "You don't often hear of couples retying the knot. It's kinda sweet."

"Yes . . . so let's put the whole thing to rest, okay? I'm tired of rehashing it. And I told Olivia the same thing last night. Jake is with Gwen right now, and I'm sure it's for the best. Onward and upward." Daphne held up her coffee mug for a toast.

Sabrina clinked her coffee mug against it. "That's right. Onward and upward. Hey, I was just reading this week's newspaper. Did you know that next weekend is Founder's Day?"

"I saw the article but haven't read it yet." Daphne took a sip of coffee. "I haven't been to a Founder's Day celebration in years. But as a kid I loved it. Mostly for the carnival rides and cotton candy. It'll be fun to see how it's evolved over the years."

"Sounds like they'll have a lot of interesting activities. The mile-long antique sale is on Saturday. I'm dying to go to that. And there's a barbecue and dance on Saturday night. I wonder if Mick and Collin would like to be our escorts."

That did sound fun, but Daphne had no desire to call the guys up and ask them out. She might be a modern woman in some ways, but not when it came to asking out a man. That's where she leaned toward old-fashioned. Very old-fashioned.

"So are you open to that?" Sabrina asked.

"What?"

"Going to the barbecue with Mick and Collin?"

"Well . . . sure . . . but they haven't exactly asked."

Sabrina set her empty coffee cup on the table with a wink. "Don't you worry your pretty little head. Sabrina will work out those details."

"But I hope you don't—"

"Like I said, honey, I'll take care of it." She stood, smoothing the front of her pale yellow capri pants. "Just you plan on being available, ya hear?"

"You got it." Daphne agreed. It was pointless not to.

"I got the impression you are into Collin."

"He seemed nice enough." Daphne studied Sabrina. "Were you more interested in Mick?"

"I must admit that my first impression of him—that morning when he showed up in your lovely garden—oh my, you could've knocked me over with a feather."

"Really?"

"You know what I thought when I looked into his eyes—those ocean-blue eyes—I thought this man is everything that Edward was not."

"You knew him that well that quickly?"

"I have very good instincts." She giggled. "Well, sometimes I do. Not with Edward. Although my instincts had probably been warning me about Edward. I just wasn't listening."

Daphne nodded and took a slow sip of coffee.

"But when I met Mick . . . well, I just felt myself getting swept away." She looked intently at Daphne. "Do you know that most people know if they're in love within the first three minutes of meeting a person?"

"I've heard something like that before."

"That's exactly how I felt about Mick. I knew. It didn't even take three minutes."

Daphne nodded again, biting her tongue as a variety of concerns flashed through her mind. Was Sabrina serious? And if so, was this a rebound romance for her? And what about Julianne Preston? Should Daphne warn Sabrina about the beautiful landscape artist who worked for Mick? Daphne liked Julianne and appreciated her design skills, but the young woman was a force to be reckoned with. But even as Daphne considered these possible obstacles, she wondered why trouble Sabrina?

After all, Sabrina was a grown woman, perfectly capable of thinking for herself. Besides that, Mick and Julianne were not an official couple. Sure, they did things together sometimes and it seemed that Julianne wanted to be with Mick. But it also seemed that Mick wasn't moving too fast in her direction. Daphne's theory was that Mick was still playing the field. He had the kind of good looks that drew lots of female attention. He probably felt confident that there were still plenty of sheilas to choose from. Including Sabrina. And Daphne hadn't missed him carefully checking out her new neighbor. He was Johnny-on-the-spot when Sabrina put out the call for yard assistance. And if Sabrina and Mick were meant for each other, why would Daphne want to stand between them? It's not like she wanted to pursue Mick . . . did she?

On Sunday, Sabrina went to church with Daphne and afterward, Daphne took her up to meet Pastor Andrew, explaining how they were neighbors.

"And Daphne has been so good to me." Sabrina winked at the pastor. "She really understands the meaning of *love thy neighbor*."

He smiled at Daphne. "That's very nice to hear."

"Sabrina only moved here last week," Daphne told him. "From Georgia."

"I thought I heard a Southern drawl," Pastor Andrew said to Sabrina. "Anyway, welcome to Appleton. And welcome to our little church. I hope you'll come again."

"I just might take you up on that. It's very different from what I'm used to back home. But I really like it. You have an interesting way with words, Pastor Andrew."

"Thank you . . . I think."

"Oh, I meant that as a compliment."

"I told Sabrina about your singles group too," Daphne said. "I thought she might like to try it out."

"Yes, please consider coming. We're always happy to see a new face."

"Thank you, I'll keep that in mind."

As they walked out to the parking lot, Daphne told Sabrina a bit about Pastor Andrew. "I have great respect for him. He's really genuine and transparent. The first time I heard him speak was at the singles group. He talked about his own life and how he'd had his heart broken a few times. But it was his words about how we need to trust God with being single that really helped me. He's really come to terms with it. I'm not as far along that road as he is, but I'm trying."

"Do you mean to say that Pastor Andrew is single?"

"That's right." Daphne got into the car. "And he's not looking for a mate. He's trusting God." She shook her head as she started the car. "I wish I had that much faith. Sometimes I do."

"Have you ever considered Pastor Andrew as husband material?"

Daphne laughed.

"Well, a girl could do worse," Sabrina said. "He's nice looking in a pastoral sort of way."

"What's that mean?"

"You know . . . quiet . . . reserved."

"He reminds me a little of Ralph Fiennes."

"Yes! I can see that." Sabrina giggled.

"But no, I'm not thinking of him as husband material. I prefer to think of him as pastor material."

"Maybe so, but you could keep him on the backup list."

"Backup list?"

"Well, you know . . . May will come rolling along and you'll want a backup list. Just in case."

Daphne sighed. Between Sabrina and Olivia, she shouldn't be too worried about finding Mr. Right. On the other hand, maybe she should be more worried.

"My house is really coming together," Sabrina told her as they got out of the car. "I think I'll be ready for company in a few days."

"That's great."

"So what are you doing today?" Sabrina asked as they stood in the driveway. "Any big plans?"

"My dad and his girlfriend are coming for lunch."

"Ooh, that sounds fun. Something with family." Sabrina smiled but her eyes looked sad. "I won't keep you. I better check on Tootsie."

Sabrina was already across the street when Daphne called out to her. "Hey, do you want to join us?"

"You mean have lunch with you and your family?" she called back hopefully.

"Sure. It's at one. Want to come?"

"I'd love to! And I'll bring something. What can I bring? I don't mind running to the store either."

"I'm just grilling chicken," Daphne said. "And fixing a green salad."

"How about if I pick up some dessert?"

Daphne nodded. "That'd be great. I hadn't planned anything, but my dad will be thrilled." As she went into the house, she wasn't sure that inviting Sabrina was such a good idea. Usually lunch with her dad was their special time. But since he'd insisted on bringing his girlfriend today . . . well, maybe it didn't matter. It wasn't that Daphne didn't like Karen. Mostly she was just unsure as to Karen's intentions. At first she'd assumed that Karen was only pursuing Dad for her own real estate gain. But after the purchase of his condo unit and the sale of his house, Karen was still sticking around. So maybe Daphne was wrong about her. Still, she'd never crashed one of their lunches before.

Sabrina showed up at a quarter to one. "I hope you don't mind I came early. I thought maybe you could use help."

"Sure, that'd be nice."

Sabrina held up the pink box. "Boston cream pie."

"Oh my goodness. Dad loves that!"

"And I left Tootsie at home," Sabrina said as they went into the kitchen. "I thought you might appreciate that."

"Thank you. A little dog underfoot can be troublesome . . . especially with older people."

"Is your daddy elderly?"

"Not exactly. I mean he's seventy-two, but he's a young seventy-two."

"And his girlfriend?"

"Karen's pushing sixty. But she keeps herself up pretty well. She could pass for fifty."

"That's so cute." Sabrina set the pink bakery box on the counter. "Your daddy having a girlfriend."

Daphne frowned as she returned to chopping a cucumber. "I guess . . ."

"You don't like his girlfriend?"

"Maybe I just don't know her well enough." Daphne pointed to a colander of loose-leaf lettuce and spinach. "Would you mind rinsing that for me?"

"Not at all."

As they worked together, Daphne told Sabrina about how her mom died when Daphne was young. "It was like I forced myself to grow up—probably too soon—and I tried to handle the housekeeping and cooking." She sighed. "In fact, it was only here—at Aunt Dee's house—that I felt like I got to be a child."

"Your aunt sounds like she was a wonderful lady."

Daphne scraped the cucumber slices into a bowl. She hadn't

confided the true status of Aunt Dee to Sabrina yet. But since it was no longer a secret, she would go ahead and tell the story. At least that part of the story.

"So your Aunt Dee was really your *grandmother*." Sabrina just shook her head. "Very interesting."

"Which explains why she left everything to me."

"You mean *if* you secure a husband by May," Sabrina reminded.

"Yeah."

"Does your dad know about that part of the will?"

"No. And that's exactly how I want to keep it. My dad was already playing matchmaker with me when I first came here. He needs no extra encouragement."

"Really? Did he have some good prospects?"

"Just Ricardo. Dad loves Ricardo."

"Hmm . . . maybe Daddy knows best."

Daphne pointed out the kitchen window, where a yellow convertible Mustang was pulling in front of the house. "That's them now. Let's change the subject, okay?"

"You got it, honey."

Hugs and greetings were exchanged and Daphne quickly made introductions. "Sabrina, can you get them something to drink while I put the chicken on the barbecue? There's lemonade and iced tea in the fridge."

"I'm on it," Sabrina cheerfully assured her.

As Daphne carried the platter of marinated chicken breasts outside, she was grateful for Sabrina joining them today. Not only was she a good conversationalist, she was a great buffer too. And for some reason whenever Karen was around, Daphne felt she needed a buffer. As she laid the chicken on the hot grill, she wondered what Aunt Dee would say about Dad and Karen. Would she suspect that Daphne was simply jealous and overprotective? Would she be supportive of what seemed a blooming romance? Perhaps Daphne needed to write to Dear Daphne for advice on this one.

Back in the kitchen, the three of them were chatting merrily. As Daphne rinsed her hands, she heard Sabrina let out a little shriek. "Oh my goodness!" she exclaimed. "What a lovely piece of ice!"

Confused, Daphne turned around to see Sabrina holding Karen's left hand in her hand, staring at what appeared to be a very big engagement ring. *"What?"* Daphne glanced at Dad, but he just made a sheepish shrug. "Dad? Is there something you want to tell me?"

"As a matter of fact . . ." He chuckled. "I asked Karen to marry me last week. As you can see, she agreed."

"As usual, the master of understatement," Karen teased him.

"So . . . you . . . you're really getting married, then?" Daphne said uneasily.

"Yes. Karen wants to have the wedding in autumn," Dad told her.

"I was thinking early November would be fun," Karen said. "A fall wedding with rich fall colors—golds and russets and plums. Don't you think that would be pretty?"

"That sounds absolutely beautiful," Sabrina said. "I can just imagine the gorgeous flowers."

"It wouldn't be a big wedding," Karen explained. "We're both beyond that at this stage of the game. But I'd like it to be pretty . . . and memorable." She looked fondly at Dad. "I don't plan on doing this again. Not anytime soon, that is." She laughed.

He grinned at her. "You just tell me when and where, Karen, and I'll be there." He turned to Daphne. "I didn't mean to spring it on you quite like this. But I hope you're as happy about it as I am."

"Yes," she said a bit unsteadily. "Of course, I am. If you're happy, I'm happy. Congratulations—to both of you."

"Oh my, November is not that far off," Sabrina said to Karen. "Are you sure that's enough time?"

"I plan to send out a save-the-date note next week. *If* we can pinpoint the date." Karen looked at Daphne. "Do you have any conflicts in November? Any trips planned?"

Daphne shook her head as she poured dressing over the big bowl of green salad. "Not at all. I'll be around."

"Oh good. Then I think I'll go with the first Saturday of November." Karen flipped through the calendar hanging on the fridge, then took a pen and circled the day. "There. That way you won't forget."

"Daphne wouldn't forget her own father's wedding," Dad said.

"No, of course not." Daphne pasted a bright smile onto her face. "I thought we could move this outside. I've set the backyard table for lunch. It's lovely out there in the shade."

She led her small procession out to the backyard. This was good news. Really, it was. She had often worried about Dad being alone in his old age. Of course, that was when she lived far off in New York. But even so, she was happy for him. She really was! Really.

Chapter 9

Daphne had never enjoyed feeling confused. Even as a child, she'd gone to great lengths to eliminate the underlying causes of confusion—demons like chaos and disorder and uncertainty. Whether it was laying out her clothes for school the night before, or writing the weekly menu plan for her and Dad, she was usually on top of it. These habits continued into adulthood. Sometimes to the extent that she worried she might be a borderline control freak or even suffer from OCD.

However, she'd felt much more relaxed since coming to Appleton. And really, she made significant strides in the art of "letting go." She'd even started to think of herself as fairly laid-back. Until recently that is. Recently she'd been concerned that she was returning to her old ways.

So as she often did, she wrote a letter to Dear Daphne. Oh, she was fully aware of the foolishness of these letters—at least to someone who wouldn't understand. And although she was thinking of Aunt Dee when she wrote the responses, Aunt Dee was not communicating to her from the grave. But to her these letters were cathartic and therapeutic. And they always went into a special private file for her eyes only.

> *Dear Daphne,*
> *For some reason I feel as if a fuzzy blanket of confusion is lying upon me. I am wishy-washy and torn over the simplest of choices. This morning it took me thirty minutes to make up my mind whether I wanted eggs or granola with yogurt. Eventually I settled for a piece of toast. It's like my mind is muddled and confused. At first I thought it was because I was recently disappointed in love. Then I thought it was because my dad's getting married. Now I wonder if I'm just putting too much pressure on myself to find Mr. Right and get married too. Please advise.*
> *Befuddled and Bewildered*
>
> *Dear B & B,*
> *Assuming your condition isn't medically related (and I have reason to believe this is true), I encourage you to take a quick inventory of yourself. Are you feeling anxious? Anxiety can lead to confusion. If you're anxious, ask yourself what's behind it. Often anxiety is simply feeling like you've lost control of a situation. Perhaps that's how you feel about your broken relationship, as well as your father's upcoming marriage. You also mention that you feel "torn," which sounds as if you're divided in some way. The*

*Bible describes a double-minded person as very
unstable—think train wreck. If your anxiety stems
from being unable to control things, focus on what
you can actually control. The list is usually very short.
You can control things like what you eat for breakfast
or whether to take a walk—in other words, you
control yourself. But you cannot control other people.
Not even God does that! The sooner you accept this
lack of control, the less confused you will be.*

Daphne

She saved the letters in her private file, then taking her own advice, she did something within her control. She went for a walk. She wasn't really sure where she was going, but after a few minutes she decided to walk to town and pick up a few things. With her basil coming in so well, she longed for some linguini with pesto.

"Hello, Truman," she said as she went into The Apple Basket. "How's it going?"

"Pretty good." He grinned from behind the counter. "But I haven't seen much of you lately. Where you been hiding yourself?"

"I haven't been in as much because my garden's been providing so well." She told him about her canning day with Mrs. Terwilliger. "My pantry looks like I'm set for winter."

He made a mock frown. "Pretty soon you won't need me at all."

"No way. Just so you know, I've given up canning. And I'm not into growing and grinding my own wheat yet. Or making homemade olive oil. Or growing pine nuts."

He laughed. "That might be a challenge."

"Which is why I'm here. I've got lots of basil and—"

"You are making pesto!" he finished. "And if you need some olive oil, you should try this." He held up a dark bottle. "I just started carrying some of this extra-virgin stone-pressed oil from Italy that's really special. Want a sample?"

They were talking about gardens and food and recipes, and Truman told her about a veggie quiche he'd made for his mom's bunko club. "It was killer, if I do say so myself."

She smacked her lips. "You are going to make some lucky girl a fine husband someday, Truman Walters."

He gave her a sly grin. "And how about you?"

She tried not to act shocked—was he flirting with her? Or had she simply misunderstood? "Well . . . uh . . . yes," she stammered, "I might make some man a good wife someday too. Although not everyone is as appreciative of cooking as you and me." She smiled as he handed her the receipt.

"Enjoy that pesto," he called out as she was leaving.

"Thanks. And I'll bring you in some of that surplus basil too."

Next she went to Bernie's Blooms to see if Olivia was around. "She's making a delivery," Stella told her as she set a tall bucket of sunflowers next to the front door. "She should be back soon."

"I'll just look around while I wait," Daphne said.

"Sure." Stella pointed to a table near the counter. "Check out the new linens we just got in. They're really retro. Straight out of the forties and fifties."

As Daphne was perusing the linens, gathering a small collection for her kitchen as well as some for a housewarming gift for Sabrina, Olivia came into the shop. "Hey, Daph, I was just thinking of you." Olivia reached out for a hug. "I hope we're still friends."

"Of course we're still friends." Daphne frowned. "Why wouldn't we be?"

Olivia gave her a half smile, then turned to call out for Stella. "Can you manage the shop for a while longer? I want to take Daphne to lunch." She peered at Daphne. "If that's okay with you? I mean it is lunchtime."

Daphne laughed. "You're right, it is. I'd love to have lunch with you."

"No problem," Stella called out as she emerged from the back room.

"Eat my leftover pasta, if you want," Olivia told her. "It's in the fridge."

"Thanks." Stella reached out for the linens in Daphne's arms. "Want me to hang on to those until you come back?"

"Sure." Daphne handed them over.

"Midge's okay?" Olivia asked as they went out the door.

"Perfect."

"Good." Olivia linked her arm into Daphne's as they crossed the street. "I'm really sorry for how I laid into you the other night."

"That's okay."

"No, it's not okay. Jeff overheard me and after I hung up, he assured me that I was perfectly horrible to you."

"Oh . . . you were just concerned."

Olivia rolled her eyes. "I'm glad you're so gracious." She nodded to an outdoor table. "Want to sit out here?"

"Absolutely."

After they were seated, Ricardo came out. "Hello, ladies." He smiled at them, then looked directly at Daphne. "You're both looking lovely today."

Olivia laughed. "You must have overlooked me, Ricardo. I am a mess."

Daphne looked more closely at Olivia. With her pale face and dark shadows beneath her eyes, combined with her faded T-shirt and old jeans, she wasn't really looking her best.

"You are always lovely, Olivia," Ricardo assured her.

Olivia shrugged. "Anyway, you're right about Daphne. She *does* look good, doesn't she?"

Ricardo nodded but looked slightly embarrassed as he handed them their menus. "Would you like beverages?"

They told him their order and he nodded with a stiff smile. "I'll send Kellie out to take your order." He peered at Daphne. "You will not have to wait forever this time."

She just laughed. "That's okay. Olivia and I have some catching up to do."

His smile grew more natural. "Thanks."

As he went inside, Olivia tilted her head toward the door. "Now seriously, Daph. What is wrong with that guy? If I wasn't happily married, I'd be going after him myself. And I saw him looking at you. Can't you tell he likes you? I know he wants to ask you out. But it seems like you're always unavailable. And trust me, he knows it."

"Oh my." Daphne took in a big breath. "That's a lot to take in."

Olivia looked sheepish. "Sorry, I didn't mean to go off on you like that. Good grief, that is exactly why I wanted to talk to you. I'm sorry for being so over-the-top the other night. And I want to explain what's—"

"Here you go, kiddos." Kellie set their drinks on the table with a big smile. "Ready to order yet?"

They scrambled a bit, trying to figure out what they wanted, but before long Kellie was on her way. "She seemed extra attentive," Daphne observed.

"Yeah. Ricardo probably read the riot act to her last week."

Daphne studied Olivia as she took a sip of her iced tea. "Are you feeling okay?" she asked as she set the glass down.

Olivia let out a long sigh. "That's what I want to talk to you about."

Daphne remembered how Olivia's older sister Bernadette had been struck down with cancer several years ago. "What's *wrong*?" Daphne asked in a weak voice.

"Nothing is really *wrong*," Olivia said quietly. "I've just been feeling a little under the weather the past couple of weeks."

"Have you been to the doctor?"

She shook her head. "No, not yet."

"But what if it's—"

"I took an EPT last week."

"Huh?"

"It's a home pregnancy test."

"Oh?" Daphne felt a surge of hope.

She nodded. "Yep. I am. I took the test several times. I couldn't believe it."

"That's wonderful! Congratulations!" Daphne remembered her best friend Beverly back in New York . . . and how she was pregnant too. And how her pregnancy had pushed Daphne to the back burner. Still, Daphne didn't want to go there. *Remember, you cannot control this.*

"It is wonderful," Olivia said. "Jeff is over the moon."

"I'll bet."

"But I've been a mess." Olivia frowned.

"Why?"

"At first I thought I had some kind of summer flu. But it was only in the morning, then I was pretty much okay."

"Morning sickness?"

She nodded. "And then I've had these crazy mood swings." She held up her hands helplessly. "Which I think is why I went off on you that night at The Zeppelin and then later on the phone."

"Oh, now that you mention it, it did seem odd. Out of character."

"My hormones have been running amuck on me."

"Well, all is forgiven, Olivia." Daphne smiled. "I'm so happy for you."

"I'm happy too." Olivia shook her head. "That is when I'm not having a crying jag."

"I'm sorry. That must be hard."

"It should get better soon. They say it doesn't usually last beyond the first trimester."

"When's the baby due?"

"First week of March." Olivia lowered her voice as a couple sat at the table nearest them. "But we're keeping it under our hats. Even our parents don't know."

"Well, I'm honored you told me."

"Jeff said I should, in order to explain my craziness the other night." She laughed. "It was bizarre, like I thought I was your mother or something—trying to protect you from the Aussie boys. Later on that night, I had a good cry over it."

Daphne reached over to pat Olivia's hand. "Thanks. I really appreciate that you love me that much."

Ricardo brought their food out to them, carefully arranging it on the table, then remaining for a long moment. "It's good to see you two together," he finally said. "Something comforting about old friendships that survive the years. You know?"

"I do know," Daphne said.

Olivia nodded.

"Well, enjoy." He gave her a slightly sad smile as he tipped his head and left. "Bon appétit."

"Was that odd?" Daphne asked Olivia after he was gone.

Olivia frowned. "Yeah . . . sort of. Did Ricardo seem unhappy to you?"

"Maybe . . . a little."

"I'll have to ask Jeff to talk to him, see what's going on."

"Maybe Kellie's driving him nuts," Daphne said in a joking tone.

Olivia laughed. "You could be right."

As Daphne walked home from town, she was thinking about Ricardo. Was it possible Olivia was right? Could Ricardo have some interest in her? Or was there another reason he was feeling blue? She walked slowly by his mother's house. She hadn't seen much of Maria recently. Was she having some health problems?

As Daphne reached her own yard, she peered into the free produce box to see there were still a few items in it. Had Maria been by? And if not, why not? If anyone in the neighborhood enjoyed cooking, it was Maria. So Daphne dropped off her groceries on the porch, then went back to the garden to fill a basket with some surplus produce. She marched it down the street to the Martoni home and knocked on the door.

"Daphne!" Maria Martoni said happily. "What a pleasant surprise."

"I brought you some things from my garden."

"Oh, you dear girl." Maria peered into the basket. "How beautiful. Thank you so much!"

"I've had the free-produce box in my front yard," Daphne explained, "but I haven't noticed you picking anything up. I thought perhaps you were under the weather or something."

"Oh no, I've been fine. Just a little housebound lately. I've been working on a quilting project."

"You're a quilter?"

"I'm still learning. I took it up several years ago. Would you like to see my current project?"

"I'd love to."

Maria led her through the dimly lit house. It looked exactly as Daphne remembered since childhood. From the crucifix on the wall by the stairs to the forest-green floral furnishings in the front room. "I turned the downstairs bedroom into my quilting room." Maria opened the door to a bright and inviting room. "Better light in here."

"I can see that."

Maria picked up a quilt top in a rainbow of colors that seemed to spiral around and around. She proudly spread it out over a twin-sized bed. "This is my latest creation."

"It's beautiful. So colorful."

"It's called 'round the world," Maria explained. "It's not the most complicated design, but I like how the colors look."

"It's very cheerful."

Maria nodded. "I plan to give it to Ricardo for his birthday in September. He always says that someday he'll go around the world. Maybe he can dream about it while sleeping under this." She glanced at Daphne. "Do you think he'll like it? Or is it too feminine? Be honest with me now. It won't hurt my feelings."

"I don't think it's too feminine at all. It's gorgeous and bright and cheerful. I cannot imagine him not liking it."

"Oh good. Sometimes I just don't understand what young people like these days."

Daphne chuckled. "You're not the only one. I get confused too."

Maria pointed at her. "But you *are* a young person. Surely you know how the young folks think."

Daphne shook her head. "Not as much as it would seem."

Maria's brow creased. "Here is what I do not understand, Daphne. I do not understand how all of you young people can be happy . . . living single and being alone. I was married at eighteen. For more than thirty years I had my dear Lorenzo sleeping by my side. He's been gone more than seven years, and I still miss him every day."

"I'm sorry. I'm sure you do."

"But you kids these days. You think nothing of being in your thirties and still not married. And what about having children?" Maria looked truly distressed. "Do you know that Ricardo will be thirty-six? *Thirty-six!* When I was thirty-six, Ricardo was in high school!" She shook her head. "No, I do not understand."

"I guess we're just not in a big hurry." But even as Daphne said this, she felt like a phony.

"But don't you get lonely? Living in your aunt's big house all by yourself? It seems so lonely. I know how lonely I get." She sighed. "I just don't understand it."

Daphne hugged her. "Well, don't be too worried. Ricardo is a wonderful guy. I'm sure it's just a matter of time before the right girl comes along."

She sighed again. "I just hope he notices when she does. Sometimes I worry that he still misses Bernadette too much . . . that he will never get over losing her . . . that I'll never have grandchildren."

To distract Maria as well as change the subject, Daphne told her about her dad and Karen's engagement as they walked to the front door. "So you see, if my dad can find someone after missing my mom for all those years, surely Ricardo will too. You'll see."

Maria nodded hopefully. "I'm sure you must be right. I don't know why I get so worked up about it."

"Especially since it doesn't help. I know for a fact since I tend to worry about things I can't control sometimes. We're better off praying about it, don't you think?"

Maria smiled as she opened the door. "You're right. For a young person, you've got your head on straight. Now if you would just get married and have children!" She laughed as she waved good-bye.

As Daphne walked home, she thought about how lonely Maria had sounded. And yet she was usually so cheerful and positive. But of course, she was expressing concern for Ricardo, identifying with him. Daphne got to her own yard and noticed Wally crossing the street back over to his house. In his arms was some produce. She smiled as she went up the porch steps. It was sweet seeing him help himself.

As she went inside, it hit her—two older single people, both widowed, both lonely, both living just a few houses apart. Was it possible they had never met? And if not, why not?

Chapter 10

So I finally get everything put away and in order, and I wanted to start planning a little shindig," Sabrina told Daphne on Friday morning. "But now my backyard is all torn apart." She shook her head as she looked across the street. "I hope they're done with the heavy equipment, Tootsie is turning into a real basket case."

"He's not the only one suffering." Daphne picked up one of the cinnamon rolls Sabrina had brought over to share on the porch.

"I'm sorry. Is the noise bothering you too?"

"Not as much as it's bothering Wally."

"That old grump?" Sabrina frowned. "It's partly his own silly fault that my yard's torn to smithereens. If he hadn't complained."

"Yes, but you needed a fence," Daphne reminded her. "Plus, hasn't the landscaping project allowed you to see a lot of Mick this past week?"

Sabrina smiled as she sipped her coffee.

"And I told Wally it would soon be done and the permanent fence would be up, and hopefully he will have nothing to complain about then."

"Did you figure out a way to get him and Ricardo's mama together yet?"

Daphne shook her head. "I mentioned her to him, and he basically told me to mind my own business."

"Old curmudgeon."

"I think he's just lonely . . . misses his wife."

"Then why doesn't he want to get acquainted with Maria? She is perfectly delightful."

"Well, I haven't given up on them. I'm trying to think of a reason to invite some of the neighbors over. I was even considering using you as an excuse."

"Moi?"

"Sort of a 'let's welcome the new neighbor' get-together. Maybe a potluck picnic."

"Or maybe I should invite everyone to an open house after my backyard is completed. It's going to be so pretty out there with the pond and fountain and outdoor kitchen and everything. I can't wait to show it off."

"I like that idea. You host the party and I'll help you."

"Mick says he'll be done by late next week," Sabrina said. "You suppose the neighbors would mind if I invited him? And maybe his crew too?"

"It's your party. Invite whomever you like."

"And if I invite Mick, I can't leave out Collin." She gave Daphne a sly look. "Mick confided to me that Collin delayed his flight in order to spend more time with *you*—under the code of silence, if you get my meaning."

Daphne made a stiff smile. It wasn't that she was displeased Collin had extended his visit. It was more that she felt pressured now, as if she needed to perform or something. And she'd never been good at performing.

"Mick said Collin will be back from his sightseeing trip later today. It sounds like he drove about a thousand miles this past week. Really packing it all in."

"I'll say. The poor guy will be all worn out."

"He better not be too worn out for tomorrow night. I'm really looking forward to the Founder's Day dance and barbecue."

"So we're still on for that?"

"We most certainly are. And I don't know if you've thought about what you're wearing, but I think you should wear that teal sundress. It's got the perfect skirt for dancing."

"Well, it's been warm enough in the evenings. Maybe I will."

"And your espadrilles too."

"So nice having my own private fashion consultant right across the street."

Sabrina ignored Daphne's sarcasm by telling her what accessories to wear. "And pin your hair up the way the stylist showed you last week." She stood and smoothed her glossy blonde hair. "Guess my work here is done now. I better go home and check on Mick."

Daphne couldn't help but chuckle as Sabrina trotted across the street in her kitten-heeled sandals. Such a Southern belle. But in the short two weeks that Daphne had gotten to know Sabrina, she knew that some of those Southern belle's feminine ways were rubbing off on Daphne. And perhaps that wasn't such a bad thing. Even Olivia, when not suffering a mood swing, had to acknowledge the improvements.

On Saturday, Daphne and Sabrina went to the mile-long antique sale together. Sabrina was on the lookout for some accent pieces for her backyard, and Daphne was just looking for the fun of it. But as they were examining an old enamel bed frame, Daphne got a feeling she was being watched. When she looked up she saw Jake on the other side of the street. At first she felt awkward, but then why? So she waved and he came over to say hello, and she introduced him to Sabrina.

"I almost didn't recognize you," Jake told her. "Something about you seems different."

Daphne shrugged. "It's probably just the straw hat and sunglasses. Trying to ward off the sun."

He smiled. "Well, you look good anyway."

"Did you have a nice vacation?" she asked a bit stiffly. "Mattie told me you went to the lake."

"Yes . . . I meant to tell you about that."

"I don't see why." She waved her hand. "It sounds like a pretty fun place. I hope you had a good time."

"It is a pretty place. We have three cabins right on the water. They've been in my family since I was a kid. We go up there the first two weeks of August every year. Nice little break." His brow creased slightly. "I—uh—I would've called you, but we don't get cell-phone service. It's actually kind of nice being cut off for a while. Jenna went through texting withdrawal. But I think that's a good thing."

"Well, unless you have an emergency." Daphne didn't know why she said that. Just trying to fill space.

"There is a landline in one cabin. And my assistant has the number in case a client needs to reach me."

Daphne brightened her smile. "Well, this client did not need to reach you. But it's good to know you're available if something comes up. And I'm glad you had fun. Now if you will excuse me." She pointed to where Sabrina was examining an old ice-cream maker.

"We're on a mission here." Okay, that wasn't exactly true, but she did not want to prolong this uncomfortable conversation for one more minute.

"How did that go?" Sabrina asked quietly as they put their heads together, pretending to be studying the hand-crank machine.

"Okay . . . I guess." She sighed. "Awkward."

"He's good looking."

Daphne just nodded, trying out the crank. "It works."

"Are you sure he's not still interested in you?"

"You know the story," she said quietly. "Vacationing with the ex . . . what does that mean? It's over. I get it. Moving on."

"Well, good." Sabrina turned away from the ice-cream maker. "I know one Aussie bloke who will be very glad to hear that."

Daphne followed Sabrina's fashion direction to the *T*. Even taking time to loosely pin up her hair. It took a couple of tries to get it just the way the hairdresser in Fairview had done, but finally she was satisfied.

"You look fabulous," Sabrina told Daphne as they met on the porch.

"So do you," Daphne assured her. "Ready?"

"Yes." Sabrina held up her phone. "Mick just texted me that they're saving a table in the beer garden."

As they got into Daphne's car, she felt relieved that she'd insisted on driving tonight. Sabrina had questioned this. "It doesn't seem like a real date if they don't pick us up at home," she'd protested.

"Well, it's the only way I'm going," Daphne replied. Daphne's thinking at the time was that if she wasn't having a good time, she would have an easy way out. But hearing they were waiting in the beer garden made her glad to have her own wheels. Not that she thought they'd get inebriated. But on the other hand, she didn't know that they wouldn't. And she would rather be safe than sorry.

The Founder's Day celebration was mostly being held in the Appleton City Park, but the closest parking place Daphne could find was down near the bank where her dad worked, which meant they had to walk a few blocks. Sabrina complained a little, but as they got closer and could hear the music playing, she cheered up.

Before long they were seated at the table with Mick and Collin. The guys were just finishing their first beers and offered to get another round for the table.

"None for me." Daphne didn't like being judgmental about drinking, but she personally did not care to imbibe. It was simply how she'd been raised.

"I'm not much of a beer drinker," Sabrina said, "but I suppose I could give it a try."

"That's a good girl," Mick told her.

"What would you like?" Collin asked Daphne. "A Coke or something?"

"Just water is fine."

He looked slightly disappointed but went off with Mick to get in the drinks line. When they returned, Daphne was feeling slightly aggravated. Not so much over the beer drinking. But because she was hungry. "That barbecued pork sure smells good," she said to no one in particular.

"It is." Mick nodded. "I still remember tasting it when I was passing through Appleton. I was charmed by the small town festival."

"It was Founder's Day the first time you came here?" Daphne asked.

"Yeah. I'd already been wowed by the agricultural potential. But I still think that pulled pork helped to cinch the deal."

"I haven't been home for Founder's Day in ages." She looked longingly toward where they were cooking the pork. "I hope they don't run out."

"It's still early," Collin assured her. "And I took a sneak peek at the pits. Looks like they've got plenty of food over there."

"But look at that line." Daphne pointed out the people already waiting for food. "Hey, maybe I should go get in line. I could save everyone a place."

"That's not a bad idea." Mick said.

"Yes, and all this talk of food is making me hungry too," Sabrina told her. "Go save us a place, Daph. We'll be along soon."

Daphne felt relieved to leave the table. She wasn't even sure why. Perhaps it was just her. Or maybe it was the beer. But for some reason she just didn't feel like she fit in with the Aussie boys tonight. As she waited in line, she looked over to where the band was playing. A few older couples were dancing, as well as some children, but the dance floor wouldn't get really full until later. Since childhood she had loved seeing the outdoor dance floor with the strings of colored lanterns gently waving in the evening breeze, couples out there enjoying the music, the night, each other. It was all very romantic.

She glanced back over to the beer garden to see that Mick, Collin, and Sabrina were laughing together. Sabrina was probably entertaining them with her usual Southern charm. Or perhaps the Aussies were sharing stories. But Daphne felt a definite disconnect— from her group as well as the celebration in general. As she stood in line, she didn't even see a familiar face nearby. If she just vanished into thin air—*poof*—she doubted anyone would really notice.

As she got closer to the front of the line, the others finally joined her. They seemed even merrier than before, and unless Daphne wanted to ruin this evening for everyone, she had better play along. But that was how she felt. Like she was playacting.

Fortunately the food was as good as she remembered, and she started to relax as the four of them joked and chatted. And she almost didn't feel like she was pretending so much. She wasn't having as much fun as she had last week at The Zeppelin, but it wasn't so bad either. And now she started seeing people she knew, and they even made room at their table for Olivia and Jeff to join them. And later, because the tables were all crowded, they made room for her dad and Karen to sit as well.

Dad seemed curious as to her relationship with Collin, but thankfully he didn't say anything about it. However, she did tell the others about her dad and Karen's recent engagement and everyone lifted their glasses to toast them.

Eventually it was getting dusky and more couples wandered out to the dance floor. However, none of the guys at their table seemed ready to budge.

"All right," Sabrina announced. "Time for ya'll to get off your hind ends and get out there on that dance floor." She patted her midsection. "I don't know about ya'll, but I need to work off all those scrumptious calories I just devoured. On your feet now, ya hear?"

"We're still finishing our dinner," Dad said.

"But we'll be out there before long," Karen promised.

The rest of them meandered toward the dance floor. But now

Daphne felt uneasy. What if Collin wasn't a dancer? She glanced nervously at him. "You do like to dance, don't you?"

He reached for her hand and nodded eagerly. "You bet I do. I even won a dance contest once . . . down in Melbourne."

And she could understand how that was possible because Collin was a superb dancer. Far better than she. Fortunately he was so good that he made her feel like she was even better than she was. "This is really fun," she told him as they took a break. "I feel like you've greatly improved my dancing skills."

"You're a natural. Stick with me and I'll wager we could win another dance contest if we wanted."

She laughed. "Well, I'm not sure about that."

"Ready for another round?" he asked as the band started a new song.

She nodded and he grabbed her hand, whirling her around in a spin, then catching her in his arms just like it was choreographed. They danced a couple more dances together, then seeing her dad and Karen, Daphne asked if he was open to switching partners. "I haven't danced with my dad in years."

Dad was happy to dance with her, but after just one dance, he asked if they could sit the next one out. "I played eighteen holes today. And I'm just not as young as I used to be."

"No problem," she told him. "I'm not either."

"Looks like Karen's enjoying your fellow."

"Collin is a very good dancer."

"I can see that." Dad's brow creased. "Is this a serious relationship?"

She shook her head. "No. Not at all. Collin is nice and all. But I can't see myself getting serious."

Dad seemed relieved. "I thought you were dating Jake McPheeters. What became of that?"

She shrugged. "We're just friends, Dad."

"Uh-huh."

"Really. He's been helpful with Aunt Dee's estate and a good friend. That's all there is to it. In fact, he might be getting back with his ex."

"Oh?" Dad's bushy brows arched. "I hadn't heard that."

"Well, it's probably a new rumor."

Dad waved at someone, and she looked behind her to see Ricardo coming their way. "Ricardo," Dad said. "Just the man. I was supposed to be dancing with my daughter and I ran out of gas. Any chance you can take over for me?"

Ricardo's eyes lit up. "Sure. You game, Daphne?"

"Absolutely." She stood and followed him to the dance floor. Although he wasn't nearly the dancer Collin was, she actually felt more comfortable dancing with him. Plus he seemed to be genuinely enjoying himself. Just as they were starting their second dance, Collin came looking for her. Ricardo seemed slightly disappointed but politely offered to dance with Karen.

Shortly after they'd exchanged partners, Daphne felt as if someone was watching her. For the second time today, she turned to see Jake staring at her. His expression was hard to read and he quickly looked away—almost as if he didn't want to get caught looking.

As she danced with Collin, she put all her energy into the steps. So much so that she knew she was showing off. As juvenile as it was, she felt certain she was doing this for Jake's benefit. And just admitting that made her feel edgy and agitated. Why did she allow him to affect her like that? Why couldn't she just get over him and move on?

Chapter 11

As the evening wore on, Collin was consuming more beer than Daphne felt was reasonable. It wasn't as if he was drunk, but he was certainly jolly . . . and loud. And it made her uncomfortable. As a result, she danced with Ricardo a couple more times and even danced with Truman once. Collin was having such a good time, he barely seemed to notice.

Then as she was taking a break and thinking about making her exit, Jake came over to speak to her. "You and Sabrina are the belles of the ball tonight," he said in a slightly teasing tone.

"Is there anything wrong with that?" She held her head high.

"No. It looks like you're having fun. I didn't realize you were such a good dancer."

"That's more Collin than me." She pointed to where he was now dancing with Kellie. Although that girl left much to be desired as a waitress, she did know how to move on the dance floor. "He's a great dancer. He can make anyone look good."

"I suppose all that beer helps loosen up the legs." Jake gave her a curious sideways glance, and she suspected he was testing her.

She simply shrugged, suppressing the urge to defend herself. Let him think what he wanted. Why should she care?

"No offense, Daphne, but I didn't realize you were into all that. I never thought of you as the party-girl type."

She narrowed her eyes. "I am *not* the party-girl type, thank you very much."

"That's a relief. Because Dee had higher expectations for you than that. I'd hate to see you let her down."

"Are you trying to advise me about my dating life now?"

"Well, I am your legal counsel." He gave an uneasy smile.

"So was that part of your responsibility when you crafted Aunt Dee's will? Were you expected to approve the guys I go out with?"

"No, no, of course not. But as your aunt's attorney, I can't help but have a concerned interest." He tipped his head to the dance floor where Collin and Kellie had taken center stage. The couple was dancing in a very intimate manner. In a way Daphne found unsettling.

She tried to conceal her discomfort as she turned back to face Jake. "Thank you for *caring*," she said coolly. She was ready to go home now. Even if Sabrina insisted on staying, Daphne was done.

"It's just that I remember how Ryan was. How he tried to take advantage of your trusting nature. I don't want to see that happen again."

"*Really?* And what do you intend to do about it?" She tossed her half-full soda cup into the trash barrel. She was so out of here.

Jake shrugged. "There's not much I *can* do about it. But as your friend, I hope you'll trust me. And, at least for Dee's sake, you should realize I only have your best interests at heart." He gave her a small smile, but his eyes seemed sad. "You can trust me, Daphne."

Now she was torn. On one hand, she wanted to tell him to butt out and go back to his ex-wife and just leave her alone. On the other hand, she treasured his friendship—more than she cared to admit. "Thank you," she said quietly. "I will keep that in mind. And now, if you'll excuse me, I'm ready to call it a night."

"You don't want to make one last trip round the dance floor?"

"Huh?" She frowned at him, then looked back to where Collin was still dancing with Kellie—looking into her eyes as if she was the only female on the planet.

"I mean *with me*," he said quietly.

She took in a deep breath and slowly let it out. "Sure, why not."

The band, which was probably getting tired by now, had ended the last number and was just starting a slow song as they reached the floor. But before they began to dance, Collin came over. "There you are, Daphne. I've been looking all over for you." He peered at Jake. "Hey, mate, mind if I dance with my date?"

Jake shook his head. "Not at all."

As Collin took Daphne into his arms, she watched Jake walk away. Would he invite another girl to dance with him? But he just kept going, and unless it was her imagination, sadness lumbered his steps.

On Wednesday morning, Daphne took her coffee out to the garden. Sabrina would probably be watching for her to be on the front porch, hoping to bring her coffee over to join her. But today Daphne just wanted to be alone with her thoughts. As much as she liked Sabrina, sometimes her nonstop chatter was just too much. Especially in the morning.

She was just finishing up when the garden gate creaked. Worried that it might be Sabrina, she actually considered hiding behind the raspberry bushes.

"Good day," called a male voice with a distinct Australian accent.

Daphne cringed. Hopefully it wasn't Collin. She'd been trying to avoid him since Saturday night. She believed that he'd shown her his true colors. As a result her interest in him had dwindled considerably. But she wasn't sure how to let him know. Holding her breath, she peered around the corner and was relieved to see it was only Mick.

"Oh, it's you."

"That's not a very cheery welcome." He sat in the chair across from her. "That the best you can do for your garden guy?"

She smiled. "Actually, I was glad it was you." Now she frowned. "I was afraid it was Collin."

"So you've gone cold on my mate?"

She gave him a sheepish shrug. "Sort of."

He nodded. "I reckon I knew that."

"He's just not my type, Mick. He's a nice guy and all that, but he's not really for me."

"Too bad." He shook his head. "Old Collin thinks the world of you."

"Oh dear."

"What is it that you don't like about him, Daph?"

She thought hard. "To be honest, the biggest problem for me is the beer drinking. I'm just not like that."

"Ah . . . I see."

She peered at him. "I didn't even think you were like that, Mick."

He chuckled. "Well, I'm not as much like that as I used to be. Back in Sydney, I mean. You do understand that Australia is the beer-drinking capital of the world, don't you?"

She laughed. "I might've heard that before."

"I really cut back after moving to the States. Not completely, mind you. But I like having a clear head in the morning. Helps me to focus on my work." He set his thermal coffee cup on the table. "Having Collin around has been a bit of a challenge for me too."

For some reason this was reassuring.

"Collin likes his beer." Mick gave her an uncertain look. "And he likes the sheilas too. I reckon you noticed."

She nodded. "He's a fun guy. And interesting too. But I felt like I saw a different side of him . . . and, well, I just know it would never work."

"Can't say I'm surprised."

"I don't suppose you could let Collin know that I'm not, uh, that into him, could you?"

Mick frowned. "I learned long ago that the best way to keep a mate a mate is not to interfere with his love life. Sorry, Daph, you'll have to sort this one out yourself."

She sighed.

"While we're on this topic, I should let you know that I'm not as interested in your neighbor as she appears to be in me." He glanced over his shoulder as if he thought Sabrina might be lurking in the bushes. "In fact, I ducked over here to get away from her." He shook his head. "I reckon that little sheila could talk the leg off of a mule."

Daphne laughed. "That's why I'm back here too."

He chuckled. "We are quite a pair, aren't we?"

She nodded. "But there is a comfort knowing you're in the same boat. You know what they say—misery loves company."

"Yeah. And I already promised Sabrina that Collin and I would come to her house for a barbecue this Friday. I can't think of an easy way out of that one. I know you're supposed to be there too."

"Fortunately, she's inviting a lot of other people too. So it's not like a dinner date for four. That would be awful."

"Oh, well, that's a relief. I can deal with a crowd easy enough. No worries."

On Friday afternoon, Daphne went over to help Sabrina prepare for her get-together. "Your backyard looks fabulous," Daphne said as they were setting some things up outside. "So inviting and fun."

"I can't wait until the sun starts going down so I can light all these tiki torches. And even though it's warm, I still plan to turn on the fire pit. Just for ambiance. Won't it be lovely?"

"Absolutely." Daphne frowned at the amount of beverages Sabrina was loading into the small outdoor fridge. "Do you think you'll really need all that?"

"Oh yeah." Sabrina stood up straight. "At my last count, more than thirty people are coming. I think it was up to thirty-seven."

"Thirty-seven?" Daphne was stunned. "I didn't realize you knew that many people in town."

Sabrina grimaced. "I'm not sure I really do know them."

"What?"

"Saturday night, at the Founder's Day dance, I guess I invited almost everyone I met. At least that's what Mick told me."

"Seriously?"

Sabrina nodded. "Yeah . . . it's a little embarrassing."

"How do you know all these people are really coming?"

"Apparently, I gave them my phone number, told them to RSVP."

"And they did?"

She nodded as she closed the fridge door. "I didn't even recognize most of the names. I suppose I was a little under the influence that night."

Daphne shook her finger at Sabrina. "I wish I'd known. I could've intervened for you. Friends shouldn't let friends invite drunk."

Sabrina laughed. "Well, I just keep telling myself that these strangers are simply friends I haven't really met."

"Let's hope so."

"And a number of them were your friends too, Daphne. I invited your dad and Karen. As well as our neighbors. So they're not all strangers." She grinned. "And of course, there's Mick and Collin. They're certainly not strangers."

Daphne hadn't really confided to Sabrina about her true feelings for Collin. But perhaps it was time. So she explained the situation.

"You're kidding?" Sabrina frowned. "You're dumping him just because he drinks a little beer?"

"No, it's not just that," Daphne said. "It's the whole thing. He's a nice guy, but he's not the guy for me."

Sabrina just shook her head. "Don't forget that your clock is ticking. Just since I've been here, you've frittered away three weeks on Collin. And now you're saying he's not the guy. At this rate, you might find yourself both man-less and ring-less—by December."

Daphne rolled her eyes. "December isn't the drop-dead date for me."

"If you want to plan a nice wedding it is."

"Maybe I don't care about a nice wedding."

"Seriously?" Sabrina looked doubtful. "But you've never been married before. Why wouldn't you pull out all the stops for one now? Just imagine what a perfect wedding you could have in May. Mick was just telling me which flowers will be in bloom by then."

"That's true, but I'm not sure I care." Daphne set a bowl of tortilla chips on a table. "I think I'd rather focus on having a perfect marriage . . . more than a perfect wedding."

Sabrina patted her on the back. "That's what I really like about you, Daph. So down-to-earth and practical. Not like me. But you're just what I need in my life."

Sabrina was not exaggerating about the number of guests she'd invited. Not only was her lovely backyard full, her house was crawling with people too. Daphne was relieved there were so many. It made it easier to avoid running into Collin. And her most-recent plan for letting him know her true feelings was to keep her distance. She was also keeping her distance from another guest. She'd been surprised to discover Sabrina had invited Jake, but then considering the rest of the guest list, it made perfect sense. Daphne had exchanged a formal but slightly cool greeting with him, then kept herself busy with other people.

"I'm so glad you came," Daphne told Wally shortly after he arrived. She'd gone out of her way to invite him several times this past week, finally persuading him that since Sabrina had made such an effort to contain Tootsie, he could at least make an effort to show a little appreciation. Besides, she'd pointed out, there would be food.

"I don't plan to stay long," he told her as she led him into the house.

"Well, you can't leave before you get something to eat." She linked her arm in his and led him to the dining room where all the food was laid out buffet style. And since he'd arrived late, there was no line. She handed him a plate and pointed out the dishes that were really good. Staying with him as he filled his plate, heaping it high, she chatted pleasantly. Then when he was done, she invited him to come outside. "Just wait until you see what she's done to her yard. It's beautiful."

He glanced around the crowded yard, barely nodding. "It does look better. But where is that nasty rat dog?"

"In a back bedroom. I insisted that it was the kindest thing to do." Daphne giggled. "I think Sabrina may have given him a doggy tranquilizer."

"Too bad she didn't give him a whole bottle."

"Oh, Wally." She gave him a dismal look. "I'm sure you don't mean that."

"There's no place to sit out here," he said with a frown.

"I saved a place for you." She led him over to where Ricardo and his mom were seated at a little table. She'd already clued Ricardo into her little plan and although he was skeptical, he agreed to play along. "Do you know the Martonis?" she asked as they both sat down.

"You run the diner, don't you?" Wally said to Ricardo.

"That's right." Ricardo pointed to his mom. "And this is my mother, Maria. She lives down the street."

Wally nodded to Maria. "I think I've seen you around the neighborhood. Pleased to meet you."

As Wally ate, Daphne explained how he'd been her favorite English teacher. "He actually helped to inspire me to become a writer." She smiled at him and his expression seemed to warm up. "I didn't even realize he was my neighbor. I was living in New York when he'd moved to the neighborhood. I was pleasantly surprised to find he was living just across the street."

"The house belonged to my late wife's parents," he explained. "After she passed on . . . well, I suppose I became somewhat of a hermit."

"Oh, I know what you mean," Maria told him. "I was the same way after my husband died."

"I try to get her to come to the restaurant just to be among people," Ricardo said. "You'd think I could lure her out with a free meal. But the problem is, she's such a good cook, the restaurant doesn't tempt her."

"Nonsense. I eat at your restaurant two to three times a week, Ricardo." Maria explained how she could lose herself in a quilting project. "I get so caught up in it that several days might pass and I realize I haven't left my house."

"That's when I get worried," Ricardo confessed.

"You should be thankful," she told him. "My quilting helps to take my mind off of other things. It's a good escape."

"That's like me and my books," Wally said. "I can read for hours and hours."

"But being isolated like that," Ricardo said to his mom, "doesn't seem healthy to me."

"That's because you're young. You don't understand how older people are." She looked at Wally. "Do you have children who tell you what to do too?"

He smiled. "My daughter. She calls me about every other day to make sure I'm eating right." He forked into the potato salad. "Sometimes I lie to her, just to get her to leave me be."

And suddenly, almost like magic, these two older people were chatting and comparing notes and even laughing together. It seemed that a real friendship was being forged right before Daphne's eyes. Was there romance in the air? Maybe not. But perhaps what these people needed more than that was companionship.

Daphne couldn't help but feel a sense of accomplishment to think that she, in a small way, had helped to facilitate it. Too bad she wasn't more adept at creating such miracles in her own love life.

Chapter 12

"I don't know how to thank you for helping my mother to meet Wally," Ricardo told Daphne on Sunday afternoon. She and Sabrina had come to the diner after church, and it seemed that Ricardo couldn't have been more pleased to see them.

"They really seemed to hit it off, didn't they?" Daphne smiled as he set their iced teas on the outdoor table.

"I had to leave early the other night, to close up here. But Mom came here for breakfast and she looked happy." He grinned. "Truly happy!"

"I'm so glad. And Wally seemed pleased to meet her too. I think that's the first time I've seen a genuine smile on his face. I mean since back in high school."

"It gives me hope," Ricardo told her. "I'm in your debt, Daphne."

She laughed. "No, you're not. I'm just glad two sweet but lonely people have found each other."

"Your lunch is on the house," Ricardo said as he was going.

"But you—"

"No arguing," he said over his shoulder.

"Wow," Sabrina said without enthusiasm. "I'm glad someone is enjoying a happy little romance."

Daphne reached over and patted Sabrina's hand. "Come on, you'll get over this."

Sabrina let out a slow sigh. "I just don't see where I went wrong. Mick and I were having such a good time. I feel totally blindsided."

"Maybe it's just a case of chemistry. Like it was with Collin and me. I just wasn't hearing any bells."

"But I was hearing bells," Sabrina protested. "Every time I saw Mick, my chemistry was working just fine."

"But it's a two-way street, Sabrina."

"Tell me something I don't know." Her lower lip protruded. "I just feel so utterly let down . . . deflated. You know?"

Daphne nodded. "I do know."

Sabrina forced a weak smile. "Yes, I suppose you do. We've both been unlucky in love lately. At least you can commiserate with me. I'm not sure how I'd feel if I thought you and Collin were madly in love and planning your wedding right now."

"Knowing you, I believe you'd be happy for me."

Sabrina's smile grew stronger. "You're right. I would."

"And it's not like you're in any rush to get married," Daphne reminded her. "You don't have any big deadline looming ahead for you, do you?"

"No, of course not. In fact, when my divorce was finalized, I promised myself not to even consider marriage for at least five years." She slid her straw into her tea. "I guess being around you made me think that I needed to hurry things up too." She giggled. "Silly ol' me."

"I think we should both just take a nice little break," Daphne said.

"A break?"

"From being so focused on dating . . . and men . . . don't you think?"

Sabrina laughed. "You won't hear me agreeing to anything like that anytime soon." She pointed into the diner. "And unless I'm mistaken, there's a guy in there who would like to get better acquainted with you. That is, if you would just give him half a chance."

"Ricardo?" Daphne glanced in the window. "He's just grateful for his mom's sake."

"Looked like more than that to me."

"Well, we are friends, Sabrina."

"Friendship seems like a good foundation for romance."

Daphne nodded. "I totally agree."

"Hmm." Sabrina got a thoughtful look. "Speaking of friends, I feel like Collin has been a friend to me. If you're certain you're finished with him . . . maybe I should take the boy out for a spin."

"Really?" Daphne blinked.

"Well, I was so in love with the idea of vacationing in Australia again," she said dreamily. "Seeing it with someone who was from there. Perhaps I was just dreaming about the wrong man."

Daphne tried to wrap her head around this. "You really think you're that interested in Collin?"

"I might be." Sabrina grinned. "He's definitely a good dancer."

"Well, after I told him I didn't see a future for us, he sounded like he'd be heading back to Australia—"

"So you told him after all?" Her expression was a mixture of surprise and hopefulness. "Were you planning to tell me?"

"Sorry. I spoke to him at your little soiree." Daphne shrugged.

"How did Collin take it?"

"He was perfectly fine."

"Oh, good." Sabrina's lips curved into a smile.

"But if you want to make a move on him, you better not waste any time." Daphne said this in a teasing tone, but she could tell by Sabrina's expression that she was already considering it. Really, was she that desperate?

Sabrina wrinkled her nose. "On second thought . . . maybe not."

"Why not?"

She shrugged. "I just remembered Pastor Andrew's sermon. Remember how he talked about not running ahead of God? And how we sometimes do that and mess everything up?"

"Yes. Those were good words."

"Maybe I just need to slow down a little."

Daphne nodded. "You and me both."

"Then what about Jake?" Sabrina asked pointedly.

"What about him?"

"Just before he left the other night . . . I overhead him asking you to meet him for coffee on Tuesday. What's up with that?"

"Oh, that's nothing. Just a business meeting."

"You know that for a fact?"

"I'm pretty sure that's what it is." Daphne replayed their brief conversation from the previous evening. "Jake said he needed to speak to me regarding something in Aunt Dee's will."

"Maybe he wants to declare his undying affection for you and propose marriage. That would have something to do with the will, wouldn't it?"

Daphne rolled her eyes. "I am 100 percent certain that is not going to happen."

"But you'd be happy if it did happen." Sabrina scrutinized her closely. "Wouldn't you?"

Fortunately, Daphne did not have to answer that stupid question because Ricardo was coming out the door with their food. And the truth was, Daphne was unsure. Would that make her happy? Or had she simply imagined it would? As Ricardo chatted amicably, neatly arranging the plates on the small table, Daphne wondered if Sabrina really had picked up on something real. Was Ricardo interested in something beyond friendship with her?

"Thanks, Ricardo," she said warmly. "But you really don't have to comp our meal. I insist you—"

"*Please,* Daphne." He looked directly into her face. "Let this be my thank-you. Even if nothing develops for my mom and Wally, I love that you made the effort. And I know it made her happy. At the very least, she's made a friend." His dark brown eyes implored her. "Please, allow me to express my gratitude."

She smiled. "Well, when you put it like that. How can I possibly refuse?"

"Thank you." He tipped his head. "Enjoy your lunch, ladies."

"See," Sabrina said quietly after he went inside. "If that's not genuine romantic interest, I am completely out of touch."

Daphne just shook her head. Sabrina's determination could be exhausting sometimes. "Time will tell. In the meantime, I'm taking a break. A man break." Naturally Sabrina just laughed.

On Tuesday morning, Daphne walked to town to meet Jake for coffee. Even though it was only late August, she thought she could feel autumn in the air, and she wanted to make the most of the last days of summer. Jake was just getting out of his car when she reached the coffee company.

"Good timing," he said as they met at the door. "How are you?"

"I'm doing well." She waited for him to open the door. "Enjoying this lovely morning."

They ordered their coffees and went to a table in back. Jake had his briefcase with him and she was ready for him to open it and start spreading papers on the table—the way he had done at their first meeting. But instead he set the briefcase under his chair and just looked at her. "I feel like I need to apologize to you."

"Apologize?" She frowned. "For what?"

"I'm not sure exactly. But I think I've offended you somehow. And it seems that every time we talk, I end up offending you even more."

She tilted her head to one side, weighing her words. "Well, you were a little nosy the other night. At the Founder's Day dance."

"You mean by expressing my opinion in regards to your date?"

Unwilling to admit that he'd stepped on her toes—especially since he'd been correct—she simply shrugged.

"I only spoke up because I care about you."

She waited as the barista set their coffees on the table. "Yes, I get that," she said slowly. "And you're worried I'm going to disappoint Aunt Dee somehow. You feel it's your responsibility to see that I don't make a great big fat mess of my life." She sighed. "But honestly, it seems like I haven't done anything too terrible so far. Perhaps you could simply trust me to handle things myself from here on out. Or is that even possible?"

He looked somewhat taken aback. "Wow . . . I guess I really did offend you."

"I'm sorry," she said stiffly. "Now it seems I've offended you."

He peered over his cup of coffee at her. "It's just that I thought . . . well . . . that we were friends."

"I thought so too." She pressed her lips together.

"As your friend, am I out of line to be concerned for your welfare?"

She shook her head, then sipped her coffee. She felt herself softening and wasn't sure that she wanted to.

"And like I said, I believe I have your best interests at heart."

"Yes . . . and so does my dad, but he doesn't meddle with my life nearly as much as you do."

"Ouch." He frowned.

"Sorry, Jake. But I'm a little weary of your big-brother act."

"I understand. But as your aunt's attorney, I feel a responsibility. I see you as a vulnerable woman that could be taken unfair advantage of."

"Yes, well, if you're talking about Collin, rest assured. I sent him packing." She stirred a little more cream into her coffee. "Literally. Yesterday Mick informed me that Collin is booked for Sydney on Saturday." She held her coffee cup in the air. "Happy trails, *mate*."

Jake chuckled. "Well, that's a relief."

She frowned. "So did you really think my taste in guys was that off? That I couldn't figure it out for myself . . . eventually?"

"I didn't know what to think. I was floored when I saw you with him. It just seemed all wrong. I couldn't live with myself if I didn't say something."

"So, will you be shadowing me on all my dates from here on out? Can I expect you to pop up whenever I'm with a guy, expressing your venerated opinion? Because if that's your idea of—"

"Daphne." He shook his head. "I get it. I know you're vexed. And I'm sorry, okay?"

She sighed. "Okay."

"Anyway, I've come up with *another* plan."

She felt an unexplainable surge of hope. Was this about them? "Another plan?"

He nodded. "I've been compiling a list of suitable suitors. Local guys I don't think you've had a chance to meet yet. Respected professionals who—"

"What?"

"It's just because I understand your dilemma, Daphne. I know the pressure you're under to get this figured out. Can't say I blame you either. There's a lot at stake. Anyway, I got to thinking . . . if I'm really your good friend, why wouldn't I help you out in any way I can? We can sort of speed things along."

"Are you totally nuts?"

"Not at all." He looked slightly offended.

"So you want to set me up on dates?" She suppressed the childish urge to dump her coffee over his head. "With other men? *Seriously?*"

"You really think it's a bad idea?" He seemed genuinely hurt. "For a friend to help a friend? Surely you're aware of online-dating websites, where complete strangers match people up. Wouldn't being helped by a trusted friend be a whole lot better? That's how it used to be done—back in the good old days."

"I think you've lost your mind, Jake. And FYI, I have no intention of utilizing a dating website either."

"So you wouldn't even consider my golf buddy Anthony Wells? He's a *doctor*." The way he said the word *doctor* felt like he was dangling a carrot in front of her nose. "And he's good looking too."

"So why is he single?" She frowned. "What's wrong with him?"

He grinned at her. "I like that. You're developing a good sense of skepticism. It gives me hope."

"Seriously, what's wrong with him? Why does a good-looking doctor have difficulty getting dates? Why is he single?"

"Tony's wife left him for a plastic surgeon about a year ago."

"Oh."

"But if you're not interested." Jake leaned back in his chair, smugly folding his arms in front.

"Oh, Jake." She glared at him. "Why are you doing this to me?"

"Because I care about you."

"Or because you think I'm unable to find a man on my own."

"Nothing is further from the truth, Daphne. I'm afraid you'll find all kinds of men. You're a beautiful woman and by all appearances you are rich and successful and, forgive me for saying so, quite a catch."

She considered this. Maybe it actually made sense . . . on some levels. Still, it was insulting.

"I just want to make sure you get to meet some good prospects. I'd feel terrible if you settled for some beer-guzzling womanizer—"

"You're suggesting that Collin is a womanizer—?"

"I watched him, Daphne. He was dancing with a lot of pretty girls the other night. Seemed to enjoy it too. Besides that, he left you to your own devices most of the time. Not very polite if you ask me. But maybe I'm old-fashioned."

"For your information, I was the one who was avoiding him."

"Oh?" He looked doubtful.

"I was! I had already made up my mind about it. Even before dinner, I had pretty much decided I'd had enough of him, *okay*?"

Jake seemed pleased. "Well, I never accused you of having bad judgment. It's more a case of attracting the wrong sorts."

"How can I be sure your Dr. Tony isn't the wrong sort?"

"By meeting him."

"But I just told Sabrina that I'm taking a break from men and dating."

"You don't have to date him. Just meet him for coffee. If there's nothing there, what have you lost? A few minutes of your time?"

She considered this. Really, if Jake was just a friend and only a friend, this would seem like a perfectly natural conversation. It's just that she had once thought he was more. However, if she wanted to prove to herself—and to him—that they were only friends, perhaps she should accept his challenge to meet his doctor friend. And what if he really did turn out to be a great guy? At the very least she might manage to make Jake jealous. No, that was the wrong motive.

"Okay, fine," she said abruptly. "I'm happy to meet your friend."

He looked surprised. "Great. Want me to set it up?"

"That depends."

"On what?"

"On whether or not you'll be hiding in the shadows observing."

He laughed. "I promise you I won't do that."

"Okay . . . then go ahead. See if your friend is as keen on your idea as you are."

"Anthony is on staff at St. George. Maybe you could meet up with him there. That way it really won't feel like a date."

"Fine." She finished the last of her coffee. "Is that all you wanted to talk to me about?"

"Well, yes . . . that's pretty much it."

"Then if you'll excuse me, I need to work on the column today."

"How's that going?"

"Don't you read the newspaper?" she said a bit haughtily.

"Uh, yes, of course."

"Then you should know exactly how it's going."

"Right. So you don't miss having me as your middleman as much as you thought you would?"

She shook her head as she stood. "Apparently not."

"I'll let you know about Anthony," he said in what seemed a halfhearted tone. Perhaps he was having second thoughts, or maybe he was worried that Dr. Tony wouldn't be interested in her.

She forced a smile and thanked him for the coffee, turned, and walked away. Heat rose up her neck and flushing her face as she went outside. It was partly from anger, partly from humiliation. Who did Jake think he was? What audacity—offering to set her up with dates? Did he really think she was some poor, pathetic loser, unable to attract a guy without his help? Was she that repugnant and repulsive? The nerve of that man!

Of course, as she got closer to home, she began to see it a bit differently. Replaying Jake's words, she realized he'd been partially complimentary. He had actually called her *beautiful* . . . but then he negated that by saying she had the "appearance" of being rich and successful. How insulting. Although to be fair, it was true. It was an appearance—she was neither rich or successful, she was simply riding on Aunt Dee's coattails. And Jake knew that.

Maybe he was right. It did seem entirely possible that she could attract the wrong sort of guy without even knowing it. In fact Collin might very well have been that sort of guy. But how would she have discovered that if she hadn't given him the time of day? And yet wouldn't she have been happier not to have wasted her time on him? As she went into the house, she was feeling completely confused. Maybe it was time to write Dear Daphne again.

Chapter 13

As Daphne went out to her car on Friday, she really wanted to pull the plug on this thing. There had to be a graceful way out.

"Hey, neighbor," Sabrina called out as she crossed the street. Tootsie, dressed in a red-and-white striped T-shirt, was on his leash today. "Where you off to?"

Daphne quickly explained about her blind coffee date.

"A blind date? Who set you up?"

Daphne frowned. "Jake."

Sabrina's pale brows arched. "Interesting."

"Jake was concerned I was attracting the wrong sort of men." She rolled her eyes. "So he arranged for me to meet his doctor friend Tony."

"A *doctor*? That's fabulous. My mama always wanted me to marry a doctor. But why so glum? What's the problem with him?"

"The problem is me. I feel ridiculous."

"Well, you *look* hot." Sabrina nodded with approval.

"Hot?" Daphne frowned. "I was going for conservative."

"Okay. You look hot in a conservative way."

Daphne jingled her car keys nervously. "I'd really like to just call the whole thing off. Except I don't have Dr. Tony's phone number. Wonder what he'd think if I was a no-show."

Sabrina gave her a gentle shove toward her car. "No way. You are going to go meet Dr. Tony. If you don't like him, you can always set me up with him for another blind coffee date."

Daphne chuckled. "Maybe I should take you with me. Let him choose."

"Now you're just being silly." Sabrina waved her hand. "I want to hear all about it. Hey, why don't you come over for lunch when you get back? I made portobello raviolis last night and they are yummy."

"Sounds good. I'll bring some leftover salad."

"It's a date." Sabrina tugged on Tootsie's leash. "Taking my little boy out for a morning stroll." She made a little finger wave. "Ya'll have fun now!"

"Right," Daphne muttered as she got into the car. She ran her hand over the shiny steering wheel. "Bonnie, you're a good old car, but are you worth the effort I'm making to keep you?" Daphne continued talking to herself as she drove to the hospital. "It's just coffee. You'll make some small talk, tell him you are pleased to meet him, and then be on your way. Twenty minutes max."

As she walked into the hospital, she had a flashback that took her back nearly thirty years. She had just turned five the first time she walked through this lobby. Aunt Dee had dressed her up in her Sunday best and drove her here. Mom had been in the hospital for about a week by then. Daphne hadn't really understood why exactly, although she had been aware that Mom was sick. She just hadn't realized how sick. It was her first time being in the hospital and the last time she saw her mom. Daphne shuddered—it all seemed like just yesterday.

She was still shaking off the flashback as she entered the cafeteria. Jake had e-mailed her yesterday regarding this meeting, saying Tony would be by the windows, with blond hair and a white doctor's coat. She spotted a man who seemed to fit the description. Then trying not to feel nervous, she got herself a cup of coffee and carried it over to him. Fortunately he was reading a newspaper and didn't even notice her.

"Excuse me. Are you Tony?"

He looked up and smiled. "That's right. And you must be Daphne."

"Yes," she told him as she sat down. "It's nice to meet you."

"Nice to meet you too." He folded the paper and set it next to him.

"When Jake called me about you, I thought he was pulling my leg."

She nodded. "It took me by surprise too."

"But after I thought about it, I decided it was a good idea. And I knew I could trust Jake." He grinned. "And he was right. You are very pretty."

Her cheeks warmed. "Thank you."

He glanced at the clock on the wall. "And I only have about fifteen minutes before a staff meeting. So I suppose we should get right to it. Why don't you tell me a little about yourself?"

So Daphne told him about working for *The Times* in New York, then how she moved back home after her aunt's death. "I never thought I'd want to go back to small-town living, but I am actually loving it."

"So what do you do . . . I mean for a living?"

"Well, I'm working on a novel. And I do some other writing . . . for newspapers."

"Ah, freelancing. Sounds like a good life."

"Not quite as demanding as being a doctor. Jake said you're on staff here. I imagine that might be stressful."

"It's a little more pressure than private practice. But it's rewarding too. I've been here about five years now. Sometimes I think I'll go back to private practice, but I know I'd miss the action. I enjoy working with other medical professionals around me." He continued to talk about his work there and some interesting cases where he made what sounded like some brilliant diagnoses.

"Sounds like St. George is very lucky to have you."

He shrugged. "I try to earn my keep. But sometimes it's a challenge." He told her about how he and an older doctor had gone head-to-head. "So much of his training was antiquated, but he had seniority over me. I had to put up with the old codger for three long years, and I was actually ready to give this place up permanently. But then the administrator talked him into retiring. That was a happy day. For everyone. Since then I've really enjoyed my work a lot." He looked up at the clock again. "And as enjoyable as this has been, I need to excuse myself."

They both stood and she was a little surprised to see that he was a few inches shorter than her. And she wasn't even wearing heels. They shook hands and started walking out together. But just outside of the cafeteria, he turned to face her, asking if he could see her again.

"Sure." She felt off guard.

"How about dinner?"

"Okay . . . why not?"

"I get off work at six today. How about seven?"

"Tonight?"

"Are you busy?"

"Um . . . no."

He pulled a business card out of his coat pocket. "Here, call my cell number and leave me a message about where you live. I'll pick you up at sevenish. Okay?"

She nodded, watching as he gave her a quick wave, then hurried toward the elevators. She stood there for a moment just staring. Had she really agreed to go to dinner with him? She looked at the business card in her hand and shook her head. So much for chitchat and parting ways.

She walked out to her car. Why did she feel like dragging her heels? After all, Tony was a perfectly nice guy. Educated and professional and confident. He was well spoken and seemed to have a positive attitude about life. He really enjoyed his work. *And* he liked her.

Even so, he didn't feel quite right. Not right for her anyway. She couldn't even think of a rational reason why she felt so certain of this. And now she would be forced to spend an entire evening with him. She felt like calling Jake and complaining. But not only did that seem juvenile, it was downright ungrateful. Still, she felt irked that Jake had been behind this. What could he have been thinking?

As she drove home, she chided herself for being too judgmental. She was being far too hasty. Good grief, she hardly even knew the poor man. How could she write him off so quickly? Why not give him the benefit of the doubt? Get to know him better . . . before she decided it was hopeless. She had no plans for the evening. What was wrong with sharing a meal with a nice guy? If nothing else, she would find out for sure whether she was right or wrong about him. What if it turned out he truly was Mr. Right . . . and she never gave him a chance to prove it?

She parked the car in the driveway and, without getting out, pulled out his business card and called him. She went straight to voice mail and gave him both her phone number and address. "I'm looking forward to it," she said before she hung up. And really, she was looking forward to it, wasn't she?

"He sounds great," Sabrina said as they sat in her backyard eating lunch. "And he must like you. He's not wasting any time."

"Uh-huh." She nodded as she chewed a ravioli.

"But you still don't seem very excited."

Daphne set her fork down. "I just don't think he's the guy for me."

"Why not?"

"I honestly don't know."

"But the way you described him—he sounds absolutely wonderful."

"I know. And I hope I'm wrong. Maybe I was just nervous. They say the brain doesn't work as well when you're anxious or stressed. Maybe that's what was going on."

"Oh yeah." Sabrina nodded. "I can never think straight when I'm upset."

"Anyway, after tonight I should have a better idea."

"What does he look like?"

"Kind of fair. Blond hair, blue eyes. He reminds me of the guy who played Niles on *Frasier*. Remember the younger brother?"

"I always adored Niles. Oh, Daphne, it sounds like Tony is really cute." She sighed. "And he's a doctor. I think you hit the jackpot."

Daphne chuckled. "Oh yeah, he's a few inches shorter than me too."

Sabrina's brow creased as if imagining this. "Well, you got to admit you're pretty tall for a woman. And some guys like their women tall. I'll bet you two look sweet together. Why don't you snap a photo of yourselves together at dinner and send it to me?"

"No thanks." Daphne firmly shook her head. "I am not into that. Not at all."

Sabrina frowned. "I suppose I'll just have to play the snoopy neighbor with my nose pressed against the window. Didn't you say he's coming around seven?"

Seven came and went. It was a quarter to eight when Tony finally showed up. "I'm sorry for being late," he said when she opened the door. "I had to cover for another doctor. Her son got hurt at sleepover camp and she had to go get him."

"That's okay."

"Well, that's a doctor's life." He shrugged as he came into the house. "At least when you work at a hospital. Still, I wouldn't trade it for private practice." He looked around the foyer. "Nice place."

As she got her purse, she explained that it had been her aunt's house. "But I redecorated it."

"Looks good." He nodded. "I like it." As they went outside, he told her about his condo. "We sold the house after the divorce. Neither of us wanted it anymore. And now I live closer to the hospital. So that's pretty convenient." He opened the driver's door of a small hybrid car. "Of course, it can be inconvenient too." He called over the roof. "I'm usually the first one they call when they're short staffed."

She opened the passenger side door and got in. Okay, it wasn't that terrible—that he hadn't opened the door for her. But for some reason it really bugged her. As he rattled on about the goings-on at the hospital today, she remembered how he hadn't stood when he met her in the cafeteria. And how he hadn't called to say he was running late either. They probably didn't teach etiquette at med school.

"So this little four-year-old was so worked up," he said. "She thought that having a broken arm meant she was going to lose the arm completely. Turned out she'd accidentally broken a figurine a few days ago. The arm had come off." He laughed. "So she assumed hers would come off too."

"Poor thing. That must've been traumatic."

"You should've seen her face when we finished with her cast. She picked hot pink for it. And she was so proud of that cast she was just beaming."

"That reminds me of when I was little." She started to tell him about the flashback she'd had at the hospital this morning, but before she could finish, he was talking about another patient, explaining how the old woman had taken a permanent marker to her leg.

"She'd written 'Replace this hip and not the other one' in bold black letters." He laughed. "Can you believe that?"

She nodded, but she was still reminiscing about her childhood . . . and how she equated the hospital as a place people went to die. She had been about to tell him about how she'd been seven when her father was hospitalized with an appendicitis. She had been certain he was going to die. Fortunately Aunt Dee had set her straight on that misconception. And Dad had come back home just a couple days later.

By the time Tony parked his car at The Italian Kitchen, she realized that he had two favorite topics of conversation: 1) his job and 2) himself. Besides that, his listening skills were not highly developed. That seemed an unhandy trait for a doctor. Weren't they supposed to listen to their patients?

As they were seated in a booth, the strikes were quickly piling up against Dr. Tony. And once again, she felt irritated at Jake. Surely he must've known that his good friend was both self-centered and ill-mannered. Didn't he say they played golf together? Or maybe guys didn't pay attention to those kinds of details with their golf buddies. However, Jake wasn't like Tony. He wasn't self-centered, and even though he could be pushy at times, he was not ill-mannered. It stood to reason that he would've realized Tony would not measure up to Daphne's expectations. What was he thinking?

"You're not very hungry?" Tony asked when he noticed that she sent her entrée back only half eaten.

"I think my salad filled me up," she fibbed. The truth was, the salad had been as disappointing as this date. Why would any self-respecting chef serve limp iceberg lettuce with anemic tomatoes and wilted cucumbers when there was so much delicious fresh produce to be found this time of year? But then she'd never been a big fan of this restaurant in the first place. Of course, he hadn't asked her about that either.

"I eat most of my meals at the hospital. Some people complain about the food, but it's cheap and handy—and good enough for me." He plucked up a piece of bread. "So when I go out to eat, I really try to enjoy it. And fortunately I'm playing golf tomorrow. So I can work off all these carbs."

"With Jake?"

"What?"

"Golf," she explained. "Are you playing with Jake?"

"As a matter of fact, I am. Tee time is eight."

"Give him my regards." She genuinely smiled as she considered what her true regards would actually be. She would love to give Jake a big piece of her mind. And next time she saw him, maybe she would.

Tony continued talking about himself and his work and even his golf game. She nodded or made polite comments at appropriate intervals, but it was clear he didn't really need her to keep this conversation going. He was a one-man show.

"Well, because of that early tee time, I can't make a late night of it," he said as they finished dessert. "I hope you don't mind."

"Not at all." She set her spoon down. At least the ice cream had been good. Although it would be difficult to mess up ice cream.

He continued to chat as he drove her home. To keep herself from screaming, she silently counted. By the time he came to her street, she had reached 134.

"Now, here I've gone on and on about me and my work." He pulled in front of her house. "My ex-wife used to complain about this all the time."

"Oh?" She tried to act surprised.

"Yeah. She was always telling me I was too obsessed with work. She used to say I didn't need a wife because I was already married—to my job." He laughed wryly. "And maybe that's true. But she ended up marrying another doctor anyway. I guess some people never learn."

Daphne wanted to point out that not all doctors were as

self-absorbed as Tony. Instead she just nodded. She'd spent so much time nodding tonight that she felt like a bobble-head doll. "Thank you for dinner," she said mechanically as she reached for the door handle. "You don't need to see me to the door."

Okay, she seriously doubted he even planned to, but she wasn't taking any chances. She got out and scurried up to her porch, then turning and smiling stiffly, she gave him a little wave and hurried into the house. Hopefully he got the message.

Chapter 14

Sabrina showed up the next morning, eager to find out about the big date. But if she was disappointed by what she heard, her facial expressions did not show it.

"I'm glad you find this so amusing." Daphne leaned over to pull a weed growing in one of the decorative pots on the porch. "But you could at least show a little sympathy. I think that might've been the worst date I've ever been on."

"Maybe you should've listened to your instincts."

Daphne blinked. Hadn't Sabrina strongly encouraged her to go out with Tony? "From now on, I *will* listen to my instincts."

"So you're really not interested in Dr. Tony?"

"Not in the least." She sat back down in a rocker. "Even if my leg had been chopped off and I was bleeding to death and Tony was the only doctor at St. George, I would tell him to keep away from me."

"You would not!" Sabrina looked horrified.

Daphne chuckled. "Well, I'd think about it."

"So how about introducing him to me?"

Daphne frowned. "Oh, Sabrina, you wouldn't like him."

"How do you know that?"

"Because he is thoroughly unlikeable. Take it from me."

"You better watch what you say, neighbor. How would you feel if I met your Tony and we fell in love and got married and found ourselves living across the street from you? Then what would you say?"

"I'd say don't bring your husband over to my house for coffee."

Sabrina handed her empty cup to Daphne. "That is downright unneighborly, Daphne. But I will not hold it against you. As long as you help me to meet Tony."

"Sabrina, are you nuts?"

"Not at all. The way you described Tony makes me think that I would really like him. In fact, he and I are probably a lot alike. Everyone tells me I talk too much. And you have to admit, I'm pretty self-absorbed. We just might be a match made in heaven."

Daphne just shook her head.

"Come on, please, tell me how to meet my own Dr. Dreamy."

"Just a minute." Daphne went into the house and dug through her purse until she found Tony's business card. She walked back outside and handed the rumpled card to Sabrina. "Here. Go ahead and call him yourself. You'll probably have to leave a message. Just tell him I gave you his number because I thought you two might like each other. See if he calls you back."

Sabrina hugged her. "Oh, thank you, Daphne. You are a true friend."

"Let's see if you still feel that way *after* you have a date with him. That is, if you really decide to go through with this crazy plan. I do not recommend it."

After Sabrina left, Daphne felt a little concern for her neighbor.

It almost seemed as if Sabrina was trying to imitate Daphne's frenzied dating life. Because it wasn't as if Sabrina needed to get married anytime soon. Why didn't she just slow down a little and enjoy this era of her newfound freedom? Why was she in such a hurry? Maybe Daphne should remind her of this. Or maybe Sabrina would figure it out for herself. One date with Tony might help straighten her out!

After lunch, Daphne turned on her computer and started pulling *Dear Daphne* letters onto the screen. Her goal was to get two more done before Monday. The first one was fairly easy to answer. It sounded like it was written by a young teen, which was good since the syndicate was trying to attract a younger market.

> *Dear Daphne,*
>
> *Why does love have to hurt so much? I fell in love with "Brent" this summer and I thought he loved me too. But now he won't even speak to me. I don't know what I did wrong. I asked my best friend to talk to him and she said Brent just doesn't like me anymore. But how could he have loved me a month ago and not like me now? And when will this pain go away?*
>
> *Aching in Amarillo*

> *Dear Aching,*
>
> *I'm not sure there's a good answer for why love hurts so much. But it's partly because we open our hearts and make ourselves vulnerable when we're in love. That makes it easier to get hurt. And sometimes that happens. Unfortunately, the only way to avoid this kind of pain is to never fall in love again. But that's not much fun. What I can tell you is that it*

really does get better with time. Also you are not
alone. Almost everyone on the planet has been hurt
by love at some point in time. So welcome to the club!
And don't forget the old saying—"It's better to have
loved and lost than never to have loved at all."
  Daphne

Daphne chuckled as she saved that one. The girl sounded so downhearted and discouraged, but Daphne would wager that by the time the letter made it into print, probably just as the new school year started, *Aching* would be off falling in love with another boy.

She skimmed and read through about a dozen letters before she found one that caught her eye.

  Dear Daphne,
  I've known "Tom" for about six years. We've
  dated off and on during the whole time, but he is
  usually the one who breaks up first. I always promise
  myself I won't go back with him after a painful
  breakup. But last spring I started seeing him again.
  My friends think I'm a complete fool. But I still
  believe he is the one for me, and I can imagine us
  being happily married. So much so that I recently
  started hinting about weddings. The problem is, Tom
  shows absolutely no interest in marriage. Am I nuts
  for staying with him?
    Crazy in Costa Mesa

  Dear Crazy,
  I'm curious as to why you always break the

*promise you make to yourself—never to go back with
Tom. I assume you wouldn't make that promise unless
you were really hurting at the time. Do you forget the
pain during the intervals of being apart from Tom?
Even if you believe Tom is the one for you, it seems
obvious he doesn't share these sentiments. So if your
goal is marriage, you seem to be barking up the wrong
tree. And unless you get some kind of masochistic
pleasure from being hurt every time he breaks up,
I suggest you start keeping that promise to yourself.
The next time he breaks your heart—and I suspect
it won't be long—love yourself enough to leave Tom
for good. And maybe—if you're not too distracted to
see it—the real Mr. Right might be around the next
corner.*

Daphne

Daphne made some quick edits, then sent the files off to her syndication editor. Satisfied, she leaned back in her chair and stretched her shoulders. Done. At least until next week anyway. Her confidence in writing the advice column had increased these past few weeks. It probably had to do with no longer funneling them through Jake. It was as if she was standing on her own two feet now. Well, she might still be wearing Aunt Dee's shoes, but at least she didn't need Jake's approval anymore. If she wasn't feeling so irked at him about Dr. Tony, she might be tempted to drop him a casual e-mail to thank him for forcing herself to take those new steps. And okay, if they were really friends like he kept saying—why not?

She opened her e-mail again and started writing him a note.

Hi, Jake.

I wanted to take a moment to express my appreciation for your help with the Dear Daphne column. Initially you were just what I needed to help build my confidence as I stretched my wings. And I'm a little embarrassed to remember how I fought back when you told me I was ready to fly solo. Turns out you were right, and I just felt I should let you know. I want to say a sincere thank-you.

However, you are not right about everything, counselor! And I do not wish to express even the tiniest grain of gratitude for how you set me up with Dr. Tony. That was a complete fiasco. Perhaps Tony told you all about it during your golf game this morning. So much for your matchmaking skills!

Your Friend,

Daphne

She let out a big sigh as she hit Send. Hopefully he would take the hint and stay out of her love life. Not that she had a love life at the moment. But she hoped he would take the hint and butt out. She shut down her computer, got a glass of iced tea, and went outside for some fresh air. Lucy and Ethel followed her out and Daphne eventually wandered back to the garden to cut some herbs. Temperatures had been dropping slightly, and afternoons were no longer as scorching as they'd been a couple weeks ago. And the plants in the garden seemed to be relishing this weather. In fact, she couldn't imagine how it could look any prettier.

With a basket filled with basil, thyme, rosemary, and oregano, she sat on the garden bench and just soaked in the beauty. If anyone had told her—last summer when she was still living in the sweltering city—that she would be sitting here in Appleton, in a quiet and peaceful garden perfectly content, she would not have believed her. And yet . . . here she was.

She inhaled the fragrance of the aromatic herbs. Heavenly. She loved this place—this garden, this house, this town. But did she love it enough to marry purely for convenience? Besides, even if she ended up poor and struggling to get by, she could still grow a garden, couldn't she? And if she had a garden, she would always feel rich. She leaned back into the bench, letting the sun wash over her face. Delightful.

"Hello? Daphne, are you back here?"

Sitting up straight, she knew that voice. "Jake?"

"Oh, there you are." He came into the garden with an uneasy expression. "Sorry to intrude on you like this. Do you mind?" Dressed casually in a white polo shirt and khakis, she could tell he'd probably just finished his golf game.

She waved her hand to a chair. "Make yourself at home." She sighed. "I was just enjoying how pretty it is back here."

He looked around as he pulled out a chair and sat across from her. "It really is something. Aunt Dee would've loved it, don't you think?"

She nodded. "I think of that often. It means a lot that it was originally her plan to have this back here. I just wish she'd gotten to enjoy it."

"She would be happy just knowing how much you enjoy it."

"Yes, but I was just thinking . . . Even if I ultimately lose all this—the house, the car, the garden—well, I'll still be just fine. And no matter how poor I am, I can still have a garden. Mick has helped me to learn about plants and soil and all that. So even on my own, I think I can do it. Not as grand as this one. But I can do something. I'm sure of it. And I even know how to preserve the food too. This has all been a good learning experience. No regrets."

"You make it sound as if it's over. Are you giving up on finding Mr. Right?"

She gave him an exasperated look. "After last night's date . . . yeah, maybe so."

"I read your e-mail about Tony on my iPhone after we finished our golf. I tried calling the house and your cell, but you didn't answer. And since I was already in town, I decided to stop by. I just felt like there was something you should know . . . about Tony."

She waved her hand. "There is nothing you can tell me about Dr. Tony that would change a thing, Jake. Even if you told me he'd just won the Nobel Prize or a billion dollars or anything. I would still have absolutely no interest in that man." She narrowed her eyes. "Why on earth did you set me up with him in the first place?"

He shrugged. "Sorry about that. Sounds like you had a really horrible time. What went wrong?"

"You mean besides the fact that he talks too much, never listens, is in love with himself—and in his own words, married to his job? Well, other than that he was delightful. We had a perfectly lovely time."

Jake grinned. "And speaking of lovely, what I wanted to tell you is that Tony thinks *you* are lovely."

"*What?*" She was flabbergasted.

"Tony talked about you a lot while we golfed. Went on about how pretty you are, how intelligent—"

"How would he possibly know about my intelligence when I

hardly got a word in edgewise? Maybe he meant I was smart enough to know when to keep my mouth shut. And that was continually."

Jake laughed. "Maybe he assumed you're smart because you're a writer."

She rolled her eyes. "I'm surprised he could even remember that."

"Honestly, it sounds like you and Tony went on two completely different dates. He had a great time and you sound like you were being tortured."

"Of course he had a great time." It felt rather good to express herself like this. Almost made up for the wasted evening. "He got to choose where we ate, he got to control the entire conversation, he remained focused completely on himself. Meanwhile I simply listened, or pretended to, while I bided my time and tried not to start planning my revenge on you for setting the whole thing up."

"If you didn't like him, why did you go out with him? I mean, you did meet at the hospital for coffee, didn't you?"

"Sure, we met. And he seemed okay, but looking back I realize he was pretty self-absorbed even then. But I probably excused it because we were on his turf. It seemed natural that he was distracted with his place of work. However, a red flag did go up in regard to his manners. Rather his lack of manners."

"What do you mean?"

"Call me old-fashioned, but I like it when a gentleman stands to greet a lady—especially when meeting her for the first time. And I like it when a fellow opens the car door for me. Sure, I can do it myself. But that's just the way I was raised. My dad taught me to have higher expectations."

Jake nodded. "I have to agree with you on those things too. Maybe I'm old-fashioned. I had no idea Tony was such a Neanderthal."

She chuckled. "Well, that's a little extreme."

"Anyway, I'm sorry."

"I forgive you. But now what do I do about Tony? I can't believe he'd still be interested in me. I was pretty chilly at the end of the date last night. I never expected to hear from him again."

"He's planning on calling you."

She cringed. "Why? Why would he do that?"

"Because he's attracted to you. He said you're the first woman who's really interested him since his wife left."

"That's sweet, but honestly, it's probably only because I kept my mouth closed so much. I was way too tolerant of his bad manners. If I'd really expressed how I was feeling, he would have no interest in seeing me again. I assure you."

"Unless he likes a girl who plays hard to get."

"Well, I am hard to get. At least when it comes to Dr. Tony." She pointed at Jake. "And since you got me into this mess, I think the honorable thing to do would be to get me out of it."

"You want me to talk to him?"

She nodded eagerly. "I think you owe me that."

Jake looked uneasy.

"Come on, just let him down nicely. You can do it."

He groaned as he slowly stood. "I wish I'd known about how you felt before our golf game. It would've been a whole lot easier if I had. As it is, I feel like I may have encouraged him."

"Encouraged him?"

"Well, he was singing your praises . . . What did you expect me to do? Disagree? What kind of friend do you think I am?"

"Oh, Jake." She shook her head. "With a friend like you who needs—"

"I know, I know." He held up his hands. "I'll go do damage control now. I guess I deserve this."

She wanted to ask him why he'd ever stuck his foot into her life in the first place. Of course, she wanted to ask him a whole lot of other things too. Questions that she would never allow past her lips. But why couldn't he have just left well enough alone? And why couldn't he leave her alone too?

Chapter 15

For the next several weeks, Daphne went underground. At least that's what she told herself as she put all her energy into working on her novel, as well as getting ahead on the advice column. Naturally, Sabrina couldn't understand why Daphne was staying holed up in the house like that, but Daphne felt it was the best way to regain her personal peace as well as to keep the men in her life at arm's length. To accomplish this, she would speak plainly to her well-meaning neighbor.

"Please, don't take this wrong," she'd told Sabrina a couple weeks ago. "But I am taking a break from men and dating—and that means I don't want to talk about it either. I'm happy to visit with you over coffee and whatever, but if you start in on me about some eligible bachelor, or if you attempt to play cupid, I will send you packing."

Sabrina's eyes had grown wide. "That sounds serious."

"You got that right. I'm dead serious. I plan to get my head back into my suspense novel. Without distractions. That means I'll be keeping all men at a safe distance for a while."

Not that any men were calling these days. Not even Tony. Fortunately Jake had been able to persuade the good doctor that Daphne had absolutely no interest in getting "better acquainted." And to Sabrina's dismay, Tony had balked at being pursued by her as well. In Daphne's mind that was a win-win situation for everyone.

The only time Daphne went out was to spend time in the garden, visit with a neighbor, or make a quick trip to the grocery store. And this solitary life suited her just fine—or so she was telling herself. "I think I would make a really good hermit," she confessed to Sabrina as they sat at her kitchen table. Because it was cool and damp outside, they had moved their coffee chat indoors today.

"No, you wouldn't. A hermit lives all alone, never speaking to anyone. You wouldn't last a week living like that." She giggled. "And I wouldn't last a day."

"You wouldn't last an hour."

"That depends on whether I could send and receive texts." Sabrina pointed out the kitchen window. "Hey, speaking of hermits, there goes Wally. Do you think he's on his way to see Maria?"

"I'm certain of it. I've observed them walking together quite a bit lately. And Wally has looked exceptionally happy."

"So he's given up being a curmudgeon after all." Sabrina let out a happy sigh. "I'm glad *someone* has discovered that it's not good to be alone."

"I'm not saying I want to be completely alone." Daphne paused to check on the zucchini muffins baking in the oven. Her cousin Jocelyn, Mattie's mom, had given her the recipe. "I'm just saying I enjoy a slower, more peaceful sort of life."

"Meaning a life without a man in it?"

Daphne scowled at her neighbor. Sabrina was well aware that this topic was not welcome in this house. "Have you forgotten my new house rules?"

"Sorry. But I can't help but wonder what will happen to you. And the truth is, I worry about you. In fact I worry about *me* too."

"Why?"

"I don't want to wake up next summer, look across the street, and see a perfect stranger living in your house." Sabrina looked truly sad. "I just don't know what I'd do if you had to move away, Daphne."

"Oh, you'd be all right. I wouldn't be the least bit surprised if you were remarried by then anyway."

"Ha! At the rate I'm going, I'll probably be an old maid for the rest of my days."

Daphne laughed. "I don't think you can be an old maid if you've already been married."

"Fine then, I'll just be a pathetic, old divorcée who lives with her dog."

Daphne refilled their coffee cups. "You know sometimes I get a little mad at Aunt Dee for doing this to me. Why couldn't she have just left me her estate without all these conditions?"

"Because she loved you. She wanted you to have the happily-ever-after life she felt she'd missed out on."

"But sometimes it feels like being tortured. Like I'm just doing my time, waiting for the ax to fall. Sometimes I want to just throw my hands in the air and say 'forget it' and go live my own life somewhere else."

"I thought you liked Appleton."

"I do. I love it."

"And this house and everything? Don't you like it too?"

"Of course. You know I do. But at the same time there's so much pressure." She sighed. "If I didn't have to think about it, like I've been trying to do lately, it's not so bad." She pointed her finger at Sabrina. "And that's why I banned this topic from this house."

"I know. My bad." She frowned. "Sorry."

"Whenever I get too focused on finding Mr. Right, everything seems to go wrong. That's exactly what happened when I first moved here in May," Daphne confessed. "It was like I was so desperate to get married, I couldn't see straight. After a month or so of frenzy, I sort of stepped back and decided I was going to trust God to direct my life. And honestly, I felt as if I was finally in a really good place . . . in July."

"Right before I moved in?"

"Yeah, I guess it was around then."

"Meaning I messed you up?"

The oven timer went off and Daphne got up to remove the muffins. "I don't think I can blame it on you." She set the pans on top of the stove. "Although July was going pretty well for me. I felt happy and relaxed and I was just enjoying life. But then I got all into hypermode again."

"But I thought that was because Jake jilted you by taking his ex on vacation with him?"

Daphne frowned. "In the first place, I don't think Jake really jilted me. It's just that we were only friends. I had misunderstood. But you're probably right. That did sort of make me feel desperate again."

"And rightly so."

Daphne looked up from where she was removing the hot muffins, setting some on a plate. "You think I should be feeling desperate?"

"No, of course not, honey. No one should feel desperate. But just the same, aren't you the least bit concerned that the clock is ticking? I mean December is less than three months away now."

Daphne shrugged. "That doesn't matter to me. Besides, May is still a ways out there. That's the real drop-dead deadline."

"Yes, but—"

"I know, I know. Both you and Olivia believe it takes at least *six months* to plan the perfect wedding. But I can't get trapped in that kind of thinking. Look at Karen and my dad. They're putting together what sounds like a fairly nice wedding in just a couple of months. At least Karen's excited about it. Not sure my dad cares." She set the warm muffins on the table and sat down.

"Mmm, those look good." Sabrina reached for a muffin, carefully peeling back the paper. "See, just one more thing I'll miss if you're not here next year. You're such a good cook." She broke off a piece and popped it in her mouth. "Yummy. I'll have to make sure to get the recipe from you *before* you're gone."

Daphne rolled her eyes as she picked up a muffin. "No hurries there."

They quietly munched on the muffins, but Daphne could see Sabrina was still fretting about something.

"What is wrong with us?" Sabrina exclaimed.

"Wrong with us? What do you mean?"

"I mean you and me, honey."

"I don't think anything is wrong with us, Sabrina. I think we are just fine."

"Do you know what day this is?"

Daphne thought hard. It was easy for her to lose track of the days when she spent so much time writing. Was it Thursday . . . Friday . . . ?

"It's *Saturday*," Sabrina declared.

"Oh, well, okay. It's Saturday. What's your point?"

"My point is, what are you doing tonight?"

Daphne shrugged.

"Getting into your pj's and watching Turner Classics with Lucy and Ethel," Sabrina said in a flat tone. "You don't have to tell me. I know it's what you do almost every night."

"So."

"Doesn't that strike you as disturbing? Look at you, Daph. You're only thirty-four. You're gorgeous. You're smart. You're available. But you have spent the last few Saturdays—and Fridays—home alone with a couple of elderly felines. Anything wrong with that picture?"

"What about you? You've spent your Saturday nights with an aging Chihuahua, watching *Housewives of Atlanta* or Beverly Hills or wherever."

"I've been more into New Jersey lately. Somehow those women make me feel better about myself."

Daphne smiled.

"But here's the deal, Daph. You and I blew through several perfectly nice, not to mention attractive, single men not long ago. Mick, Collin, Tony . . . just to name a few."

Daphne chuckled. "I think you may be blowing this out of proportion."

"Maybe, but this morning I was remembering when I was in my twenties. Back then I always had a bunch of hopeful admirers clustering around me. And I was the one who left a trail of broken hearts behind. Now I can't seem to attract a single living breathing male to save my life. I honestly fear I may have lost my touch."

"Oh, come on."

"Seriously, it's very discouraging. I couldn't believe that Dr. Tony wouldn't even give me the time of day. I told him it was just for coffee and I even offered to make it my treat. I sent him a very nice photo and everything. But he said 'no thank you' so quickly, it made my head literally spin."

"Literally?" Daphne laughed to imagine Sabrina's head rotating round and round. "That must've hurt."

"You know what I mean. Tony treated me as if I had a bad case of cooties. And the photo I sent him was really a good one too."

"Well, if you ask me, I think you dodged a bullet with that guy. Be thankful."

"So you say, but I was perfectly willing to make this discovery on my own. Not that I was given the chance. But that's not all. I wasn't going to tell you, but just a few days ago—remember when you refused to go to town to have lunch with me on Wednesday—well, I went to Midge's all by my little ol' lonesome. And I hate to admit it, but I flirted shamelessly with Ricardo the whole time I was there. I practically begged the poor man to ask me out. Am I pathetic or what? Can you believe it?"

Daphne actually did feel a bit shocked. "And what did Ricardo say? How did he react?"

"Of course he was sweet and polite. Just like always. But that was it. Absolutely no interest. Totally humiliating. That is when I really started to question myself. I honestly think I've lost my appeal."

"Maybe you're just trying too hard."

"I'm sure Kellie would agree with you. Oh, if looks could kill. Seriously, she looked like she was about to invite me out back to settle things. I cannot understand why Ricardo keeps her on." Sabrina finished the last of her coffee and stood. "Anyway, thank you for listening, honey. Sometimes it feels therapeutic to whine and complain a little." She grinned. "At least I know I'm not alone in my dating dry spell. Thanks."

"You're welcome . . . I think." Daphne wondered what had happened to her previous banning of any talk concerning men and dating and her deadline. Although to be fair, this had been more about Sabrina's unfortunate love life than Daphne's.

"Anyway, I promised to take Tootsie for a nice, long walk this morning." She giggled. "And who knows, maybe I'll stumble into Mr. Right in the park."

"Good luck with that."

"I know . . . you're probably right." Sabrina shook her head. "I'm starting to worry that you and I may be fishing in too small of a pond."

Daphne set the cups in the sink with a clunk. "I'm *not* fishing, Sabrina. *Remember?*"

"So you say now. We'll see what you're saying a few months from now when we're in the middle of winter and the prospects are even gloomier."

After Sabrina left, Daphne went to her office, prepared to lose herself in chapter twenty-seven of her novel. She felt like the book would be finished in about ten more chapters or so. But since she'd never really done this before, she wasn't absolutely sure. She also wasn't sure what she would do with the novel when it was done. Aunt Dee's old publisher might look at it, simply because of the Penelope Poindexter books Aunt Dee had penned for them. However, Daphne's book was not a romance. No bodice ripping happened in her story.

Daphne wasn't sure she wanted anyone to actually read her book. What if it stunk? How humiliating would that be? Still, determined to at least finish it, she pressed on. One of her secret goals in pushing forward with her novel was the hope of independence. If only she could successfully contract a novel, she might feel like she was strong enough to stand on her own two feet. And then she could start planning for her future and stop worrying about the frustrating demands of Aunt Dee's will.

Later on Saturday, just as Daphne was comfortably—and predictably—attired in her favorite flannel pj's, with Ethel and Lucy nestled close to her, a steaming cup of chamomile tea at her elbow, and the remote aimed for the TV, her dad called.

"Home alone again?" he asked. "On a Saturday night too?"

"Have you been talking to Sabrina?"

"Not lately. Why?"

"Nothing." She tossed the remote aside. "It's just that she was over here earlier today, reminding me of my lackluster love life."

"Good for Sabrina. I'm been worried about that too. For a while I was worried I might have to ward off some of the fellows with a baseball bat. And now it seems like you're spending every night alone."

"I'm not alone." She stroked Lucy's fur.

"Oh? You have someone over there? I'm sorry. I'll let you go."

"No, I just meant the cats. And really, they're good company."

"See! That's just what I'm talking about. You've got me worried, sweetie."

"Please don't worry about me, Dad." She told him about how focused she'd been on her novel the last few weeks. "At the rate I'm going, I might finish it by the end of the month."

"That's great, Daphne. But I'm still worried."

"What exactly are you worried about?"

"That you are turning into your Aunt Dee."

"Thanks. I'll take that as a compliment."

"I suppose, in a way, it is a compliment. Except that I know Dee had regrets. It had never been her intent to become an old maid. Initially she got trapped into it." He let out a sigh. "Of course, I never realized it back then. Never fully appreciated the sacrifices she made for me. Never knew why she worked so hard."

"You mean because she was your mother, helping to support you?"

"Yes. I'm still working that all out in my head. But I am grateful. I wish I could've told her before she passed."

"I know, Dad. Me too."

"When Dee and I used to have lunch—almost every Thursday— she would open up a little with me. Especially in her final years. And trust me, she had plenty of regrets. She admitted that she was lonely too. More lonely than any of us ever realized."

"Yeah, Dad. I kind of know about that."

"How do you know? Have you found something she wrote? A journal?"

"No. Nothing like that. Jake McPheeters filled me in a little. Back in May, you know, when he told me about the inheritance."

"Oh yes. Well, that makes sense."

She could hear a questioning tone in his voice, as if he was suspicious. Naturally, this concerned her. What if he started questioning the conditions of Aunt Dee's will? What if he figured things out? The last thing she needed was for Dad to start pushing her toward available bachelors or setting her up on blind dates. "Well, I think it was just because Aunt Dee and I have some commonalities and—"

"That's my point, Daphne. *You do.* And I just know Dee would be disappointed if you followed too closely in her footsteps. Especially when it comes to being an old maid."

Daphne forced a laugh. "Okay, first of all, I'm only thirty-four, Dad. That hardly qualifies me for old-maid status. Besides that, 'old maid' is kind of a derogatory term—not just insulting to me, but Aunt Dee as well. I prefer to remember her as an independent, intelligent, confident woman. I'd be proud to end up like her."

"That's sweet, Daph. But I'm still concerned. Karen thinks you're becoming antisocial and—"

"That's a little harsh. Just tell her I'm finishing my novel. I'll be out in circulation again after it's done. Probably about the time of your wedding. How's that coming by the way?" This would be a good distraction technique.

Dad groaned. "Don't ask."

"Why not? What's wrong?"

"The guest list. It keeps growing. It's like the creature from the Black Lagoon that's threatening to swallow Appleton."

She laughed. "Oh, dear. I'm sorry."

"It's not funny. I offered to pay for half the wedding. But that was when I thought it was a *small affair*."

"Why does it have to be big?"

"That's what I'd like to know too. Karen says it's because she has so many business contacts. And I understand that. She's been doing real estate since the nineties, and she probably knows everyone in town. So she invites one old client and then she has to invite another. It just keeps going and going. Then I hear she's going to invite someone who is just a casual friend of mine, and then I feel guilty as if I should invite someone else who's been a closer friend. Can you see how it goes?"

"Yes, unfortunately. I'm sorry."

"And Karen really wanted to have a sit-down dinner, but when you pay by the head . . ." He let out a long sigh. "I guess I should be thankful you're not getting married anytime soon."

She gave a nervous laugh.

"So really, why am I calling you up and pressuring you about your love life?" he teased. "Forget everything I just said, Daph."

"I'm happy to."

"And I'm not worried about you becoming an old maid—excuse me. Well, you know what I mean. Anyway, Karen did ask if you would join us for lunch tomorrow. She wants to talk to you about some of the wedding stuff. Do you have time to meet us at the country club after church?"

"Sure, I can come out of my cave long enough to do that."

"Great. See you then."

As Daphne hung up the phone, she replayed Dad's words about being glad she wasn't getting married in the near future. She should be grateful for him stepping away like that. Except that the idea of her dad and Karen planning a big pull-out-the-stops sort of wedding left her feeling sort of lost . . . sort of left behind. What if she *did* find Mr. Right? And what if she *did* want to get married, say, within a year or maybe even eight months? Would she then be limited to a dozen guests and chicken-salad sandwiches and a DJ? What kind of wedding could she realistically afford?

She glanced down at her old and faded Hello Kitty pj's, ones she'd had since college, then dismally shook her head. Get real. At the rate she was going, what were the chances she'd ever have a wedding anyway? At least not anytime in the near future.

Chapter 16

I think you'd make a lovely bridesmaid," Dad told Daphne as the three of them were finishing up their lunch. Karen had spent the last fifteen minutes encouraging Daphne to round out her bridesmaids to five by joining the wedding party.

"I think I'd be more comfortable being a groomsman," Daphne said quietly.

"*Oh?*" Karen looked slightly offended.

"I'm sorry." Daphne tossed Dad a nervous glance. "I didn't mean it to sound like that. It's just that I haven't really gotten to know you very well, Karen. And, you see, I've known Dad my whole life."

Karen nodded. "I suppose that makes sense. But I don't see us having any female groomsmen, do you, Don?"

"It's your wedding." Dad shrugged as he reached for his water glass.

"It's *our* wedding," she reminded him for what seemed about the tenth time in the past hour.

"I know. I know." He patted her hand. "But you're the bride, dear. It's up to you. Besides, if Daphne doesn't want to be in the wedding party, we can't very well force her."

Karen's mouth twisted to one side. "No. You're right. We can't force her. I just wanted this to feel like a real family celebration. But it seems like the wedding party is a little unbalanced. It consists more of my family than yours." She turned back to Daphne. "My two sons have barely met your father, yet they are willing to stand up as groomsmen with him. And my brother as well."

Dad nodded. "That was convenient for me since I only had two buddies who seemed right for the wedding."

"So I had just hoped . . ." Karen's voice trailed off.

"Okay," Daphne agreed with reluctance. "If you really want me, I'm happy to participate."

"Really?" Karen's face lit up.

"Yes. It'll be fun." Daphne forced a smile. Okay, it might be fun watching her dad getting hitched from close up.

"But why were you so reluctant?" Dad asked.

She shrugged. "Maybe I just thought you were asking me to be polite."

"No," Karen assured her. "We want you there." She reached into her oversized bag and removed a large three-ring binder. "This is my wedding planning book." She opened it on the table. "Everything for the wedding is in here." She flipped through pages, showing photos of the cake and the flowers.

"Those flowers are gorgeous," Daphne told her. "You're so smart to pick a fall wedding."

"And these are the dresses." Karen flipped to a page where a dark-haired model wore something that resembled puffed pastry in a purplish shade that reminded Daphne of an uncooked hot dog. "I wanted to go with cocktail-length dresses," she explained. "That way you can wear it later."

"Oh." Daphne nodded. "Right."

"They're a little spendy, but being able to use them again helps to offset the cost. Don't you think?"

Daphne had to bite her tongue to keep from saying what she really thought—that the dress was absolutely hideous and she would look like death warmed over in that color. "And you're certain this dress design will look good on all your bridesmaids?"

"Oh yes. And the reason I needed to nail this down with you today is because Monday is the final day for placing orders. You'll have to go in to Frederica's tomorrow to be measured. You can do that, can't you? I mean since you don't have a real job."

"Sure," she said quietly. "I can do that."

"And tell her your shoe size too." Karen flipped to the next page. "I think these will be just perfect with the dresses."

Daphne stared at the plain-looking satin pumps. The heels were low and the toes were rounded. They looked like something her Aunt Dee might've worn.

"Naturally, they'll be dyed to match the dresses."

"Naturally." Daphne gave her another stiff smile.

"Oh, I'm so glad you want to be part of this." Karen beamed at her. And suddenly she was telling Daphne about the shower her sister was planning and the bridesmaid party for when they tried on their dresses. "And, of course, we have the bachelorette party." Karen winked at Dad. "My sister Diane has already lined up some really great surprises for me on that night."

"Sounds like fun." Daphne glanced at Dad, who was obliviously watching someone teeing off outside as Karen continued flipping through her thick book.

"My niece Kenzie made this notebook for me. She's been helping with all the plans. She's only twenty-six, but she just started a new wedding planning business in town. Maybe you've seen her ads in the paper. *Weddings 4 Hire.* She uses the numeral four instead of the word."

"Clever." Daphne nodded.

"First time I saw the ad, I thought of *gun for hire,*" Dad admitted. "I asked Kenzie if she'd ever planned a shotgun wedding, and for some reason she didn't think that was too funny." He chuckled.

"Not everyone has your highly developed sense of humor, Dad."

"Thank goodness." Karen laughed.

"Well, if that's that." Daphne set her linen napkin next to her plate. "I think I'll excuse myself. I haven't been home since before church, and I suspect my kitties are missing me by now."

Karen and Dad exchanged worried glances. As if they were still concerned that she was turning into some kind of social misfit.

"I hope to get my novel finished. Before all the wedding activities start happening."

"Then you better hurry," Karen said. "The first fitting is in a couple of weeks. And according to my sister, the shower is less than a month from now. I gave Diane your address and phone number. She said she might invite the bridesmaids to help out with some things. I hope you don't mind."

Daphne forced another smile. "Not at all." Then feeling more desperate and driven than ever, she hurried out of there and drove directly home. It felt as if her dad's wedding was suddenly encroaching on her novel—not to mention her life! A part of her realized this was not normal thinking. After all, it wasn't as if she had a life. Or much of one. Not only that, but in all honesty, she had no deadline for her book. Not like she did with the advice column. But just sitting there and listening to all that wedding talk had reminded her of how badly she wanted to make this book a success. And if she could do that, she would finally be free from jumping through the hoops of Aunt Dee's will. As she went into her office she wondered—what would Aunt Dee say about all this?

> *Dear Daphne,*
> *This question isn't exactly about my love life. Or maybe it is. My main problem is that my father is remarrying, and I am feeling out of sorts about the whole thing. It's not so much that I dislike my stepmother-to-be. I don't really know her. However, I do resent the expectation that just because it's my dad's wedding, I must be involved. Is it fair for them to pull me into their wedding festivities against my will? Or am I just being selfish? Or even worse, maybe I'm envious. Especially considering that I'm thirty-four and have never had a wedding of my own. Am I having wedding envy? If so, what should I do?*
> *Annoyed in Appleton*

> *Dear Annoyed,*
> *It's understandable that you're feeling unsettled over your father's upcoming nuptials. It is clearly stirring up a lot emotions for you. But perhaps you are looking at this from the wrong angle. Maybe you*

should ask yourself: Is your father happy? And if he's happy, shouldn't you be happy for him? Shouldn't you be willing to celebrate this special day with him? Also, his decision to take the plunge (marriage) might be challenging your own choices. Maybe it's time to ask yourself if there is some deep-down reason you're not married. Maybe it's time you got more honest with yourself regarding the answer.

Daphne

If Daphne was annoyed before she wrote those silly letters, she was even more annoyed as she hit the delete button on them now. Seriously, Dear Daphne clearly did not know what she was talking about! Instead of wasting precious time writing silly letters, she should be working on her suspense novel. After all, she had power and control over everything that happened in her fictional world. If a character was aggravating her, she could simply have her knocked off.

Whether it was to escape her own pathetic past and present or her desperate attempt to press toward her future, Daphne wrote furiously for the next week. And by midday on Thursday, she could actually see a light at the end of her book tunnel. Many of the mysterious threads were magically weaving themselves together—promising a satisfying ending. And unless she was mistaken, this novel would be finished in just a couple of chapters. Although she couldn't say for certain it was good—she had a feeling it might be. And, after doing some research she decided that if Aunt Dee's publishing house, or any other traditional houses, declined to contract her book, she might take it directly to the Internet and publish it there herself. She'd been hearing good things about authors who'd gone that route. Maybe it could work for her. Anyway, it was worth a shot.

It was barely three when she called it a day. She was just turning off her computer when the phone rang. It was Sabrina and she sounded slightly frantic. "Oh, Daphne, I hope I'm not disturbing you. I know you're probably in the middle of a big scene in your novel, but I just couldn't wait. Do you mind?"

"Not at all. I was just shutting it down." Daphne felt slightly guilty as she remembered how she'd chided Sabrina before for calling in the middle of the afternoon a while back. "What's up?"

"I want you to go to Fairview with me tomorrow. Can you get away?"

"Oh . . . I don't know." Daphne looked around her cluttered and dusty office. "I had really planned to do some housework tomorrow. I'm afraid I've let things go around here. And it's getting pretty bad."

"*Please,* Daphne. You've barely been out of the house for nearly a month now. Just come to Fairview with me tomorrow, okay?"

"Why? What's the urgency?"

"I really, really need you to help me pick out a new sofa. That one I brought with me from Atlanta is taking up way too much space in my tiny living room. I've got to scale down. And you have such a good eye for furnishings. Please, come and help me?"

"I don't know. I really need to get some clean—"

"Please, Daphne. I'll drive and I'll treat you to lunch. And I won't even take Tootsie along if you'll just come with me. Just this once. I'll help you clean house in repayment if you like."

Daphne ran her finger over the desktop, creating a trail through the dust. "Well, okay. Not that I'll let you come clean for me. But when you sound so desperate—how can I refuse? Besides I still owe you one for the day you helped with my makeover." Daphne cringed to look down at her grubby sweats, running her fingers through hair that was in need of some serious help. Fortunately Sabrina couldn't see her right now.

"Fabulous! Let's leave around noon, okay? We'll have lunch first. That way we'll be fortified for the rest of the day."

"Sounds like a plan."

"Girls' *day* out," Sabrina chirped happily.

As Daphne hung up the phone, a small figure in the front yard caught her eye. She peered out the window to see a child bending down to scoop up a big orange cat. Blinking in surprise Daphne looked again—the cat was Lucy and now it appeared as if the child was carting the poor thing away.

"My goodness!" Daphne hurried to find her shoes and then dashed out the front door to stop the catnapping juvenile. She spotted them several houses down. That child was making good time.

Daphne jogged to catch up and then fell into step next to what turned out to be a very scruffy-looking little girl. She didn't appear to be more than six or seven. "Hello there," Daphne said curiously.

The girl looked up with big brown eyes and a dirty face. "Hello?"

"Where are you taking that cat?"

"Home," she answered nonchalantly, as if accustomed to stealing cats on a regular basis.

"But *why* are you taking it?"

"Because he's my friend and he wants to go home with me."

Daphne placed a hand on the girl's thin shoulder. "Maybe you've confused this cat with another cat. This cat's name is *Lucy* and she belongs to me."

The girl looked worried now. "Oh?"

"Here." Daphne reached down to rescue Lucy from the catnapper's arms. "I'll take her for you."

The girl reluctantly released the cat, then shoved her hands into the pockets of her baggy jeans in a dejected way. "I just wanted a cat," she said quietly. "To be my friend. I didn't know he . . . I mean, she belonged to someone else."

Daphne studied the girl. Her dark brown hair looked as if it hadn't seen a comb in weeks and her thin blue T-shirt was dirty and torn. "It's okay. I'm sure Lucy enjoyed the attention. Where do you live anyway?"

"That blue house." The girl pointed to a run-down house with an overgrown yard.

"Have you lived there long?"

"No. It's my grandma's house. I came to stay with her so I could go to school."

"What's your grandma's name?"

The girl frowned. "Why? Are you gonna tell on me?"

"No, not at all. I was just curious." Daphne smiled. "I'm Daphne by the way. And I live in the house where you picked up Lucy. I have another cat too. Her name is Ethel and she would be brokenhearted if she lost Lucy. Lucy is her best friend."

"I wish I had a best friend."

"Do you know any kids in this neighborhood?" Daphne looked up and down the street, trying to remember if anyone around here had young children.

"Not really. Except for stupid old Roland and he throws dirt clods at me whenever I walk past his house."

"That's not very friendly."

"I know."

"What's your name?" Daphne asked.

The girl's brow furrowed as if she just remembered something. "I'm not supposed to talk to strangers."

Daphne laughed. "A little late for that, don't you think? But in general, it's probably a good rule. However, since you were caught taking my cat, I think it's okay to talk to me. But if you like I could meet your grandmother first."

"No . . . she's sick."

"She's sick?" Daphne frowned at the sad-looking blue house.

"Yeah, she has to stay in bed a lot."

"I'm sorry." Daphne looked down at the girl. "Who takes care of you?"

Her bony shoulders shrugged. "I take care of myself."

"Oh . . . I see."

"Sorry about taking your cat."

"That's okay." Daphne petted Lucy who seemed content to be held like this.

"My name is Mabel Myers," the girl said quietly.

"Mabel Myers?" Daphne nodded. "Well, that is a nice name."

"Daphne is a nice name too." Mabel smiled shyly.

"Hey, Mabel. Do you like pumpkins?"

Mabel's eyes grew wide. "You mean like for jack-o'-lanterns?"

"Yes. I have a garden that's got lots of pumpkins. And I was going to take some of them and put them on my porch. Maybe you'd like to help me."

"Can I?"

"Sure. If it's okay with your grandma. And if you help me, I can repay you with a nice big pumpkin to put on your own porch."

"My own pumpkin?"

"Yes. Maybe you'll want more than one. But first I need to talk to your grandma and make sure she doesn't mind."

Mabel frowned. "But she might be sleeping."

"How about if you go find out?" Daphne looked down at Lucy. "I'll take Lucy home, then come back to check on you. If your grandma is awake and says it's all right, you can come back and help me. Okay?"

"Okay." Mabel nodded eagerly.

Daphne ran Lucy back home. What on earth was she getting herself into? Yet at the same time she felt so sorry for little Mabel, she couldn't let her down. What was her situation? And what was wrong with the grandma?

When Daphne got back to Mabel's house, the front door was ajar. "Hello?" Daphne called into the house. "Mabel?"

When no one answered, Daphne pushed the door open wider and stepped inside. The first thing that hit her was the smell. Stale and musty and dirty. As her eyes adjusted to the darkness due to the closed drapes, she could see that the room was cluttered and messy. Indeed, it did seem as if the occupants here must be sick to let it get into this dilapidated condition.

"Mabel?" Daphne called out quietly. "Are you—?"

"That's her right there," Mabel announced as she led a frail-looking woman into the living room. "See, Grandma? That's the lady who's going to let me have a pumpkin if you say it's okay. That's Daphne."

"Hello," Daphne said uncomfortably. "Sorry to barge in on you like this." She quickly explained the situation and where she lived and about her garden.

"Dee Ballinger's house?" the woman questioned.

Daphne explained about being Dee's niece. "Well, actually I'm her granddaughter, but it's a long story."

"Can I go with her?" Mabel asked eagerly.

"Yes . . . that's fine."

"I can write down my phone number if you like," Daphne offered.

The woman raised her hand. "That's all right. I'm not worried about Mabel."

"Can I get your name?" Daphne asked. "I mean since we're neighbors and all."

"Yes, of course. I'm Vera. Vera Myers." She waved her hand toward her raggedy bathrobe. "As you can see, I, uh, I have been sick. Probably shouldn't have offered to keep Mabel." She put her hand on Mabel's head. "But I'm all she has now."

"Can we go now, Grandma?" Mabel asked impatiently.

"Yes, yes. Go." Vera looked at Daphne with sad eyes. "Thank you."

As they left, Daphne was filled with questions . . . about Vera and Mabel and what seemed a rather sad and desperate situation. But seeing how happy Mabel was to be out of there and looking forward to gathering pumpkins, Daphne held back on questioning her too much.

Soon they were cutting the pumpkin stems, loading them into the wheelbarrow where Mabel used a bucket of water and a rag to wash the dirt off the pumpkins. Then they lined pumpkins up and down both sides of the stairs leading to the porch, as well as beside the door.

"That looks so pretty," Mabel declared as they stood back to admire their work. "Do lots of trick-or-treaters come to your house?"

"I don't really know," Daphne admitted. "I haven't been here for Halloween in years."

"My other house—where I lived with my mom—we didn't get any trick-or-treaters there."

"Did you go trick-or-treating?"

"No . . . Mom wouldn't let me."

"Well, some people think it's not safe sending children out like that . . . going up to stranger's doors. But Appleton is a pretty small town. I'm guessing there's still a lot of trick-or-treating going on around here. I'll be sure to have candy on hand."

Mabel's eyes lit up. "Maybe Grandma will let me go trick-or-treating."

"How old are you?"

"Seven. Almost eight. I'll be eight in December."

"What grade are you?"

"Second." She scowled. "They tried to make me be in first grade again . . . 'cuz I missed so much school when I lived with my mama. But I can read real good. So they let me go in second."

"Do you like to read?"

"Yeah. I love to read."

"Maybe you'll want to borrow books from here." Daphne pointed toward the house. "My aunt had a good collection of books I used to read when I was your age."

"I thought you said she was your grandma."

"She was kind of an aunt and grandma. You know?"

"Yeah." Mabel nodded as if she understood.

"You worked really hard," Daphne said. "Maybe you'd like a snack before you go home."

Mabel's eyes lit up. "*Inside* your house?"

"Sure, come on in. We'll see what we can rustle up." Daphne looked down at Mabel's muddy tennis shoes. "But we'll leave our shoes on the porch, okay?"

"This is a real pretty house," Mabel said as they went inside.

"There's a bathroom right there." Daphne pointed to the powder room. "Go and get those hands nice and clean and I'll see what we can have for a snack."

Unsure of what seven-year-olds liked to eat, Daphne set out apple slices and cheese and ginger snaps as well as a glass of milk.

"Wow." Mabel sat down at the table. "This is a really nice snack."

"Well, you worked hard." Daphne sat across from her. "Eat up."

Mabel eagerly ate as Daphne nibbled and watched with curiosity. The child was clearly hungry. "Who fixes food at your grandma's house?"

Mabel shrugged as she chewed.

Daphne told Mabel about how her mom died when she was even younger than Mabel . . . and how Daphne learned to cook at a young age. "So I could take care of my daddy and me."

"My dad's in prison."

"Oh . . ." Daphne sighed. "I'm sorry."

"And my mom," Mabel spoke quietly, as if she wasn't sure. "Well, she's like your mom."

Daphne felt a lump in her throat. "I'm sorry, Mabel."

"Grandma says she's with the angels." Mabel picked up an apple slice. "But I wish she was still here with me."

"I know how you feel."

After Mabel had eaten enough, they went back outside and loaded the wheelbarrow with seven pumpkins—since Mabel was seven—as well as a nice selection of produce Daphne hoped the grandmother would know how to fix. Then as the sky was turning rosy and dusky, Daphne helped Mabel push the wheelbarrow down to the blue house.

As they walked, Mabel chattered away happily. It was obvious she'd enjoyed their afternoon and that a new friendship was being formed. A friendship that would require more than Daphne was used to giving—and yet she didn't feel concerned. In fact, she was looking forward to getting better acquainted with Mabel.

Chapter 17

The next morning as Daphne did some overdue housecleaning, she was still thinking about Mabel. Since it was Friday, Mabel would probably be in school right now. Still, Daphne wondered what she might possibly do to help the child. She wanted to think of ways to be involved without being overly intrusive. It was clear that Mabel needed some help with her personal hygiene and clothes. And who knew what the child was eating? Daphne was so caught up in thinking about Mabel, that she was totally surprised when Sabrina showed up at her door, reminding her that they had made plans for a girls' day out today. "And you do not look the least bit ready for it." Sabrina frowned.

"I'm so sorry." Daphne set the dusting cloth down. "I'll run and change right now. It won't take but five minutes. I promise."

"Well, at least put on something cute and festive," Sabrina called up the stairs. "I'm taking us to a pretty swanky place."

Daphne hurried to clean up and dress. Why had she agreed to this little outing? Oh, it wasn't that she didn't like the idea of furniture shopping or being with Sabrina. It was just that she would rather stay home. She would rather clean house and work in the garden and write in her book than get dressed up and go "out." This was probably the result of being such a hermit and cloistering herself up like she'd done these past weeks. Not unlike Stockholm syndrome (something she'd written about in her novel) but in this scenario, she was her own prison keeper. For that reason alone, she knew she needed to get out. It's just that she didn't want to.

"I'm sorry, kitties," she told Lucy and Ethel before she went downstairs. "I won't be back for a while." Daphne was fully aware of how pathetic and boring her homebody life might appear to the casual onlooker (like Dad or Sabrina). Here she was talking to cats and preferring housework to lunching with a friend—gladly settling for her hermit lifestyle. But the isolation didn't concern her that much. Perhaps that was because deep down inside she felt worried that it was all going to disappear soon. Next May to be exact. Daphne's real fear was that when her most-pressing deadline arrived—and she would still be unmarried—this peaceful simple life would all go up in smoke. She would be forced to leave Aunt Dee's house and everything else behind. But just like Scarlett O'Hara, Daphne didn't have to think about that today.

As Sabrina drove them to Fairview, Daphne told Sabrina all about their young catnapping neighbor and her rather tragic little life.

"Oh, my. The poor thing." Sabrina shook her head. "Do you think there's anything we can do to help her?"

"I hope so. Mabel's really a sweetheart."

"*Mabel?* Her name is Mabel?"

"Yes." Daphne chuckled. "Seems an unusual name for a little girl."

"Sounds like an old lady's name."

"Although it kind of suits her too." Daphne told Sabrina about the pumpkins and how excited Mabel was to take home seven of them. "But I really want to do more for her. It's obvious that her grandmother is unable to properly care for her." She described Mabel's hair and clothes and how hungry she seemed. "Maybe after we find your couch, we can stop by a Walmart or something and pick up a few things for Mabel."

"Maybe so." Sabrina described where they were going to lunch. "I read about it online. It sounded really good. I got us a reservation and put it into my GPS so we won't get lost." A few minutes later, Sabrina pulled up to what looked like a very nice restaurant.

"This is so chic and uptown," Daphne said as they were being seated. "I almost feel like I'm in Manhattan."

"That's right, you lived in Manhattan."

"Well, not actually Manhattan. I lived in Brooklyn. But I worked in Manhattan."

Sabrina listened attentively as Daphne described working for *The Times* and what it was like living in New York.

"That must've been so exciting."

"It was," Daphne admitted. "At first anyway. I had big dreams. But then I got kind of stuck . . . after I got my heart broke."

"With Ryan?"

Daphne blinked in surprise. She was shocked Sabrina could even remember his name. She'd told her a little bit of the Ryan story a couple of weeks ago over coffee.

"And then you really didn't date much after him?"

"Yeah. It took a while to get over that. For years I still imagined that Ryan was the love of my life."

"Until he showed up in Appleton." Sabrina grinned.

"Yes. Funny how a small town can show a guy's true colors much more effectively than a big city. It's like people can hide themselves in the busyness of New York. You think you know them . . . but you really don't. At least that's how it seemed to me."

"Atlanta was a little like that for me. So different from the sweet little town I grew up in. I suppose I was a lot like you . . . pretty naive."

"At least you had more experience with men. Sounds like you dated a lot before marrying Edward."

"I suppose, but that didn't seem to help my judgment much." Sabrina shared a little more about her family and growing up with a distant father, who she later learned was having affairs. "I guess it kind of affected my radar about guys in general. At least that's what my shrink told me."

"You went to a psychiatrist?"

She nodded. "Yeah. I pretty much flipped out after I realized I'd never have kids. Even having Tootsie didn't help that much. So Edward made me see a shrink. But she was actually pretty good."

"You've been through a lot."

Sabrina smiled. "I guess so. But doesn't that make us who we are? Anyway that's what Pastor Andrew said last Sunday. Right?"

"That's right. I keep reminding myself of that line. I even wrote it on an index card and stuck it on my fridge. 'Focus on each step of the journey and eventually you'll reach your final destination.'"

After a thoroughly delightful lunch, Daphne found she was eager to help Sabrina find the perfect sofa. After a couple of hours of shopping, they discovered a furniture store with lots of good options, and it didn't take long until they both agreed on a traditional design in a celery green chenille. "This will be gorgeous with your area rug," Daphne told her.

"And everything else in there. So much better than that oversized sectional."

Before long the sofa was written up, paid for, and arranged for delivery, and Sabrina and Daphne were on their way.

"Perfect," Sabrina proclaimed as they exited the store. "I think we should celebrate." She pointed to a brick building across the street. "McMahan's," she said eagerly. "That's my maiden name! We have to go there."

As they went inside, Daphne could tell it was a brewery, but Sabrina seemed so excited about finding this place that Daphne just went with the flow, following Sabrina to a pub table and sitting down.

"Why is there a number on the table?" Daphne asked as she picked up the folded card with a nine penned on it.

Sabrina made a funny face, then shrugged. "Maybe it's for the waiter."

"Or maybe this table is reserved for someone." Daphne looked around but all the tables had numbers. Sabrina might be right.

"Or maybe they're playing some kind of game." Sabrina picked up the drinks menu. "You know for happy hour, I remember being at a place where they had this elimination game and you won prizes like free pizza. It was really fun."

"Oh yeah." Daphne nodded. "That makes sense."

"What do you want to drink?" Sabrina asked. "Looks like they have a huge selection of beers."

"I'll just have coffee," Daphne told her.

"Good idea," Sabrina agreed as the waiter approached. "Two coffees, please. With cream and sugar. Thanks."

It wasn't long until he returned with their coffees. "You guys here for the—"

"That's right," Sabrina said quickly. "We're here for all the festivities."

"Will there be prizes?" Daphne asked.

His brow creased. "Well, I guess some people might think they've won a prize. But from what I've seen in the past, you usually go home with a—"

"Could I get some Sweet'N Low?" Sabrina asked.

"Yeah, sure."

"I didn't know you liked sugar substitutes," Daphne said as the waiter left.

"Sometimes I do." She patted her midsection. "Especially after a big lunch like we had today."

The room was starting to fill as the waiter returned with some packets and the noise level was increasing. "Looks like this is a popular place." Daphne stirred cream into her coffee.

Sabrina looked uneasy now, as if something was wrong.

"Do you feel okay?" Daphne asked her.

Sabrina bit her lower lip. "I have to explain something."

"What is it?"

Sabrina picked up the card with the nine on it. "This is your number."

"We can share it," Daphne said.

"No." Sabrina pointed to a nearby table where no one was sitting. "That's my number. I'm ten."

"Ten?" Daphne was confused.

"You see . . ." Sabrina made a nervous laugh. "We each get our own table in this game."

Daphne frowned. "What kind of game is this?"

"Have you ever heard of speed dating?"

"Speed dating?"

Sabrina winced. "Yeah. It seemed like a fun idea."

"What are—?"

"It's a quick, easy way to meet some available bachelors, Daphne. I knew you would never agree to it, so I took the liberty of arranging it myself." She glanced at her watch. "It will begin in about five minutes and—"

"You cannot be serious. You signed me up for speed dating without even telling me?"

"I knew you'd act like this," Sabrina said quietly. "But just you wait, when it's all over with, you'll be thanking me."

Daphne was flabbergasted. "Are you saying that you cooked this whole day up? Needing a new sofa? Offering to take me to lunch? Driving over here? Just so we could do this?"

"I did need a new sofa. And I wanted to have lunch with you. You've been way too much of a hermit and—"

"But you lied to me, Sabrina."

"Just a teeny-weeny little white lie." Sabrina held her thumb and forefinger barely apart. "I didn't know how else to get you here."

Daphne narrowed her eyes. "And I thought you were my friend."

"I am your friend. You know I am. But I really wanted to do this. And I felt certain you would want to do it too. Except that you'd act like this. I mean, as much as I love you, honey, and I surely do, you can be such a stick-in-the-mud sometimes."

"A stick-in-the-mud?" Daphne blinked.

"Oh, you know how you are. If left to your own devices, you might never meet Mr. Right. Can you blame me for trying to give you a little ol' boost?"

"A boost? Or a kick in the—"

"It's only because I love you, Daphne. And I don't want to lose you as my neighbor. I honestly don't know what I'd do without you across the street." She smiled hopefully. "Please, don't be mad." She tipped her head to where a couple of guys were coming in the door. "And check out some of the guys you're going to meet. Don't they look like they might be worthwhile?"

Daphne just shook her head.

"And think about it. Each fellow will only take five minutes of your time. Remember how much you hated that date with Dr. Tony? How you said it lasted forever? Well, this is a quick, painless way to avoid—"

"Can I have your attention?" A middle-aged man by the bar was ringing a bell and slowly the room quieted and everyone was looking at him. "Welcome to McMahan's *Fourth Friday Fast Finds.*" He chuckled. "Otherwise known as speed dating. For those of you who are new here, I will share the ground rules. Women, you should already know your number and you should be seated at your table. Men, you have your cards with numbers and time slots. It is up to you to find the right table at the appropriate time. Each mini date will last exactly five minutes. No more, no less. If you know you want to get better acquainted with someone, you simply request his or her phone number. But then you must move on. Is that clear? No lingering at a table just because you want to. Anyone who doesn't play by the rules will be eliminated."

Everyone acknowledged that was clear, and giving Daphne a quick wink, Sabrina moved to her table. Daphne had never really known the meaning of the old adage "fit to be tied," but that was just how she felt right now, like they'd have to tie her down to keep her here.

The man rang the bell again. "Whenever you hear this bell ringing like this, fellows, you know it's time to move on. I'll give you one minute to get to your next table, but when you hear that bell ring again, it's time to begin. And don't forget, since I'm the owner of this pub, if anyone needs a drink or a refill, just hold up your hand and the waiter will see to you." He held up a stein of beer as he looked over the crowd with a big grin. "You're a great-looking bunch of kids. Here's to you finding the love of your life tonight!" He clanged the bell. "Let the games begin!"

Chapter 18

Before Daphne could jump down from her stool and make a quick exit, a bookish-looking young man with dark, curly hair and tortoise-framed glasses sat across from her. "Hi, uh, Number Nine," he said in a nervous tone. "I, uh, I'm Jack Brandt." He stuck out his hand to shake hers. "I'm, uh, I'm happy to make your, uh, your acquaintance."

"I'm Daphne Ballinger." She peeled her hand away from his slightly sweaty palm. "Nice to meet you too." Okay, she felt sorry for him now. "To be perfectly honest, I'm kind of in shock about this speed-dating thing. You see, my friend over there, Number Ten, she sort of kidnapped me into coming here today. I had no idea we were doing this. She got me to come to Fairview under the guise of sofa shopping, if you can believe it."

He looked worried. "Oh, so you don't really want to find some-one here? Want me to go, then?"

"No, that's okay." She shook her head. "Remember what the emcee said. You have to play by the rules or get eliminated." She forced a smile. "And you probably don't want to risk that. Anyway, you seem like a nice guy. So why don't we just play along. Go ahead and tell me about yourself."

"Oh . . . yeah . . . well, there's not much to tell. I graduated from college last spring, but the only job I can find is in a convenience store. I live in my mom's basement and I—"

"Hang on, Jack." She held up her hand to stop him. "If you want to succeed at this speed-dating thing, you might need to sound a little more positive about yourself and your life."

He looked slightly confused. "How do I do that? I don't want to lie. I mean, I am what I am. If a girl doesn't like that, she—"

"Why don't you start by telling me about something you really enjoy doing?"

He frowned as if thinking hard. "Well, I do play the banjo. I like that. And I really like folk music and bluegrass."

"Really? Are you in a band or anything?"

"Some of my buddies and me—we've just started up this blue-grass band. We've had a couple of gigs already and it's been pretty fun." It was like she'd uncorked him and he went on telling her about how they wanted to record an album and attend some of the folk festivals around the country.

"That sounds very cool," she told him just as the bell clanged. "Now, if you just talk about that kind of thing—not your mom's basement—you might garner some interest."

"Thank you. That was really helpful. But you never got a chance to tell me about your—"

"Move on," a muscular guy with a shaved head was telling Jack. "Time's up, bud."

Jack vacated the stool and Mr. Baldy sat down, grinning widely at Daphne. He was just telling her his name, but the bell rang and she didn't quiet catch it. "I live over on the west side," he said quickly. "In a condo I bought a few years ago. It was a short sale so I got a killer deal on it. I work at Bob Brown Motors. In sales. I'm only thirty and the youngest sales manager Brown's ever had. But that's because I was top salesman for three years running."

"Congratulations." She set down her coffee cup, preparing to speak.

"I guess I'm a natural when it comes to cars and trucks. Probably because I've always loved anything with wheels. I think I've owned about twenty different rigs during my life. Right now I'm driving a Dodge Ram 2500 that's loaded. I also have a 300—talk about luxury. Both are less than a year old too. But hey, you can't very well be a top salesman and go around in a lame set of wheels, can you?"

"I guess not."

"Oh yeah, I have a Harley too. Can't leave that one out." Mr. Baldy chuckled. "Sorry to talk so fast, but five minutes isn't long." He glanced at his watch. "Why don't you tell me about yourself now?" He paused to take a sip of his beer. "I like redheads."

"I'm thirty-four," she said slowly.

"That's okay. I like older women too." He laughed. "Hey, it's not like you're a cougar or anything. You'd have to be forty or thereabouts, don't you? But I did have a cougar going after me once. She was like fifty but dressed like she was twenty. Pretty weird stuff."

Daphne nodded. "Anyway, I live in Appleton with two elderly cats named Ethel and Lucy." She waited for him to react.

He frowned. "Really? Cats? I have a Doberman named Butch. He'd probably like your cats. For lunch." He laughed. "Just kidding."

She gave him a stiff smile. "I'm a writer and I work from my home. In fact, I'm pretty much a hermit these days. I don't like getting out that much. My friend over there, Number Ten—"

"Oh yeah, she is really hot." He stared at Sabrina, then down at his card. "She's next for me. And I've been keeping my eye on that one. Can't wait to meet her." He talked some more about himself, and then to Daphne's great relief the bell rang.

"Good luck," she told him.

"Who needs luck?" He jerked a thumb toward his chest. "When you got all this?"

"Right." She raised her hand, hoping she might get her coffee refilled before the next round. But already a short, slight man with sandy hair sat across from her. And then the bell rang. Thomas Grant was a nice enough fellow. An accountant, he seemed polite and well spoken, and he gave her plenty of opportunity to tell him about herself—and just to make herself clear, she explained that she was doing this against her will. Then just as the interview wound down, she suppressed the urge to yawn, holding up her hand again . . . hoping to get some coffee.

"It was a pleasure to meet you, Daphne," Thomas said after the bell rang. "Any chance I could get your phone number?"

"Well, I . . ." She pursed her lips. "I, uh, I don't think so. I don't want you to waste your time on me and I'm not really looking for—" The bell rang again and the next "contestant" slipped onto the stool.

"Hi, I'm Harrison."

"Hi, Harrison, I'm Daphne," she said a bit wearily. "And I'll warn you, I was brought here against my will." She pointed to Sabrina. "My friend over there tricked me."

He glanced at Sabrina, then made a funny grin. "Welcome to

the club." Now he pointed across the room. "My friend Josh roped me into doing this with him. I'm trying to be a good sport, but my patience is starting to wear thin."

"Me too." With short light-brown hair and clear blue eyes, he was nice looking. Dressed casually in a chambray shirt and jeans, it wasn't like he was trying to impress anyone. "What do you do, Harrison?"

"For real?" He looked concerned.

"You mean you've been lying to these women?"

He gave a sheepish grin.

She shrugged. "That's fine. You don't have to tell me."

"Okay, for some reason I don't mind telling you. I'm an architect."

She studied him curiously. "And that's something you're ashamed of?"

He laughed. "No, not at all. But sometimes saying I'm an architect—only around certain kinds of women—can be similar to being a doctor or a lawyer. It's like some women's radar goes off."

Daphne laughed. "So what have you been telling women you do? Work at a gas station?"

"Close. I've been saying I'm an auto mechanic."

She looked down at his hands. "Those don't look like a mechanic's hands."

"Hmmm . . . good point. Guess I should keep them out of sight. But the truth is, I'm kind of a mechanic. I've been restoring an old MG in my spare time. At the rate I'm going, it should be driveable by the time I reach fifty."

"How old are you?"

"Thirty-seven."

"I'm thirty-four. And it feels like I'm a little old for this crowd. So far you're the first one who's older than me."

"So what do you do, Daphne?"

She considered this. "You mean for real?"

He shrugged. "It's up to you. But I was honest."

"I'm a writer."

He looked impressed. "Interesting. What kind of writing?"

"Some freelance newspaper stuff. And I'm nearly finished with my first novel."

"Cool." He nodded. "Any good?"

"I have no idea. Sometimes I think it is. But then . . . well, I don't really know."

"But kudos to you for going for it." He smiled. "I'm impressed."

She was just explaining how she'd recently relocated to Appleton when the bell rang.

"Wow, that was fast," he said as he stood.

"Yeah. For a change." She smiled.

"So, I didn't really plan on this, but are you interested in sharing your phone number?"

"I, uh, I guess so."

As the next guy stepped up, Harrison pulled out his phone and she quietly recited the numbers for him. "Thanks." He smiled brightly. "I enjoyed chatting with you."

"Yeah." She nodded nervously. "Me too."

The bell clanged again and he went on to Sabrina's table. The next guy was in his twenties and so covered with tattoos that she wasn't the least bit surprised when he told her he owned a tattoo shop in town.

"So you're kind of like a walking advertisement?" She feigned interest.

"Yeah, pretty much." And then he proceeded to tell her about each tattoo and when and where he'd gotten it and who had designed it and the meaning behind it and finally—thankfully—the bell rang.

Daphne continued working her way through the remaining five-minute "dates," trying to act interested for some of the sweeter ones and not bothering with the ones who seemed so full of themselves, they didn't even notice anyway. But as she sat there sipping on luke-warm coffee, she kept thinking of Harrison. And once in a while she would glance around the room, spot him, and try to decide whether or not he was showing the same kind of interest in the other women as he'd shown to her. Was he telling them he was a mechanic or an architect? Unless it was her imagination, he just seemed to be putting in his time.

When the final guy finished up his five minutes, Daphne looked over to where Harrison was talking to his friend Josh. Then Harrison's phone must've rung because he was talking to someone. And then he seemed to be telling Josh good-bye. As he hurried out, Daphne realized she didn't even know his last name. And she hadn't gotten his number.

"How did that go for you?" Sabrina asked in a slightly weary tone.

"Long and exhausting." Daphne reached for her purse.

"I'm sorry. I guess you were right. It was a waste of time. You ready to go?"

"Absolutely."

"Sorry I dragged you into this against your will," Sabrina said as they left McMahan's. "It seemed like a good idea . . . at the time."

"So you really had a bad time?" Daphne felt sorry for Sabrina as they walked toward the car. After all, she'd invested so much into this day. It was too bad. "You didn't meet *anyone* you liked?"

"Oh, maybe there were a couple worth getting to know better." Sabrina sighed as she unlocked her car.

"Well, there were certainly a number of guys who were looking forward to meeting you," Daphne told her. "A lot of them thought you were the hottest thing in the room."

"Really?" Sabrina brightened.

"Yeah. One guy—I didn't catch his name, but he was a car guy with a shaved head—he couldn't wait to meet you."

"Mr. Motor-head." Sabrina groaned as she started her car. "Puleeze."

"Or you could call him Mr. Motor-mouth."

Sabrina laughed.

"I'm sorry it was a bust for you," Daphne told her.

"Who knows, maybe it wasn't. I actually gave out my number a few times. I mean, you never know. Five minutes is pretty fast. But truth be told, that seemed like a whole lot of work for very little pay-off. And I'll be the first to admit you were right."

"Maybe."

"*Maybe?*" Sabrina's brows arched as she stopped for the traffic light. "You mean you met someone of interest?"

"There was this one guy," Daphne said slowly. "I didn't even catch his last name. But his first name was Harrison."

"You mean Harrison the mechanic?" Sabrina asked without much interest. "Nice looking and polite. But a mechanic? Really?"

Daphne laughed.

"What's so funny?"

"He's not really a mechanic, Sabrina."

"What? Then why did he say that?"

Daphne shrugged.

"What is he *really*?" Sabrina frowned as she drove through the intersection. "A bum? A criminal? Why would someone lie about his occupation? Did he even tell you what he really does?"

"He's an architect."

Sabrina's eyes lit up. "Well, now that's much better than a mechanic. But why didn't he tell *me* that? Isn't that kind of rude? Why be so secretive? It's not like he's in the CIA or FBI."

"Harrison and I could relate," Daphne explained. "He was there against his will. Seems that his buddy roped him into it. Harrison was just trying to be a good sport without putting everything out there. Can't blame him for that."

"Okay. I guess that makes sense. So did you get his number?" she asked eagerly.

"No." Daphne shook her head. "And like I said, I didn't even get his last name."

"Daphne!"

"But he asked for my number," she said hopefully.

"Good. So maybe this day wasn't a complete wash after all."

"Maybe not."

"At least I found my sofa."

"And we had a nice lunch together," Daphne assured her. "And really, Sabrina, despite all my complaining about the speed dating, which was mostly truly horrible, I had a good time today. And you were right, I did need to get out. Thank you."

"Who knows? Maybe this Harrison dude will turn out to be Mr. Right. He was nice looking enough. And well mannered. And an architect too." Sabrina sighed. "Wow, Daphne, you might've just hit the jackpot!"

She laughed nervously. "Well, I won't be holding my breath. He may never even call."

"If Harrison does call—and if you guys do go out and you hit it off and you wind up marrying him—then you will have me to thank, won't you?"

"Yes, I'll be forever in your debt and we'll name our firstborn after you," she teased.

But as they drove home, Daphne hoped that Harrison would call her. She did want to get to know him better. And not because he was an architect either. At least she didn't think so. However, what if he *had* been a mechanic? Would she have felt equally interested? Then she had to ask herself—did she really think of people like that? Was she truly that shallow? Did she measure a man's worth by his job or career? Or did she judge him strictly by his character? The truth was, she wasn't even sure.

Chapter 19

Due to feeling discombobulated over the whole speed-dating gig, Daphne had completely forgotten her plan to shop for something for Mabel on the way home from Fairview. But perhaps that was for the best. Daphne didn't want her enthusiasm to insult Vera. Or even worse, she didn't want to make Mabel feel inferior—as if something was wrong with her appearance. She didn't want them to feel as if they were her charity case or she was looking down on them. So on Saturday morning, she made a batch of zucchini muffins, and while they were still warm, she filled a basket and carried it down to the forlorn little blue house and knocked on the door.

"Daphne?" Mabel smiled as she opened the door wide.

"I brought muffins for you and your grandma. Is she sleeping?"

"I don't know." Mabel led Daphne into the messy living room where the TV was quietly playing cartoons. Right in front of the TV was a shabby blanket and pillow and a bowl with the remnants of colorful dry cereal in the bottom.

"I'll put these in the kitchen," Daphne told Mabel. Like the rest of the house, the kitchen was cluttered and messy . . . and smelly. Daphne longed to open the drapes and the windows to let some light and air in, but it wasn't her place.

"Here's Grandma," Mabel told Daphne as she came into the kitchen with Vera. Still wearing the same faded pink bathrobe, Vera peered curiously at Daphne.

"Sorry to barge in again." Daphne held up the basket of muffins. "But I wanted to share these with you." She rambled on about her garden and how she had so many zucchinis she had to do something with them.

"Thank you," Vera said in a weak voice.

"And I wanted to invite Mabel to come over again," Daphne told Vera. "If it's okay."

Vera just nodded. "It's okay. If Mabel wants to go."

"Yes, yes." Mabel jumped up and down.

"I thought we might go to town," Daphne told Vera. "If you don't mind."

Vera waved her hand. "That's fine."

"Can I get you anything while we're out?" Daphne offered. "From the grocery store? Or is there anything Mabel needs?"

"I, uh, I don't really know." Vera frowned, putting a hand to her forehead.

"Are you unwell?" Daphne asked. "Do you need to go lie down?"

"Yes . . . I think so." Vera started to shuffle out of the kitchen. "Do whatever you think is best," she mumbled. "Mabel can tell you what we need. Thank you."

"We're out of milk," Mabel declared.

"Yes . . . milk . . . we're out . . ." Vera kept going.

"Let's make a list," Daphne suggested. "Do you have any paper and a pencil around here?"

Mabel took off like a streak, returning with a school tablet and a purple felt pen. Together they looked around the kitchen, making a list of basic food supplies. And as they made the list, Daphne attempted to straighten a few things up, tossing some spoiled foods into the garbage and washing off a section of countertop next to the sink. With the list completed, she looked down at Mabel's food-stained T-shirt that she'd probably slept in. "Is that what you're wearing today?"

Mabel shrugged. "Yeah . . . I guess."

Daphne pursed her lips. "I think you can do better. How about if we look in your room and find something cleaner to wear."

"Okay." Mabel led Daphne down a hallway and into a small room where boxes and junk were stacked around the walls with just enough space left for a twin-sized bed.

"Is this all your stuff?"

Mabel shook her head. "No. It's my grandma's."

"Oh?" Daphne opened a closet to discover it too was filled with boxes and junk. "So where do you keep your clothes?"

Mabel pointed to a laundry basket piled with kid-sized clothes.

"Oh?" Daphne peered down at the heap. "Are these clean?"

Mabel shrugged.

Daphne picked up a pair of jeans and, judging by the dirt-encrusted knees, decided this basket was definitely not freshly laundered. She perused through the squalid pile, finally unearthing a pink sweatshirt that, though wrinkled, was stain-free. She handed it to Mabel. "This will work."

Mabel didn't argue as she switched shirts.

"Do you have a comb or a hairbrush?"

"I used to have a hairbrush," Mabel said. "But I think I lost it."

"Toothbrush?" Daphne watched as Mabel's mouth twisted to one side.

"I don't know where it is."

"Let's put that on our list too," Daphne told her. "And why don't we put these dirty clothes in the washing machine before we go? That way they'll be clean when we get back and we could put them in the dryer. And you'll have some clean clothes to wear to school next week. Okay?"

Mabel gladly agreed, leading Daphne out to the laundry area in the garage. "Do you know how to do laundry?" Daphne asked Mabel as she opened the washing machine.

"No." Mabel firmly shook her head.

"Maybe it's time you learned." Daphne found a wooden crate to use as a step stool for Mabel. And with the little girl watching, Daphne explained the basics of loading the clothes into the tub and how to measure and put in the soap and how to turn on the washer. "Just like that." As they listened to the water filling the machine, Daphne explained some safety rules. "Don't ever open the lid or unload the washing machine until the cycle is completely finished." She pointed to where the dial would turn straight up when it was done. "Okay?"

Mabel nodded with wide eyes. "Okay."

"And when we get back, I'll show you how to use the dryer."

As they went back through the house, Daphne felt she needed to have a quick but honest conversation with Vera. Privately. "Mabel. I want you to do what you can to clean up that kitchen. We'll need room to unload our groceries. Put any dirty dishes in the sink and anything that's garbage in the trash."

"The trash can is full."

"Then find a bag and put the trash in it."

"Okay!" Mabel nodded like this was a good plan.

"And I'm going to talk to your grandma for a few minutes."

Mabel looked uncertain but didn't say anything.

"Excuse me." Daphne tapped on Vera's bedroom door.

"Yes?" Vera said weakly.

"May I speak to you?" Daphne entered the dimly lit room where a TV was quietly playing on a nearby dresser. It smelled as musty and airless as the rest of the house, but it seemed a bit tidier and roomier than Mabel's room. Plus it had a master bath. "I feel I must talk to you about Mabel, Vera. I'm concerned for her welfare."

Vera sat up in bed and sighed. "Yes . . . so am I."

"I can see you're in no condition to care for a child."

"No, but I'm all she has." Vera's brow creased. "You're not from CPS, are you?"

"CPS?"

"Child Protective Services?"

"Oh no. Not at all. Like I told you, I live down the street. Dee Ballinger was my aunt."

"Yes . . . I know. But I worry that CPS might come here and take Mabel away."

"I can understand that." Daphne wanted to say maybe it would be best if they did take Mabel away, but she could tell by Vera's concerned eyes that she loved her granddaughter. "The thing is, I would like to help you. I'd like to do more than just get some groceries.

I'd like to help with some cleaning and organizing. I'd like to make Mabel's room more habitable for her."

"I used that room to store things."

"Perhaps Mabel and I could move those things to the garage."

Vera looked worried but then waved her hand. "Yes. Do whatever you like with them. I certainly can't."

"So you don't mind then . . . if I help out?"

"Mind?" She let out a tired sigh. "I would be very grateful."

Daphne smiled. "Good. Now we'll be on our way and you can rest."

Daphne felt victorious as they walked back to her house. She told Mabel about how she had to learn to do things like laundry and housecleaning when she was Mabel's age. "Because my daddy worked. But my aunt taught me how to help out around the house."

"You mean your grandma-aunt, the one who lived in your house?"

Daphne smiled at Mabel's quick memory. "Yes, you're right. But I always thought of her as my aunt when I was little."

"I wish I had an aunt."

"Maybe I can be like your aunt." Daphne hoped she wasn't crossing some invisible line by saying this. But really, what was wrong with adopting an aunt?

"Can I call you Aunt Daphne?"

"I don't see why not." As they went inside the house, Daphne asked if Mabel had breakfast.

"I had Froot Loops."

"With no milk?"

"Yeah. We're out of milk."

"How would you like some eggs and toast?" Daphne offered.

Mabel eagerly agreed. And as Daphne fixed her breakfast, Mabel explained how she usually ate both breakfast and lunch at school. "On Saturday and Sunday I get hungry."

Daphne set the plate of food in front of Mabel, trying to disguise how disturbing it was to hear all this. And yet she felt she needed to know the real details. It was surprising that someone hadn't turned Vera in for child neglect, and yet where would that put Mabel? In a foster home with strangers? What if it was a worse situation? Anyway, Vera had given Daphne the green light. She wanted help. And she was certainly going to get it.

"Do you know what kind of sickness your grandma has?" Daphne poured herself a cup of coffee.

"Cancer," Mabel said soberly.

"Oh . . . I see."

Mabel looked up with worried eyes. "Is she going to die?"

"I . . . uh . . . I don't know. I mean I don't think so."

Mabel just nodded, forking hungrily into her eggs.

However, as Daphne watched her eating, she realized this was a question she needed to know the answer to as well. What exactly was Vera's condition? Was she in treatment? Remission? What?

As Daphne and Mabel piled their cart high at the Fairview Walmart, Daphne couldn't remember ever enjoying shopping as much as today. And since she'd been living rather frugally these past few months, her generous monthly allowance from Aunt Dee's will had been accruing steadily. And according to Aunt Dee's will, Daphne wouldn't be able to take any of the saved money for living expenses with her in May, in the likely event that she was still unmarried, so she felt delighted to be able to share it with Mabel.

In fact, she suspected Aunt Dee would thoroughly approve. And having seen the condition of Mabel's clothes as they loaded the washer this morning, she was well aware that the little girl was in severe need of everything. From practical school clothes like jeans and shirts to underwear and socks.

"Are those your only shoes?" Daphne looked at the dirty, worn canvas shoes.

"I think so."

"Well, it's time for some new ones." Daphne led her to the shoe department to measure her feet, but seeing the condition of her socks, Daphne knew it would be wrong to let her try on shoes. "Take those off." Daphne reached for a packet of clean socks and pulled out a pair. "Put these on."

"Will we get in trouble?" Mabel frowned.

"No, we're going to buy them anyway."

"Okay?" Mabel looked uncertain as she peeled of her soiled socks. And Daphne, trying to hide her disgust, picked them up and dropped them in a nearby trash container.

Mabel's eyes grew wide as Daphne had her try on several pairs of shoes, putting the ones that fit into the cart.

"Are we getting all of those?" Mabel asked incredulously.

"Yes. It's good to have a spare pair or two." Daphne picked up some rubber boots with pink, blue, and yellow polka dots. "What do you think of these rain boots?"

"They're pretty!"

Daphne checked the size and then dropped them into the cart

too. "And that reminds me, you probably need a warm coat and maybe a raincoat too."

With each additional item, Mabel's big brown eyes lit up. And she even let out some squeals of delight when Daphne let her pick out two sets of pajamas and a nightgown and pink bunny slippers. Clearly, the little girl felt like she'd won the lottery. And Daphne thought that seeing Mabel get so thrilled over even the smallest things, like a Cinderella toothbrush and strawberry toothpaste, was a huge payoff. They picked out more hygiene essentials like shampoo and conditioner, a good hairbrush, and even a small pink hairdryer.

Finally they went to the hardware department where Daphne got a closet rod and several packs of clothes hangers. "I think this will do for now," Daphne told Mabel as they wheeled the heaping cart up to the registers. Of course, all the Halloween merchandise was near the front of the store, and Mabel's eyes grew wide as she saw the row of children's costumes.

"Do you have a Halloween costume yet?" Daphne knew this was unlikely.

With her eyes fixed on one particular costume, Mabel shook her head.

"Well, why don't you pick one out while the selection is still good?"

"Really?" Mabel looked up in disbelief.

"Sure. Which one do you like?"

Mabel reached for *The Little Mermaid* costume. "Ariel," she said quietly. "She's my favorite."

Daphne smiled. "*The Little Mermaid* was always one of my favorite fairy tales too . . . when I was little." She helped her to find the right size and this time, instead of dropping it into the cart, Mabel clutched it to her chest as they walked toward the checkout area.

"Do you have enough money for all this?" Mabel asked nervously as Daphne got into a line for a cashier.

"Don't worry. My aunt was very generous to me so I can be very generous to you."

"I like having an aunt." Mabel grinned. "Thanks, *Aunt Daphne*."

The man in front of them turned around. "Daphne!" Jake exclaimed with a broad smile. "I thought I heard your name."

"Jake?" Daphne blinked. "What are you doing here?" Somehow Jake did not strike her as a typical Walmart shopper.

"Just picking up some essentials." He held up a shopping basket containing a variety of small sundries. He peered at her heavily loaded cart with interest. "Nothing compared to the damage you're doing."

Daphne tipped her head toward Mabel. "That's because I have help." She introduced him to her young friend.

"Pleased to meet you Miss Mabel." Jake shook the little girl's hand with curious eyes. "Did I hear you say that Daphne's your aunt?"

Mabel grinned. "She said I can call her that."

Daphne put a hand on Mabel's head. "We're neighbors, but I decided to make Mabel my honorary niece."

"Nice." He nodded as if he approved.

"As we know, there's more than one way to get an aunt." Daphne inched her cart forward.

"That's true." For a long moment he stared deeply into her eyes—almost as if he wanted to say something but was holding back.

She waited, experiencing a warm rush of pleasure combined with a self-conscious uneasiness. "Your turn to check out, Jake." With relief, Daphne pointed to the cashier who was waiting for him.

"Yeah . . . right." He started to unload his items onto the counter.

She watched as he set a package of batteries, a bottle of shampoo, and several other things out, then proceeded to pay for them. With his bag of purchases in hand, he turned back and gave a little wave. "Good seeing you, Daphne. And nice to meet you, Miss Mabel."

They both told him good-bye. But as Daphne unloaded their items, she couldn't help but wonder—what was it that Jake had wanted to say to her? Or maybe she misread him. Maybe it was just her imagination.

After she and Mabel packed their purchases into every available space of her small car, she realized that they'd worked up an appetite. So they went to a drive-through and picked up sandwiches and drinks, taking their makeshift picnic lunch to a nearby park.

"This is the best day ever," Mabel told Daphne as they were throwing away the bags and paper cups afterward. "You are the best aunt in the whole world."

Daphne laughed. "And you are the best niece!"

Mabel looked longingly to where other children were playing on the playground. "Can I play for a while?"

"Sure." Daphne sat on the bench, watching as Mabel ran and jumped and climbed around on the playground equipment. Having fun, just like a normal kid. Playing and laughing with the other kids as if her mother wasn't dead or her dad wasn't in prison or her grandmother didn't have cancer. As if her little life was just peachy.

After about an hour, they went to the grocery store and got everything on their list as well as a number of other things that seemed kid-friendly and easy to fix. Then Daphne drove them back to the little blue house in Appleton. She could hardly believe how much they'd managed to pack into her car. It took lots of trips before it was all unloaded.

"I'll go see if Grandma is hungry. She likes those kinds of yogurts we got. She might want one."

"Good idea." Daphne started to unload a grocery bag. She attempted to clean the kitchen and fridge as she put food items away. However, it was going to take much more time and effort than she could give it today. But suddenly she remembered how Sabrina often said how she owed Daphne some "favors" for her help with unpacking. Daphne closed the fridge. It might just be payback time.

She got out her phone and called Sabrina, quickly explaining what was going on here and how it was getting a bit overwhelming. "I really need some help."

"You want me to come down and lend a hand?"

"Yes!" Daphne said eagerly.

"Well, why didn't you just say so? I'll be right over. What about Tootsie? Will he be in the way?"

"Maybe he should stay home this time. It's pretty messy here. I wouldn't want him to get into something that would hurt him. Plus Mabel's grandma needs quiet to rest. And be sure to put on some grungy clothes. It's a real roll-up-your-sleeves-and-get-dirty kind of project."

"Gotcha."

After Daphne hung up, Mabel reminded her of the clothes still in the washer. So they went out and Daphne showed her how to load them in the dryer. "And see if you can find that box of dryer sheets I got. I think it's still in the kitchen."

While Mabel hunted down the dryer sheets, Daphne strategized for where to store junk from Mabel's bedroom. Like the rest of the house, the garage was pretty packed, but there was an open section near the big garage door that could be put to use. And Daphne's plan was to get that little bedroom cleared out and cleaned up before Mabel's bedtime. The image of a cleaned up Mabel, wearing clean pajamas, tucked into a clean bed in a clean room was enough motivation to keep Daphne working hard.

Chapter 20

Your grandma said it would be okay to rearrange your bedroom," Daphne told Mabel as she pointed out the space in the garage. "We'll stack all those boxes and stuff right there for now. You ready to go to work moving it all out here?"

"I guess so." Mabel looked a little uncertain.

"Just think," Daphne said as they returned to Mabel's jam-packed little room. "With all this stuff gone, it will be like a real bedroom for you."

"A *real* bedroom?" Mabel echoed with what sounded like disbelief.

They were just making their second trip to the garage when Sabrina arrived. Dressed in an old shirt and blue jeans, she had a bucket of cleaning supplies with her. "Help has arrived," she announced as Daphne let her into the house.

"Thank you!"

"Where do I start?" Sabrina looked around with wide eyes.

"The kitchen is in the greatest need." Daphne pointed her toward it. "I've opened some windows in there. I guess it wouldn't hurt to open some more in here."

"Not at all."

Daphne introduced Sabrina to Mabel and explained that they were working on Mabel's bedroom. "This is no small project," she told Sabrina.

"I can see that."

Back in the bedroom, they continued to carry out load after load. Daphne made sure that Mabel got the lighter boxes. Even so it was hard work, but Mabel didn't complain once. But after it was cleared out and all the boxes and junk were stacked in the garage, Daphne could see that there was mildew on the bedroom walls. Probably due to years of being covered by all that junk. She opened the window to let in fresh air, but it still didn't seem like a healthy place for a child—or anyone—to sleep.

She told Mabel to take a break, then went outside to use her phone. She called her painter friend and started to leave a message, but then he answered. "Oh, hello, Tom," Daphne said. "I have a painting problem I thought perhaps you could help me with. I'm sure you're busy and it's a Saturday, but perhaps you could just advise me."

"What's up?"

So she quickly described the situation, including the details of how Mabel recently lost her mother and how Vera had cancer and the horrible condition of the house. "Her little bedroom probably isn't even safe and I'd just like to clean the walls so she can sleep there, but I have no idea what to use and—"

"Where is this house?"

Daphne explained how it was just down the street.

"How about if I drop by and give you a hand?"

"Really?" Daphne was so moved, she felt close to tears. "You could do that? On a Saturday?"

"Sure. I was just sitting here watching UCLA getting whooped by Stanford. I could use a good distraction about now. It would do me good to help out."

"Great. Thank you!" As Daphne closed her phone, she got an idea. If Tom was so glad to give of himself . . . who else might be interested in helping? The words: *You have not because you ask not* reverberated through her head. That was it—she would do some more asking. She looked around the overgrown yard as she opened her phone. Before long, she had called Mick, explaining the situation and asking if he could spare one of his yard guys to come over and cut this grass. To her surprise, Mick offered to come himself.

Daphne went back inside to find Mabel flopped in front of the TV with a granola bar. And considering how hard the little girl had been working the last couple of hours, who could blame her for taking a break? She went past Mabel and tapped on Vera's door again. When Vera responded, Daphne went in and explained Tom's and Mick's interest in helping out.

"I can't afford to pay them."

"That's okay. They just want to do it out of the kindness of their hearts."

"Really?" Vera's eyes were misty. "People are still like that?"

"Some of them are." Daphne smiled. "In fact, there are quite a few generous people in this town. Do you mind if I invite them to help?"

Vera sighed. "There was a time when I would've minded . . . quite a lot. But not anymore. I'm too tired and worn out to care about much of anything—except for Mabel. And even then it doesn't do much good."

"Well, you just rest. And if you don't mind, I'll do what I can to help you out, Vera."

Vera gave her a weak smile. "Thanks . . . that means a lot."

Daphne stood for a moment. How would it feel to be so helpless? "Is there anything I can get for you?"

"No, thank you. I just need rest."

"I'll tell people to keep it quiet—"

"Don't worry. When I'm this tired, noise doesn't bother me."

"Okay." Daphne reached for the doorknob.

Daphne found Sabrina still hard at work in the kitchen. "Hey, you've really made a dent in here." She pointed to the porcelain sink. "Wow, it's actually white." Daphne ran her finger over the yellow laminate countertop. "And you could even eat off of here now."

"Yes, but I think this is more than just an afternoon project." Sabrina looked at the stove clock. "How late do you want to work?"

"How about until dinnertime? Then I'll treat you and Mabel to takeout at my house."

"Sounds like a deal."

Daphne returned to Mabel's room and frowned at the nasty-looking walls. Perhaps this space had been safer before the boxes were removed. She looked down at the matted brown carpet, wondering what might be under it. She gave a corner a tug and was surprised to see that it popped right up and underneath it was a hardwood floor. Because the carpet hadn't been properly installed, it came up easily. And since the only piece of furniture in the room was the twin bed, she soon had both it and the carpet removed from the small room.

She was just dragging the rolled-up carpet out the front door, when Tom's white van pulled up. "Need a hand?" He hurried over to help her pull it down the porch and onto the overgrown lawn.

"Thank you! And thank you for coming."

Soon she was showing him the room, and before long the two of them were brushing some cleaning compound onto the wall and scrubbing it off with rags. "Now, I'll just slap some Kilz on here," Tom told her. "You go fetch your little friend so she can tell me what colors she likes."

"Sure. We'll be right back."

She found Mabel with Sabrina in the kitchen. "Tom wants to know what color you'd like for your room," Daphne told Mabel.

"What color?" Mabel looked confused.

"For the walls."

"Oh." Mabel twisted her mouth to one side. "Can he do purple?"

"I don't know." Daphne suppressed the urge to laugh. "Why don't we go talk to him."

After Daphne introduced Mabel to Tom, Mabel attempted to explain the color she wanted, but unable to make him understand, she told him she'd be right back. When she returned she had the nightgown they'd purchased at Walmart in hand. "I want this color."

"Lavender," Daphne proclaimed. "That would look very nice."

Tom opened a can of paint and Mabel frowned, pointing out that it was white. "The same color the walls are now."

"Yes, but that's because I haven't done my magic yet," Tom told her with a twinkle in his eye.

"You do magic?" Her brown eyes grew wide.

Tom pulled a plastic bottle from a group of similar-looking bottles and squirted something dark into the white paint. Then he reached for another and gave it a generous squirt too. "Now the magic begins." He stirred it with a paint stick.

"It's purple!" Mabel exclaimed. "You did it. Magic!"

"Uh-huh." He nodded as he reached for a brush and dipped it into the lavender paint. "Let's see how it looks on the wall." He brushed a large square. "What do you think?"

"It's beautiful!" she cried out.

Now he handed her the paintbrush. "Want to help?"

Her eyes grew even wider now. "Really?"

"Yep." He poured some paint into a smaller container, then directed her to a windowless wall where he'd already put a drop cloth over the floor. "Go for it." He nodded to Daphne. "Don't worry, it's a very safe paint. No fumes."

"You are like the Superman of painters, aren't you?" Daphne teased him.

"It's fun to be a hero sometimes," he confessed as he dipped a roller into the paint and rolled it on the wall.

"Unless you need my help, I'll go work on something else," she told him.

"We're good. Me and my helper got it under control."

When Daphne had removed the twin bed, she'd realized what bad shape the sheets and blankets were in, and upon searching the linen cabinet in the hall bath, she discovered more of the same. Suddenly she remembered her aunt's well-stocked linen closet and hurried down to gather some things from home.

When she returned with a laundry basket loaded with some sheets and blankets and towels, she spent some time cleaning the hall bath since this was the one Mabel used. She took all the raggedy linens from the narrow cabinet, as well as the filthy towels hanging on the towel racks, which looked as if they hadn't been changed in months, and tossed them all into a large plastic trash bag. Then she did some quick scrubbing of the fixtures, hung up fresh towels, and put the rest of the linens in the linen cabinet.

She was just about to check on Sabrina but stopped to look at the painting progress. "My goodness. You're more than half done."

"He even painted *inside* the closet," Mabel told her. "I have a purple closet!"

"It looks so bright and cheerful in here. Very pretty." Daphne knew just what this room needed and where to find it.

It was a little tricky putting the small white dresser into the back of the Corvette, but by putting the top down, she was able to set it in upright. She also put in a pastel-colored braided rug as well as a pink-and-white gingham comforter that had been Daphne's when she was a girl. She tossed in a couple of pillows as well as a set of white eyelet curtains that looked about the right size. She also put in several framed prints of flowers to hang on the wall and a small white table lamp. It wasn't a lot to outfit a room, and it left one of the spare rooms looking a little sparse, but it would help to make Mabel's room feel like a real bedroom.

Tom was completely done with the room shortly after five o'clock. "It'll take a couple hours for the paint to completely dry," he explained as he was carrying his tools out to his van. "But Mabel will be fine sleeping in here tonight."

"I don't even know how to thank you. But please send me your bill."

"This one is on the house. It's not every day I get to help someone in a situation like this." He smiled. "I admire you for doing what you're doing for this child, Daphne. I'm thankful I could be of help."

"God bless you, Tom!" she said happily.

"Oh yes, he has." He tipped his head. "See ya 'round."

By six o'clock, while Mabel and Sabrina fixed something for Vera to eat for dinner, Daphne started putting Mabel's bedroom together. "It's going to be a surprise," she told them. "So no peeking until I'm done."

"How about if I call and order up our dinner?" Sabrina suggested. "Then we can all meet back at your house—around seven, you think?"

"Perfect." Daphne reached for her purse. "Here's my card."

"Mabel is voting for pizza," Sabrina said. "I'm inclined to agree. As hard as we've all worked today, I think we could use the extra carbs."

Daphne laughed. "You're right. See you around seven."

While they were gone, Daphne put the bed into place, careful not to bump the freshly painted wall. She set it up near the window, which Tom must've washed because it was now transparent. Next she used some rags as sliders to move the white dresser against the wall near enough to the bed to work as a bedside table. On it, she placed the pretty white lamp as well as a fairy-tale book she'd nabbed on her way out of the house.

She made up the bed, topping it with the pink-and-white comforter and the two pastel patchwork throw pillows. Then she laid out the braided rug. Perfect! Finally she pulled out the tools she'd brought over and hung up the three prints as well as the eyelet curtains. And then satisfied that the closet paint was dry enough, she put in a new closet rod, low enough that Mabel could reach it.

She looked around with satisfaction. It was almost done. All she needed to do now was to haul in all the bags of clothes and shoes and things and put them all away. But it was fun work hanging the clothes on the clean white hangers, filling the dresser with socks and underwear and pajamas. Daphne couldn't wait to see Mabel's reaction to her new room. Daphne even laid out the lavender nightgown on the bed, placing the bunny slippers on the rug beneath. She felt just like Cinderella's fairy godmother as she turned on the little white lamp. It was all perfectly lovely.

"Oh my!"

Daphne turned around to see Vera looking into the room. Still wearing her faded bathrobe, her eyes were opened wide—as if she was in shock.

"What do you think?"

Vera just stared, holding on to the door frame as if for support.

"I hope it's okay," Daphne said nervously. "You did say it was all right, but I let Mabel pick out the color."

Vera's hand went over her mouth and she started shaking as if she was about to fall. And then she began to cry.

"Oh, Vera." Daphne ran over to help. "I'm sorry. Did I go too far? Is it too much? I didn't mean to overstep my—"

"No, no." Vera shook her head. "It's fine. It really is fine. I'm just so—so shocked. I never expected anything like this. How could you do this? So quickly?"

"I had help." Daphne put an arm around her, trying to support the trembling woman.

"But I—I don't know what to say—" Vera let out a choked sob. "I feel so—so guilty. This is what I should've done for her and I couldn't—"

"It's okay. We wanted to help. That's what neighbors do."

"But . . . I . . . don't know how to thank you."

"You thanked us by allowing us into your lives, by letting us help," Daphne told her.

"But it's too much. I never expected . . ."

"I know. But let's get you back to your room now. I can tell you've worn yourself out." Daphne slowly walked Vera back to her bedroom. "I really enjoyed doing this. I honestly can't remember when I've had this much fun. I mean, sure, it took some elbow grease too. But the end results were so satisfying. I'd gladly do it all over again if I needed to."

"I . . . I had no idea people could be so kind."

"Well, we all enjoyed helping you, Vera. And Mabel is a dear little girl. We loved helping her too. Thanks for letting us." She eased Vera down onto her bed. "Is there anything else I can get for you?" She glanced at the food tray, seeing that it was partially eaten.

"No, I am fine. Thank you."

"If you don't mind, Mabel is joining my friend Sabrina and me for dinner. Then we'll bring her back here for the big reveal."

"Reveal?" Vera's eyes lit up. "Like on those home-improvement shows?"

Daphne laughed. "Yes. Just like that."

"Will you let me know when you get back?" Vera asked hopefully. "I'd like to see her reaction."

"Absolutely."

By the time Daphne got home, the pizza was just arriving. Sabrina was just finishing up making a green salad to go with it. The three of them, still scruffy and dirty from their hard work, sat at the kitchen table and ate.

"I've been getting better acquainted with Mabel," Sabrina told Daphne. "Did you know she is a very good singer?"

"No, I did not." Daphne smiled. "Maybe after dinner she'll sing for us."

"And she wants to take ballet lessons," Sabrina said.

"Really?" Daphne was a little surprised that Mabel knew about such things.

But then Mabel described a cartoon where all the mice were ballerinas and went to dance school together. "I want to be like them."

It was nearly eight when they finished cleaning up the dinner things, and Daphne could see Mabel was tired. In fact, she was sure they were all tired. "Are you ready to see your new bedroom?"

"Yes!" Mabel was on her feet.

"Can I come see it too?" Sabrina asked.

"Yes," Mabel said happily. "Come with us."

So they all walked down to the little blue house and Mabel led the way to her bedroom. "Wait," Daphne said before she opened the door. "I promised your grandma she could see the big reveal."

Mabel looked confused.

"You know," Sabrina said. "When you see your room for the first time."

"I'll get Grandma."

Daphne introduced Vera to Sabrina and then they were all standing outside the door, waiting for Mabel to open it.

"Oh my goodness," Sabrina said as they followed Mabel inside. "It's perfectly lovely."

"My room!" Mabel danced around, taking time to examine every single thing, even pulling open the dresser drawers. "My very own room!"

Vera looked happy as she thanked Daphne again, then excused herself.

"It's so beautiful." Mabel ran her hand over the comforter.

"Beautiful and clean," Daphne pointed out. "But you're still a little grungy from all the housework. I think you should take a nice bath and get yourself all cleaned up to spend the first night in your lovely new room."

"And wash that hair," Sabrina told Mabel in a slightly teasing way. "Any self-respecting ballerina would want to go to bed with nice clean hair."

"If you want I'll stick around and help you with your hair," Daphne told Mabel. "It looks like it's pretty tangled up."

"And I will bid you adieu," Sabrina said.

"Huh?" Mabel frowned.

"That's good-bye in French," Daphne explained.

"Oh." Mabel nodded. "A-do to you too."

It took about an hour to get Mabel thoroughly cleaned and her hair detangled and dried, but eventually she was wearing her lavender nightgown and bunny slippers and ready to get into bed. "Can I read this now?" She picked up the fairy-tale book.

"Maybe not tonight. I'm sure you must be really tired."

"Okay." Mabel pulled back the covers and jumped into bed.

"Do you want me to wait while you say your prayers?" Daphne asked.

"Prayers?"

"Do you say prayers before you go to bed?"

Mabel shook her head. "I don't know how."

"Well, maybe we can do it together." Daphne smiled. "You just close your eyes and imagine that God is right here with you—because really he is. Then you tell him thank you for whatever comes to mind and you ask him to bless the ones you love. Or you could ask him to help your grandma get better. Just whatever it is that comes to mind."

"Okay." Mabel got a thoughtful look. "How do you start it?"

"I usually start by saying 'Dear God,'" Daphne told her. "Kind of like writing a letter. But it probably doesn't matter how you begin, as long as you begin. And it's good to tell God thanks. If you're especially thankful for anything, God likes to hear about it."

Mabel closed her eyes. "Dear God. Thank you . . . for my new room. It's really cool. I really, really love it." She twisted her mouth to one side like she was thinking hard. "God, I really, really want to thank you for Aunt Daphne. She's really, really great. And I love her a lot. I'm so glad that I have an aunt now. And thanks for Sabrina too. I'm glad she's my friend now." Mabel opened her eyes. "What else do I say?"

"Anything you want to say. God's listening."

"Can God help Grandma to get better?"

"God can do anything, Mabel."

She closed her eyes tightly. "Please, God, make it so my grandma won't be sick anymore." She looked expectantly at Daphne. "Should I say anything else?"

"If you're finished praying, you can say 'Amen.' It's kind of like saying good-bye to God—or like agreeing with him about what you just said."

"*Amen,*" Mabel proclaimed. Now she looked at Daphne with worried brown eyes. "Was God *really* listening?"

"Yes, of course."

"Will God make Grandma better?"

"I hope so." Daphne pushed the freshly washed hair away from Mabel's forehead. "But God is God. He can do what he wants. But I'll be praying for your grandma too."

Mabel snuggled down deeper into bed. "Do you go to church?" she asked sleepily.

"As a matter of fact, I do go to church." Daphne nodded as she pulled the quilt up around Mabel's chin. "Would you ever want to come with me?"

"Yes!"

"All right, then. You ask your grandma about it in the morning. If she says you can go, call me and let me know. Church starts at ten thirty, but Sabrina and I go earlier than that."

"Okay!"

Daphne leaned down and kissed Mabel's forehead—just the same way her Aunt Dee used to kiss her at bedtime. "Good night." She clicked off the light. "Sleep tight—don't let the bed bugs bite."

Mabel giggled. "There aren't any bugs in here."

"No, there certainly aren't. See you tomorrow, Mabel."

"Uh-huh," Mabel murmured drowsily.

As Daphne tiptoed out of the room and out of the house, she felt exhausted—thoroughly but wonderfully exhausted. With no regrets. What a perfect way to spend her Saturday! As she walked home in the moonlight, she thought about Aunt Dee. It was too bad her aunt's will didn't have some other options in it. Like instead of insisting that Daphne find herself a husband, why couldn't her aunt have settled for Daphne finding herself a needy little girl to help out? Didn't that count for anything? Maybe she'd call Jake and ask him about it. Not that he could change anything. But wouldn't it be wonderful if he could?

Chapter 21

On Sunday morning, Sabrina brought blueberry muffins over to Daphne's house around nine. They were just having them with coffee when Mabel showed up. Dressed neatly in the red plaid dress she'd fallen in love with the previous day, Mabel proudly announced that her grandma said she could go to church. "Grandma told me that she used to go to church too. A long time ago when she was a little girl."

"Great." Daphne straightened the collar of the dress. "So have you had breakfast yet?"

"I had cereal and milk," Mabel proclaimed. "And I made some for Grandma too."

"Good girl." Daphne held out a muffin. "Sabrina made these. Do you have room for one?"

Mabel's eyes lit up as she slid into a kitchen chair.

"Uh, Mabel . . . who cut your hair?" Sabrina frowned at Mabel's choppy-looking brown hair. Although it wasn't as tangled as yesterday, it still looked odd.

"Mama cut it," Mabel said quietly. "Back . . . before . . . she . . . uh . . ."

"Oh—well," Sabrina said quickly, "It's just that I went to *beauty* school." She exchanged glances with Daphne. "And I just *love* doing hair. You see, I thought I was going to be a beautician. Until I discovered it was real hard work. So then I went to business college instead." She ran her fingers through Mabel's choppy haircut. "And I could give you a real cute hairstyle. I mean if you want—"

"Yes!" Mabel said with a mouthful of muffin. "The kids at school might not tease me if my hair wasn't so funny looking."

Soon Sabrina returned with her haircutting tools and by ten o'clock, Mabel's hair was all tidied up with feathered bangs that sweetly framed her face.

"You look like a pretty little pixie," Daphne told her.

"Or a fairy." Sabrina peeled the tea towel off of Mabel's shoulders.

"You did a wonderful job," Daphne told Sabrina.

Sabrina nodded proudly. "Who knows. Maybe I'll take it up again—open my own salon and hire some other girls to work for me. That might not be so bad."

It wasn't until Tuesday that Daphne was reminded of last week's speed-dating debacle. "It seemed such a good idea at the time." Sabrina laughed merrily as the two of them walked toward town together. "But I assure you that is a mistake I will not make again."

"I nearly forgot." The image of the attractive architect flashed through Daphne's mind. "I wonder."

"Huh?" Sabrina tugged at Tootsie's leash as they crossed the street. Today, since there was a nip in the air, the little dog was wearing a purple turtleneck sweater. "What do you wonder?"

"Oh, just that guy. Remember the architect I met? He seemed nice."

"So you haven't heard from him yet?" Sabrina asked. "What was his name?"

"Harrison." Daphne grimaced. "I didn't even get his last name. And I didn't give him mine."

"That's not good. But you did give him your number, right?"

"Yes."

"And you're sure he hasn't called? Maybe he called when we were helping at Mabel's. Maybe he didn't leave a message."

Daphne pulled out her phone to check. "No. I don't see any strange numbers here. He hasn't called."

"Oh dear. This is not good." Sabrina scowled. "What if he lost your number, Daph? Or what if he got the numerals mixed up? It's a shame he doesn't know your last name so he could look you up. Did you tell him where you live?"

Daphne thought hard. "Yes, I'm pretty sure I told him about Appleton."

"Well, if he knows that much. *Daphne in Appleton*. He could find you if he wanted. That is, if he's persistent enough. After all, you know half the people in town. Almost anyone could send him in your direction."

"Oh, I don't know about that."

They were on Main Street and Sabrina started pointing out various businesses and listing off everyone Daphne knew, and it did start to sound as if she knew half the town.

"Okay, you're right. If Harrison lost my number, he probably could find me. If he really wanted—he could make it happen."

The next couple of days passed and Harrison did not call. And by Thursday Daphne was determined to stop sitting by the phone, so to speak, since she didn't actually *sit by the phone*. Her cell was simply lying on her desk as she worked, or in her pocket if she happened to be doing something else in the house, or working in the garden. Still, it was not ringing.

As Daphne sat in her office staring blankly out the window, she knew she should've been finished with her novel by now. And by all rights, it was very nearly done—just a few pages away really. And yet she just seemed unable to tie up the ending. And even this afternoon, instead of writing those few last pages like she'd planned, she was playing spider solitaire and gazing out the window. It was about time for Mabel to get home from school. And after she checked on her grandma, she often came here to visit with Daphne and play with the cats.

Daphne heard her cell phone ring and quickly answered without checking the number. She hoped that perhaps it was her mysterious architect friend calling at last.

"Daphne?" a woman's voice said. "This is Karen's sister, Diane. We're going to have a bridesmaid dress fitting Saturday afternoon at Frederica's. Can you be there at four?"

"Sure."

"And afterward we're going to have a little shower for Karen. Just the bridesmaids. I know it's short notice, but time's been flying past and I really wanted to do this for her. It'll be a personal shower, if you know what I mean." Diane made a nervous giggle.

"Meaning nighties and that sort of thing?" Daphne felt

uncomfortable at the idea of selecting lingerie for her dad's future bride.

"Exactly. I suppose it might seem silly at our age, but Karen is looking forward to this shower. She doesn't speak of it much, but she eloped for her first wedding. So she missed out on all this hoopla. I'd like to make it up for her with this one."

"I didn't realize she'd eloped." Daphne felt a little guilty for her lack of enthusiasm over Karen and Dad's wedding now. "Well, that makes sense why she's so into this wedding."

"She's tried to play it down, but she really wants all the bells and whistles."

"Well, I'll be at the fitting and I'll do my best to find something special for her shower." Daphne couldn't even imagine what that "something special" might be.

"Karen's registered at Frederica's here in town, as well as Victoria's Secret in Fairview."

"I doubt I'll make it over to Fairview before Saturday, but I'll do what I can here in town."

As Daphne hung up the phone, she knew for a fact she would not be shopping for her future stepmom's shower present at Victoria's Secret of all places. Really? She didn't even shop in stores like that for herself! Admittedly, she'd gone to a lingerie store once, thinking she'd try something new, but then she'd felt so self-conscious and embarrassed that she quickly left. No, it was not her cup of tea, and there was nothing she could do about that.

She was an old-fashioned girl . . . who would probably wind up being an old-fashioned old woman. She stooped down to pet Ethel, who was rubbing herself against Daphne's ankles. "Yes, it's me and the cats . . . stuck in a previous century."

Daphne had even made a hesitant call to Jake not long after their unexpected meeting in Walmart, asking about the possibility of changing her aunt's will. "What if I sort of adopted a needy child," she had said in a slightly joking tone. "You know, instead of getting a husband? You think Aunt Dee would mind?"

"Are you talking about your young neighbor? Little Miss Mabel?"

She quickly explained a bit more about Mabel's situation.

"That's a very generous idea, Daphne. But you must realize that Dee's will is a legal document. She is the only one who could change it. Obviously, that is not going to happen."

"Right . . ." Then without explaining herself further, she'd quickly apologized for bothering him and hung up.

Now a few days later, she felt like she was truly trapped in writer's block. She wasn't sure if this was about Mabel or Aunt Dee or even Jake, but for some reason she felt stuck as she stared blankly at her computer screen. Finally she just shut the whole works down. Since she was making so little progress on finishing the book, it was time to take a break.

She would walk to town and see what she could find for Karen at Frederica's, but after looking at Karen's wish list and perusing the shelves and racks, Daphne wasn't comfortable with purchasing intimate garments for her soon-to-be stepmother.

Instead she went down the street to the drugstore and selected a nice assortment of luxurious French bath oils and lotions and scented candles. She even picked up a nice box of chocolate truffles. Sure, her gift wasn't lacy or wearable, but it was romantic. And what was wrong with that?

She picked out an elegant gift bag, tissue paper, and ribbon, then took it home to assemble into a lovely package. If she were the bride-to-be, she would be totally thrilled with such a thoughtful and non-embarrassing gift. Not that there was much risk of her being a bride anytime soon.

On Saturday afternoon, Daphne walked to town for the dress fitting and bridal shower. It was a gorgeous fall day with a crisp blue sky and a slight autumnal breeze in the air. Perfect sweater weather. Since she was a little early, she stopped by Bernie's to say hi to Olivia. "How are you feeling? Over the morning sickness yet?"

"It's a little better. And I've already put on ten pounds." Olivia patted her midsection. "The doctor's not too thrilled about that."

"Well, if you can't put on weight when you're pregnant, when can you?"

"Exactly." Olivia pointed across the street. "Ricardo has chicken pot pie for the blue plate special today. Want to come?"

Daphne chuckled. "Sounds good, but I'm on my way to a fitting." She described the horrible hotdog dresses Karen had picked out.

"Oh, dear." Olivia frowned. "And her flowers are going to be so pretty too."

"Maybe you can make the bridesmaid bouquets really big," Daphne teased, "to cover up the hideous dresses."

Olivia laughed. "I'll see what I can do. Hey, take a photo of the dress and send it to me."

Daphne rolled her eyes. "Only if you promise to destroy it afterward."

"It's a deal."

As Daphne entered Frederica's, she tried not to think about the bridesmaid dress she was about to be forced to try on. Instead she greeted Karen and waited to be introduced to the bridesmaids. Interestingly, they all seemed to be in their fifties. And if Daphne was worried about looking like a pudgy hotdog in her dress, she had nothing on the other matronly ladies.

"It's called ruching," Karen explained to the women in regard to the puckered purple-ish dresses they were all squeezing into.

Daphne was one of the first ones to emerge from the dressing room. The dress seemed to fit okay, but her rolled down wool socks and brown clogs did nothing to help the effect. Not to mention that with Daphne's auburn hair, purple was probably not her best color. Staring at her pale-looking image, which truly looked as if she'd been swallowed by a hungry wrinkled hot dog, she realized that people only did this for love. And since she loved her dad and Karen was the woman he wished to spend the rest of his days with, she could bite the bullet and do this.

"Daphne?" one of the salesclerks was saying.

"Yes?" Daphne turned.

"Oh, that's her right there," the woman said to a man standing by the door.

Daphne squinted, trying to see the face of the man silhouetted in front of the glass door. "What?"

"Daphne," the man said.

"Huh?" She tilted her head to one side, trying to make him out.

"It's Harrison," he said cheerfully. "Remember from the speed dating?"

Daphne took in a quick breath. "Harrison?"

He chuckled as he came toward her. "I didn't mean to intrude on you. I met a friend of yours at the diner. She told me I'd find you here."

"Olivia . . ." Daphne put a hand over her somewhat exposed chest. "Remind me to thank her."

He laughed. "She told me you were being fitted for a wedding." He lowered his voice. "And that you weren't too thrilled with the dress."

Her cheeks flushed. "Yes, well, it's my father's wedding. Karen . . ." She glanced over her bare shoulder. "She's the bride-to-be." Now the other women were starting to emerge from the dressing area, which was causing the dress shop to resemble a wrinkled sausage factory.

"Anyway, I was in town," he said quietly. "I thought we could get together."

"Yes. I'd love that."

"How about after your, uh, fitting?"

"Yes." But now she remembered the shower. "Except I'll be tied up for about an hour. Do you think you'll still be around?"

"I can make sure that I am."

"Okay." She looked at her watch. "Around six then?"

"Where do you want to meet?"

"The shower is at, uh, Barney's," she told him.

"Great." He backed toward the door as the other bridesmaids started filling the shop. "I'll figure out where that is and meet you at six." And then he ducked out of there as if he felt nearly as uncomfortable as she.

The fitting took about an hour. Of course, Karen and her friends wanted to know about the "handsome stranger" and without mentioning speed dating, Daphne managed to explain they planned to meet up later.

Everything seemed to take longer than it should, but eventually they all made their way down the street to Barney's, which was a tavern on Main Street and not Daphne's favorite sort of hangout. Although the other women all ordered various drinks and seemed intent on making this into a real event, Daphne stuck with iced tea and tried to keep an eye on her watch.

Her plan was to excuse herself a little before six. However, the women who were getting rowdier as each present was opened and each drink was consumed insisted she must stay until the end. The presents, which were strange concoctions of black and red and lace and such, were passed around. Daphne tried to quickly shuffle the garments along to Diane sitting next to her, hoping to get this over and done with as soon as possible.

"Oh, just look at this." Diane held a hot pink lacy piece of fluff in front of Daphne, as if to model it. "I'll bet you would look hot in it, Daphne."

Just as Daphne was about to peel the skimpy garment off of her chest, she looked up to see a familiar face peering at her just a few tables away. Of course, it was her architect friend. She glanced at her watch. It was already past six.

"If you'll excuse me," she said to Karen. "My friend is here to get me."

Karen's eyes lit up when she saw Harrison waiting in the shadows. "Oh yes, Daphne, you should definitely not keep *that one* waiting." The rest of the women erupted into gales of laughter.

"Sorry to run out like this." Daphne grabbed for her purse.

Karen lifted her glass and the others followed. "Here's to Daph finding the man of her dreams too!"

"Here, here," they all echoed as Daphne scurried away.

Her cheeks were flaming by the time she joined Harrison. "Sorry. I sort of lost track of time."

He chuckled. "Looks like you girls were having fun."

"*They* were having fun. *I* was just trying to be a good sport," she said crisply as she led the way toward the door. Of course, this was how their first encounter would start out. First the humiliation at Frederica's in the hotdog dress, then to top it off with these wild women at Barney's. At this rate, she would be greatly relieved when this date—if she could even call it that—was over.

Chapter 22

"So what are you doing in Appleton?" she asked after they were seated at The Zeppelin. Since neither of them had eaten lunch, they'd agreed to share an early dinner.

"I'm one of the architects bidding on your new city hall." He reached for a napkin.

"Oh, that's right. I heard they planned to start rebuilding it this winter."

He nodded. "I already have some ideas drafted, but I felt I needed to walk around a little to really experience the whole environment." He smiled. "Appleton is a charming town."

"I couldn't agree with you more." She took a slow sip of water, still trying to calm herself down from her previous embarrassing moments.

"And it's even more charming after seeing you here."

"Well, thank you," she murmured. "I couldn't have been more surprised to see you today."

"I could see that."

She filled him in about her father and Karen and their wedding. "I know it seems odd, I mean at their age, to pull out all the stops like this. But I guess Karen never had a real wedding before." She shrugged. "My parents did though. I've seen the photos."

They talked about family history and all sorts of things. And by the time dessert was served, Daphne felt almost completely at ease. "This has been an unexpected delight." She took a sip of coffee. "I had no idea when I got up this morning that my day would turn out like this."

"I'm sure the prospect of trying on sausage dresses and hanging with the old ladies didn't sound like much fun." He chuckled.

"Do you think you'll get the bid?"

"I hope so." He grinned. "I like the idea of spending more time here."

"Does an architect have to be on hand throughout the whole building process?"

"Not necessarily on-site. But I have to be able to drop everything and pop over at a moment's notice when needed." He set down his fork. "And I'm less than twenty minutes away, so it's no problem."

They were just finishing up when Daphne noticed Jake and Jenna coming into the restaurant. Jake saw her right away and gave her a friendly wave. They even stopped by the table and she handled the introductions, explaining how Harrison hoped to be hired for the city hall job.

"And believe it or not, we met at a speed-dating thing over in Fairview," Harrison told Jake.

Jake's brows arched with curiosity and Daphne just gave him a stiff smile.

"Is that where you meet a whole bunch of guys all at once?" Jenna asked with interest.

"Something like that," Daphne told her. "My neighbor Sabrina sort of tricked me into going."

"We both got tricked into it," Harrison explained.

"But at least it seems to have worked out okay," Jenna said with a curious smile.

"We won't keep you," Jake said abruptly. "Pleasure to meet you, Harrison. Good luck with the city hall job."

"Nice folks," Harrison said as they walked away.

"Yes." Daphne nodded. "They are."

As Harrison drove Daphne home, they made small talk about the town and city hall, and Daphne shared some of her earlier memories of growing up in the charming little town. "Of course, it's changed some since then. But only for the better. I think Appleton is steadily becoming the sort of place where people like me—ones who were sick of the big city life—were happy to return to. It's been really nice getting reacquainted with folks, meeting my neighbors." She told him about meeting Mabel and her garden and the free-produce box.

"You make small town life sound very appealing." He pulled up to the house.

She nodded. "It really is."

He pointed to the produce box in her yard. "And I've always wanted to try my hand at gardening too."

She glanced out at the dusky sky. "I'd invite you to see the garden, but I'm afraid it's getting too dark to see much."

"And I need to get going. I left Heidi home alone."

"Heidi?" She studied his face.

"My German shepherd." He chuckled. "Although she's certain she's human. I usually take her with me wherever I go, but sometimes she barks when I leave her in the car. Didn't want to make a bad impression if any of the city folks were out and about today."

"Oh yes." She pointed to her house. "And my two cats—actually they belonged to my aunt, but they're in my custody now—anyway, they're probably wondering where I've been all day. I'm usually a real homebody."

He looked up at the house. "That's a pretty nice house to be a homebody in. Queen Anne Victorian?"

She nodded. "Would you like to see it?"

"I'd love to. But not this time." He looked at his watch. "If I don't get there soon, Heidi will probably start chewing up the furniture. She is very persnickety about her dinner hour, which I've already missed."

"Oh dear." Daphne opened the door. "Hopefully she hasn't done much damage yet." She smiled and thanked him for dinner. "And now you really do have my phone number." Unsure that he'd actually gotten it right, she made sure to give it to him before they left the restaurant—as well as her last name. And she'd gotten his name as well. Harrison Henshaw. However, she hadn't asked for his number. A girl could only be so pushy.

For the next few days, Daphne waited for Harrison to call. But once again, her phone did not ring. However, she distracted herself on Wednesday afternoon with finishing her novel, which other than needing a thorough editing, appeared to be finished. To celebrate, she invited Sabrina over for tacos on Thursday night.

"What is wrong with that man?" Sabrina demanded as they were cleaning up the dishes. "You have a perfectly wonderful date with him on Saturday and now, four days later, he can't even pick up the phone?"

"He's probably just busy." Daphne closed the dishwasher. "If he wants to reach me, he knows where to find me."

"You are way too patient. I would've called him by now."

"I don't have his number."

"You have his name, silly. You could look it up and call him if you wanted to."

"Maybe I don't want to."

"I know, I know," Sabrina said in a slightly mocking tone, "you're an *old-fashioned girl.*"

"And what is wrong with that?"

"As long as you don't mind being an old-fashioned old maid, it's just fine."

To change the subject, Daphne started talking about the situation with Mabel. "I spent the morning with Vera. I wanted to help her figure some things out for Mabel . . . and I found out more about her condition."

"Oh, what exactly is going on with her anyway?"

Daphne hung up the dish towel and turned to Sabrina. "She has lymphoma."

"Oh dear."

"She was treated for it before, about three or four years ago. Apparently they didn't expect her to fully recover then. But she seemed to go into remission . . . or so she had hoped. Then last summer, about a month before her daughter passed away, Vera started experiencing symptoms again."

Sabrina shook her head. "What is she doing about it?"

"She just finished chemo before Mabel came to live with her. She said she tried to appear strong to the social worker, but between the chemo and the cancer, she feels pretty helpless. She also feels guilty for having Mabel with her. She knows that Mabel deserves better."

"Poor Vera. To lose her daughter and get the cancer back all around the same time. That's so sad. Did she tell you how Mabel's mother died?"

"Drug overdose."

Sabrina sighed. "I was afraid it was something like that. Poor little Mabel."

"I know."

"So what is Vera doing about the cancer now? Radiation? More chemo?"

"The chemo made her so sick that she feels it nearly killed her. She says she's done with treatments. She's certain that nothing will help her now. She just hopes to get a little stronger so she can do a better job caring for Mabel."

"But what then? I mean, if the cancer isn't gone? Will it kill her?"

"Unless she recovers." Daphne tried to forget Vera's tear-filled eyes when she shared her gloomy prognosis this morning. "And I promised to be around to help out—with her and Mabel."

"I'll help too."

"I even offered to have Mabel over here if necessary. I mean, if Vera's condition really worsens. And Vera seemed relieved. She's worried that Mabel has already seen too much of the dark underside of life."

"Poor little Mabel." Sabrina shook her head. "But what about Vera? Is she just giving up then? She doesn't want to seek out any more medical treatment?"

"She plans to just tough it out."

"Tough it out?" Sabrina frowned.

"I know." Daphne pursed her lips. "I've been asking myself all day if there was something I could do."

"You've already done a lot."

"I know." Daphne flashed back to that moment in Vera's overgrown front yard. "You know the words that Jesus said: *You have not because you ask not?* Well, that was what gave me the idea to ask Tom and Mick to help with Vera's house. And that turned out pretty good. I even asked Wally to help Mabel with some of her schoolwork—because she'd gotten a little behind. And that's been working out quite nicely too. But now I wonder about asking a few others. For starters, I was thinking about Pastor Andrew."

"What would you ask him to do?"

"To come and talk to Vera."

"Oh . . ." Sabrina nodded. "That's a good idea. He could talk to her about life and death and heaven."

"Yes. And then I thought about some other friends who might be able to offer help or encouragement. Like Olivia. Maybe she could bring Vera some flowers. Truman might donate some healthy foods. He's such an expert on what's good for what ails us. And then Ricardo makes such good soups and—"

"See, it's like I always say, you know everyone in this town, Daphne." Sabrina laughed. "For a hermit, you sure manage to get around."

"Maybe I'm not such a hermit after all."

"You're the perfect one to coordinate these people to help Vera. Just let me know how I can help."

So they put together a quick plan and made some phone calls and in less than an hour, they had a nice little task force. For their reward,

Daphne got out a carton of mocha-fudge-nut ice cream and made a pot of decaf. As they were finishing off their treat in the living room, Sabrina looked at Daphne with a somber expression. "What happens to Mabel? I mean if Vera dies?"

"That's exactly what I've been wondering myself." Daphne set her empty dish onto the side table and leaned back into her favorite chair. "Vera told me she has a son who's trying to get out of the Marines. She thinks he'll be able to take Mabel . . . in the event of her death."

"*Take* Mabel?" Sabrina looked distressed. "Where will he take her?"

"I don't know. But Vera seems to think he will assume guardianship."

"Is this guy *ready* to be a dad? How old is he? Is he married? Does Mabel even know him?"

"Good questions." Daphne sighed. "I don't know the answers."

"I suppose Vera doesn't have any idea about how long she has. Do you think it's like a year?"

"I don't know. I wasn't sure how to ask that, Sabrina. Just getting her to open up to me like she did was no small thing. I can tell Vera has been a very private person."

"I know we shouldn't make her feel worse. But it seems cruel to put Mabel through losing another family member like that."

"Poor Vera has had a pretty rough go of it in recent years. I guess her husband left her shortly before she was diagnosed with lymphoma."

"Hey, maybe he could come back and help with Mabel."

"I don't think so. He's not even Mabel's real grandfather. And Vera is very antagonistic toward him."

"Isn't it sad how some marriages turn out?" Sabrina shook her head. "I certainly hope to do much better my next time around."

"So anyway, I'm hoping that Mabel's uncle will get here soon. Apparently he wasn't supposed to get discharged until next summer, but due to the circumstances—his sister's death and his mother's illness. Well, Vera hopes they'll make an exception and discharge him sooner since his niece is in need of a guardian."

"Do you know *anything* about him? Is he a *nice* person?"

Daphne shrugged. "Vera is his mother. What do you expect her to say?"

"Good point."

"I just feel so responsible for Mabel now." Daphne reached down to pick up Ethel, swooshing her into her lap. "I've known her less than two weeks and yet she's become a regular part of my life. Do you know that she's made a best friend at school now? A little girl named Lola. Mabel wants to invite Lola over to play on Saturday. I told her they could come here if she wanted."

"A friend. That's wonderful."

"Yes. She was so happy. I'll really miss her if the uncle takes her away."

"So will I." Sabrina let out a sad sigh.

They both just sat there in a silence for a while.

"Do you think you'll ever have children, Daphne?"

Daphne frowned. "I'd like to have a husband first."

"Yes, of course. But, say, if you got married in May like Aunt Dee has planned. Do you think you'd want to have children soon? I mean your biological clock is ticking. You can't put it off forever. They say the odds of having kids after your midthirties goes down significantly."

"Well, that's just one more thing I'll have to trust God for. If it's meant to be, it'll be."

"I sometimes wonder about adoption." Sabrina reached over to where Lucy was curled up on the couch next to her and slid the big orange cat closer. "I could imagine adopting a child, making it my own. Kind of like Mabel. I would gladly adopt her."

"Me too."

"I wish we could both adopt her together."

Daphne chuckled. "That would be interesting, but I doubt we could get children's services to agree to that. Plus there's the uncle . . ."

"Yeah, probably not. Just the same, spending time with that child has opened my mind some," Sabrina said.

"Would you consider adopting a child while you're still single? I know they allow foster kids to stay with single people. It's possible you could adopt too . . . especially if it was an older child."

"Maybe."

"I asked Jake about Aunt Dee's will. I thought maybe he could change things around, you know, tweak it a little so that instead of finding myself a husband I could adopt a child."

"Now there's an idea."

Daphne wrinkled her nose. "Jake put the kibosh on that. He can't change the will."

Sabrina laughed. "Well, it's too soon for you to give up on marrying. And don't forget, there's Harrison still. Now if we could just think of a way to get him to call."

Daphne shrugged, unsure as to whether she really cared or not.

"Or if we could get you to call him." Sabrina rubbed her chin.

"Hey, why don't you invite him here for dinner? You said he wanted to see inside your house."

"That's true."

"What if you were having a little get-together? Say, a buffet dinner for a few of your friends? You could just casually invite him. What do you think he'd say?"

"I don't know." Daphne considered this. It really wasn't such a bad idea. Except it might come across as a bit desperate.

"How about for Halloween?" Sabrina suggested.

"You mean have a Halloween party?" Daphne frowned.

"Not exactly. But you could use that as an excuse to have friends over. Your house looks so cute with those pumpkins lined up on the stairs and around the porch."

"But I promised to take Mabel trick-or-treating. And you said you and Tootsie would go too. Remember?"

"Yes, of course. And I've got Tootsie's little outfit all ready. But what if you have a party on the Saturday before Halloween?"

"That's only two days away. Kind of short notice, don't you think?"

"How about the following Saturday?"

"My dad's wedding, remember?"

Sabrina frowned. "That's right. How about the Friday before?"

"Rehearsal dinner."

"Oh, yeah." Sabrina slapped her forehead. "That's it. Who is your date for these social events? The dinner and the wedding? You can't go alone."

"I can go stag if I want to."

"Yes, I suppose *you* could do that. Or you could invite Harrison."

Daphne forced a laugh. "Oh, Sabrina, you are such a cunning little conniver. Always scheming and planning."

Sabrina gave her a sheepish smile. "Sorry. It's just the way I'm wired."

"How about you give it a rest. If Harrison wants to call me, he will call me."

"Okay, fine. But that still leaves you dateless for the wedding activities. Do you really want to be there without a guy? You do realize how pathetic that will make you look. At your old man's wedding, all by your sorry little lonesome? Poor Daphne."

"So who's your date?"

Sabrina smiled. "I'm working on it."

The next day, Daphne was putting together her column and came across a letter that seemed to hit uncomfortably close to home.

> *Dear Daphne,*
>
> *I met the most perfect guy about a month ago. Friends introduced me to "Stephen" because they were certain we would hit it off. And we did! So we went out on a totally wonderful date. Really, it was fabulous. Everything was dreamy. And as he was kissing me good night, I was planning my wedding . . . and deciding how many children to have. Honestly, this guy is that wonderful. So I waited for him to call back. I waited a week. Then I waited another week. And it is now the third week since our wonderful date. Stephen hasn't called once. I asked our mutual friends if he was okay. I thought maybe he'd died or gotten sick or something. But they*

said, "Yeah, he's fine." So why hasn't he called me? Why? And since he hasn't called me, I think maybe I should call him. I don't normally call guys because it's against my "rules." But for this guy I could make an exception. Please, Daphne, tell me what to do.

Pining in Pensacola

Dear Pining,

As hard as this will be to hear, if Stephen wanted to call you, I'm certain he would. If Stephen is as into you as you are into him, he would not waste any time in reconnecting with you. Although you were hearing wedding bells that night, I suspect Stephen was probably just hearing the "final bell" and calling it a night. My heart goes out to you, but I suggest you try to move on and forget about Stephen. As I'm sure you've heard, there are lots more fish in the sea.

Daphne

As Daphne saved this letter and response, she put a check mark beside it—her reminder to give it one last look before turning it in to the syndicate. Just in case her response was too harsh. Because she probably wasn't attempting to shoot down poor "Pining's" hopes as much as she was trying to shoot down her own. Because if Harrison wanted to call her, he certainly would. *End of story. Get over it.*

Chapter 23

On Friday morning, Daphne felt the need to get out of the house and walked to town. She would've invited Sabrina except she'd taken Tootsie to get his teeth cleaned. The air was cool and crisp and Daphne's breath came out in little puffs of fog. By the time she reached Red River Coffee, she was glad to get in out of the cold.

"Good morning," Jake said as she got into line behind him. "How are you doing?"

"Trying to get the chill off." She rubbed her hands together.

"A cup of joe will fix you right up." He grinned. "Are you alone or meeting someone?"

"I'm by myself."

"Why don't you join me?"

She hesitated. "Sure." And before she could stop him, he ordered a latte for her. "You still like those, right?"

She nodded. "Thanks."

Soon they were settled at a table by the window. "So how is my favorite client doing?" he asked.

"I'm your favorite client?"

"My most-interesting heiress to be certain."

"A *conditional* heiress."

"That's what makes it interesting."

"So how are things going with Harrison?" Jake asked. "I hear he got the city hall job."

"He did?" She tried to act nonchalant. "I hadn't heard."

"So you and he . . . you're not going out?"

"No, not really. We just happened to cross paths that day. We shared a meal. That's all."

"Really?" Jake looked skeptical as the barista set their coffees on the table and took the number placard. "So did you honestly meet speed dating?"

She rolled her eyes and took a sip.

"Yes, I remember. Sabrina's idea. How is she doing?"

"She's fine." Now to change the subject. Daphne talked about Mabel, filling him in on Vera's illness. "It's just so sad. First Mabel loses her mother . . . and it seems almost certain she'll lose her grandmother as well."

He frowned. "That is sad. Poor child."

"I really wish there was a way I could adopt her."

"Seriously?" He blinked. "As in twenty-four/seven? Day in and day out? Year round?"

"Absolutely. I really like this little girl."

"What plans does the grandmother have for her? I mean after her demise?"

Daphne told him about the uncle. "But when I asked Mabel about him, she didn't even know his name."

His brow creased. "That's too bad. I hope this child is resilient."

"She seems to be. But it'll be so sad if the uncle takes her away. She's finally settling into school. She made a new friend. They're coming to play at my house tomorrow."

"That's sweet that you're helping the child." He looked uneasy. "But I hope you're not letting your heart get too involved, Daphne. It could really hurt when the uncle comes for her."

She looked defiantly into his eyes. "Isn't it better to have loved and lost than never to have loved at all?"

"Sounds like Dear Daphne talking."

She frowned down at her half-full cup. "Maybe so." She looked up at him, locking gazes again. "Isn't there some way you could help me, Jake?"

"Huh?" He looked startled. "How? What?"

"I mean *legally*. Is there some way you could help me to get custody of Mabel?"

"Custody?"

"I know . . . it's probably a long shot. But Vera does like me. And Mabel and I just connected right from the start. The first day I met her, catnapping Lucy, I could tell she was special."

"She tried to steal your cat?"

"She was just lonely. She thought Lucy wanted to go home with her and be her friend."

"Oh."

"I just wish there was a way to keep Mabel."

"Maybe there is. Have you tried talking about this to the grandmother?"

"Not specifically."

"Maybe you should bring the subject up. And if she seems open to the idea, I could draw up something legal for her. It would actually be fairly straightforward and simple. I mean, while the grandmother is living. After that . . . well, as you know, it could get complicated."

"Okay." Daphne nodded. "I'll do it. I'll talk to Vera about this."

"It's nice you want to help this child," he said carefully, "but you should consider your own situation too, Daphne."

She scowled. "You mean Aunt Dee's conditions?"

"Yes. The clock is running. If by some chance you do get custody of this child, what can you guarantee her after May comes? I mean if you're still single."

"I am perfectly capable of supporting myself."

"But with a child? Do you have any idea how expensive that can get?"

"Poor people have children too, Jake."

He gave a sad smile. "Yes. I know all about that."

"You?" She cocked her head to one side. "How so?"

"Contrary to popular belief, I was not born with a silver spoon in my mouth." He set down his cup with a clunk. "Would it surprise you to learn I spent my early years in an impoverished home? My mother was widowed, struggling to get by. I remember lots of times when I went to bed hungry. My sister and I wore thrift-store clothes and didn't see a dentist until we were in our teens."

"Really?"

"It wasn't that our mom wasn't trying. She worked hard as a waitress."

"I had no idea."

"Most people don't. Anyway, my mom met Ralph just as I was starting high school. He was twenty-two years her senior, but he fell head over heels for her. And I think my mom saw him as her ticket out of poverty. Ralph was wealthy. Very wealthy."

"I see."

"He was a good guy and he took good care of us. Gave my mom anything she wanted and put my sister and me through the best colleges. And I believe that over time, my mom really did come to love him. She certainly appreciated his generosity. Ralph passed away a few years ago."

Daphne nodded, trying to remember why Jake was sharing so much. Oh yes, Mabel. "So you don't think I would be a very good single mother?"

"I'm not saying that. I'm only saying it's not easy." He made a half smile. "You're my client, Daphne. I care about your welfare."

"Right . . ." She frowned, wondering what this really meant.

"And that reminds me of something."

"What?"

"A friend of mine. If you're not actually dating Harrison."

"Oh no. Please, don't tell me you want to set me up on another blind date. Don't you remember how that—?"

"Hey, I told you I was sorry about Tony. I guess I didn't know him as well as I thought. But I do know Spencer. I would've told you about him sooner, but I figured I should give you time to, uh, forget about Tony."

"And you think I should trust you? After that fiasco with Tony?"

"My bad." He gave an apologetic smile. "But Spencer is not like Tony. Not at all. Besides that, Spencer is a writer too. Wouldn't it be interesting to meet another writer? If nothing else you could talk about your craft."

"What kind of writer?" she asked a bit dubiously.

"He's been working on a mystery."

"So he's not published?" She frowned, trying to determine Jake's real motives here. "You think two starving writers would be a good match?"

"He's not starving. He has a real job."

"Meaning writing is not a real job?" She twisted her mouth to one side.

"Of course writing is a real job. Look at how well Dee did in her profession. But Spencer has a career as a software designer. He works out of his home."

"Oh." She considered this. Maybe she was being too hasty to dismiss Spencer without meeting him first.

"And he's a really nice guy, Daphne. Very thoughtful. And he's interested in other people. Not a bit narcissistic like some doctor who shall go unnamed. I actually think you'd like Spencer. And hey, even if you don't fall in love, you'd at least have made a writer friend. Nothing wrong with that."

"I guess not." She felt herself softening . . . just a little.

"He nearly married a girl once, back in his twenties. But it didn't work out. He hasn't been in very many relationships since then."

"How old is he?"

"My age. About forty."

"Uh-huh . . ."

"Why don't you look him up online? Google him for yourself. If you like what you see, give me a call and I'll arrange a meeting."

"A meeting," she clarified. "Not a date. Right?"

"Sure. Whatever you want." He waved his hand. "You could meet him here for coffee. You don't like him, you walk away. End of story."

"Okay . . ." She set down her empty cup. "I'll Google him and see what I think."

So Daphne found herself meeting Spencer for coffee on Sunday afternoon. And to her surprise and relief, he seemed to be pretty much as Jake had described. He was interesting and interested. And he seemed to like her.

"Would you like to get together again?" he asked as they were getting ready to go.

Daphne considered this. Her first impulse was to decline. Not because she didn't like him. But more because she didn't feel any real chemistry. Of course, that seemed a bit silly since she had barely met the man. Was it even possible to experience any real chemistry over coffee? Although he wasn't unattractive, his looks were not especially appealing to her. His short light-brown hair was neatly cut, his gray eyes seemed sincere, his smile genuine, but it felt like something was missing.

"Or maybe it's too soon?" he said quickly. "I don't mean to rush you into anything, Daphne. I don't really know how these things work. I haven't dated in years. I've had some online friendships, but they just never seemed to get anywhere. That probably has more to do with me than the women I've met. I've been overly careful . . . if you know what I mean. My mother keeps telling everyone I'm a confirmed bachelor. Maybe she's right."

Daphne felt sorry for him. "Sure, why don't we try getting together again. I'd like to hear more about your book."

He brightened. "And I'd like to hear more about yours."

Remembering Jake's suggestion that they could at the least become writing friends, she agreed to meet him for dinner at Midge's on Thursday. And if things improved, perhaps she would invite him to be her escort for the wedding activities. Of course, she'd have to make it clear to everyone, including Spencer, that they were not seriously involved. But he would probably be a perfectly acceptable wedding date.

Of course, as fate would have it, Harrison called up later that same day. "I'll be in town all day on Thursday. I thought maybe we could get together for a bite to eat. Catch up."

"I'm sorry. I just made plans for Thursday night." She weighed her words, unsure of how much she wanted to disclose. Should she call it a date or not? "A writer friend is meeting me for dinner."

"Oh well, bad timing."

"I wish I'd known sooner. And it's been a while since I've heard from you." Was that too strong of a hint? "But I did hear you got the city hall job. Congratulations."

"Yes, I meant to call you and tell you about it. But I've been so busy getting everything ready. Construction is due to begin in November."

"That soon?"

"So I'll be in Appleton a fair amount. Hopefully we can get together one of these times. I'd still like to see your house."

"Just give me a little heads-up," she said. "And we'll see what works out."

"Maybe the following week."

"Maybe so." She hung up with mixed feelings. On one hand, she was disappointed that she was missing out on an evening with Harrison in order to spend time with Spencer. On the other hand, Spencer seemed to have better manners than Harrison. So perhaps it made more sense to invest some time in getting to know him better.

On Tuesday afternoon, Mabel toted her stuffed backpack over to Daphne's house. Since it was Halloween, the plan was to go trick-or-treating and over to the church for a harvest party, and then to spend the night at Daphne's. After seeing how weak Vera was this morning, Daphne felt it was best not to disturb the poor woman. She'd even put a sign on Vera's door to warn trick-or-treaters that someone inside was ill.

Just as it was getting dusky, Daphne, dressed as a scarecrow, and Mabel, wearing her Little Mermaid costume, went over to knock on Sabrina's door. Sabrina was dressed like a bottle of ketchup and Tootsie was wearing a hotdog bun. "Ready to trick-or-treat?" Mabel asked happily. And soon the four of them were going house to house in the neighborhood. Mabel was having such a great time, no one would be able to guess that she had so much tragedy in her life.

Eventually they headed over to the harvest party, where lots of kids were already gathered to play games and dunk for apples and get their faces painted. Mabel insisted on participating in every activity. But finally, Daphne had to remind her it was a school night and they went home.

It wasn't the first night that Mabel had slept in Daphne's guest room. Occasionally if Vera had an especially bad day, she would ask Daphne to keep Mabel overnight. And because Daphne had purchased a few child-friendly items, this spare room was slowly taking on the appearance of a child's room. But Daphne didn't mind. However, Jake's warning still rang in her ears. If she was to have a chance at getting custody of Mabel—and it was probably a long shot—it would have to be worked out before Vera passed on. And who knew how much time there was? According to Pastor Andrew, he'd been to visit Vera several times now and it wasn't looking good.

"I don't like to betray anyone's confidences," he confessed to Daphne a couple of days ago, "but Vera fears she won't make it until next summer—when her son is scheduled to get discharged."

"Can't he get discharged sooner? Or get an emergency leave or something?"

"I hope so. And I've written a letter in support of this. But since he recently came out for his sister's funeral, it's uncertain."

Daphne felt like she didn't have just one time bomb ticking away inside of her—the one that would detonate in May—she had the Vera clock ticking down as well. And if Sabrina were around to put in her two cents, she would probably point out that Daphne's biological clock wasn't slowing much either. To that end, Daphne was starting to make a plan.

Next week, after the wedding festivities were finished, Daphne would sit down and have a nice long chat with Vera. She would try to convince Vera that until this mysterious uncle could come home, perhaps it would be wise to sign over some emergency sort of guardianship to Daphne. She would list all she could offer Mabel, including not being relocated again—especially since Mabel was finally starting to thrive in school and making friends.

Daphne would explain how important Mabel had become to her and how Sabrina would be like an aunt to the child. Daphne would plead her case to the best of her ability. She would try to make Vera see that it really was in Mabel's best interest. She would even offer to have both Vera and Mabel come live with her when Vera became too ill to be alone. Vera would be welcome to Aunt Dee's first-floor bedroom. And if necessary, Daphne would get help from hospice to care for her as well. She would do everything possible to make this time as easy as she could for Vera. And for Mabel.

In the meantime, she would pray. If this was meant to be . . . it would be. If not, she would just have to get used to the idea of not having Mabel as part of her life. But for some reason, she felt certain God would not allow this.

Chapter 24

Daphne's "date" with Spencer left her feeling a little ho-hum, at least in the romance department anyway. Although Jake had not misrepresented his friend—Spencer was clearly a good guy. He was a good conversationalist and a good listener. And when they talked about books and writing, he even proved to have good friend potential too. But as a boyfriend? Not so much. She wished she felt differently about him . . . but she didn't. Perhaps it was simply a matter of chemistry.

"I insist we go dutch," she told Spencer when the bill came.

"Oh?" He looked slightly crushed. "Does that mean I failed the test?"

"Test?" She forced a smile as she laid some cash on the bill. "This wasn't a test, Spencer. In fact, I've really enjoyed getting to know you. It's fun talking about books. And I like your idea of forming a writers' critique group. That would be wonderful. Especially in winter, you know, when the nights are long."

He brightened. "That would be nice."

She stuck out her hand and shook his. "I really enjoyed your company. I hope we can continue our friendship."

He actually seemed slightly relieved. "I would like having you for my friend, Daphne. That's a lot less pressure, you know, compared to having a girlfriend."

She nodded. "So let's agree to it then. Friends?"

"Friends. And I'll talk to the other writers I mentioned to you . . . about getting that critique group together."

"Thank you." Daphne stood now, relieved that she'd driven there to meet him and didn't need to have him take her home—avoiding that awkward moment on the porch. She might still be a bit inexperienced at this whole dating game, but she had learned a thing or two along the way.

Of course, this probably meant she was going "stag" to both the rehearsal dinner and the wedding. But what did it matter? Besides, as far as she knew, Sabrina would be alone at the wedding. At least they could hang out together during the reception. And if Karen didn't mind, maybe Daphne could bring Mabel as her guest. Mabel had just told Daphne that she'd never been to a wedding before. Plus that would give Vera a quiet day on Saturday.

Daphne would give her dad a jingle. "So . . . getting any wedding jitters?" she asked after he answered the phone.

"You want my honest answer?"

"Sure."

"Okay, I suppose I am feeling a little unsettled."

"You mean you're having second thoughts? Because it's not too late, you know. Weddings have been called off at—"

"No, no, that's not what I mean. I want to marry Karen. I'm just not sure I'm up for all the pomp and circumstance."

"Oh . . ."

"But it means a lot to Karen. So I better just bite the bullet . . . like I've been doing. Better just go for it. Eh?"

"Sounds like a good plan." She explained about how Mabel would love to experience a real wedding. "Do you think it would be okay if I brought her as my date?"

Dad chuckled. "Well, I wouldn't mind in the least. Mabel is all right with me." He'd only seen Mabel a couple of times, but it made Daphne feel good to think he liked her young friend.

"Should I ask Karen about it?"

"I don't see why. You're allowed to bring a guest. Doesn't mean it has to be a man."

"That's right."

"Besides, there will be some unattached men there anyway. Might be better if you weren't with a date."

"Unattached?"

"Seems Ricardo is coming to the wedding alone. And Karen has a nephew named Calvin she's dying for you to meet. She even invited him to the rehearsal dinner."

"I see."

They visited awhile longer, but Dad strongly encouraged her to bring Mabel. "Tell her I'll even dance with her if she comes."

"Oh, Dad, she would love that."

The next morning, after Mabel had gone to school, Daphne went over to check on Vera. To her surprise, Vera was in the kitchen cleaning up the breakfast dishes. "I made us pancakes," she told Daphne. "Mickey Mouse pancakes."

"Good for you." Daphne sat on the kitchen stool. "So you must be feeling pretty good."

"I am." Vera set a pan in the sink, then sat on the stool across from Daphne. "How are you?"

"I'm fine. I wanted to come by to ask you about taking Mabel to my dad's wedding on Saturday. I know she'd like to go and I thought you might appreciate having a quiet house for a few hours."

Vera seemed to consider this. "That's not a bad idea."

"Great. My dad even promised to dance with her."

Vera smiled. "That's nice."

"Well, I shouldn't keep you." Daphne stood. "It's so great to see you up and about . . . and feeling well."

Vera reached for Daphne's hand and gave it a firm squeeze. "I owe much of this to you, Daphne. You've been a real godsend to me and Mabel. I don't know how I'll ever thank you for all you've done."

Daphne was tempted to broach the discussion of Mabel's future, but it wasn't the right time. Especially since Vera seemed to be doing so well. "I'm just thankful I get to enjoy Mabel. She is really a treasure. But I'm sure you know that."

"I most definitely do. And I just heard from Daniel—that's my son. Sounds like he gets to come home for Christmas. Not sure he'll be fully discharged by then, but he's working on it. I feel hopeful."

"That's wonderful, Vera. How lovely for you to have your son and Mabel with you for Christmas."

"What should Mabel wear to the wedding?" Vera said suddenly. "I'm not sure she has something—"

"I'd love to get her a dress. Something frilly and girly and sweet. Perhaps something she can wear at Christmas too. If you don't mind, that is."

Vera waved her hand. "I told Mabel you're like her fairy

godmother. Go ahead and find her a dress. I know she'll love it." She sighed. "I just wish I felt well enough to do those things for her."

Daphne smiled. "Well, keep getting better, Vera. It's great seeing you up and around like this."

Vera just nodded.

Daphne tried to act like there was nothing strange about having a wedding rehearsal where most of the bridesmaids were old enough for Social Security. Oddly enough, other than Dad's best man, Stewart, from the bank, the other groomsmen, Karen's sons, were all in their twenties and thirties. Maybe the newspaper could write the attendants up as a "cougar" wedding party.

Naturally Daphne kept these thoughts to herself. But as they practiced going up and down the aisle, she couldn't help but think it was a strange coincidence that she was being escorted by Ricardo.

"I'm guessing this is my dad's doing," she whispered to Ricardo as they stood in the shadows. "He's always trying to get us together."

Ricardo winked. "Nothing wrong with that."

Daphne tried not to look shocked. "Really? You don't mind being set up?"

"Not if it's with the right girl."

Her cheeks grew warm, but now it was time for them to walk up the aisle together. Karen was trying to decide if she wanted the bridesmaids coming in separately or being escorted. Because of the general age differences, Daphne would've opted for separately, but this wasn't her wedding.

After the rehearsal, they all headed over to Midge's Diner, which Ricardo had closed for their dinner. Daphne was slightly relieved that

Ricardo kept busy with food responsibilities because his words about the "right girl" were still ringing in her ears. Was he serious? This was the first time it ever felt as if he saw her as something more than just a friend. Or perhaps she'd misread him. She acted natural as she visited with various members of the wedding party, keeping one eye on Ricardo as he moved through the crowd and back into the kitchen and then out again.

Thanks to Karen, Daphne was seated next to the nephew Calvin. And, sure, he was nice enough and not bad looking, but he did seem rather boring. Or maybe he was just bored with her. Whatever the case, he seemed more interested in his iPhone than anyone there. And to be fair, Daphne might've simply been distracted by Ricardo.

Dad had mentioned that Ricardo was attending the wedding alone too. Perhaps she'd get the chance to dance with him tomorrow. Maybe she could ask Dad to lend a hand in setting it up for her. Or maybe she would become bold enough to ask Ricardo to the dance floor herself.

She remembered dancing with him last summer . . . that had been nice. She wasn't sure if her interest in Ricardo was genuine or simply desperation. It seemed the more she thought about these things, the more confused she felt. Perhaps it was best not to think on them too much.

As Daphne drove home from the rehearsal dinner, she remembered the bag still in the backseat. Mabel's dress. She had meant to try it on Mabel after school today, but time had slipped away and she'd forgotten all about it. Perhaps she'd go over in the morning to try it on. If anything it might be a bit too big, but she could simply tie the sash a bit more snugly.

As Daphne got ready for bed, she wondered how her dad

was feeling on the eve of his wedding. Was he having any second thoughts? Any regrets? He had seemed so jolly and bright all evening, she doubted he had any concerns. And even if Daphne still didn't feel like she knew Karen that well, it seemed that Dad was head over heels for her. So why would Daphne be worried? Tomorrow by this time the newlyweds would be on a plane, headed for Maui. No cares in the world. Lucky them.

It was around noon the following day when Daphne carried the fluffy rose-colored dress down the street. She knocked on the door and Mabel opened it. "Daphne. Is that my dress?"

"It is." Daphne held the garment out for her to see.

"It's beautiful!" Mabel danced around the living room, narrowly missing a cereal bowl on the floor by the TV.

"Is your grandma still sleeping?"

"Uh-huh." Mabel fingered the shiny fabric.

"Why don't you go try it on while I check on your grandma?" Daphne watched as Mabel went into her room, then quietly tapped on Vera's door. When she didn't answer, Daphne eased it open. Vera's eyes opened sleepily.

"Oh . . . hello." She yawned. "Is it time for the wedding already?"

Daphne explained about the dress. "She's trying it on right now. Hopefully it'll fit."

Vera slowly sat up in bed. "Tell her to come show me."

"I will. And if you don't mind, I'll just have her come home with me. We'll be heading over to the church in about an hour or so anyway."

"That's just fine." Vera released a weary sigh.

"And if it's okay, Mabel can spend the night at my house. I expect we'll get home around seven or so. And I know she wants to go to Sunday school tomorrow."

"That sounds like a good plan." She yawned again. "For some reason I'm extra tired today. Guess I did too much yesterday."

Before long, Mabel came into Vera's room and after a few spins and some slightly clumsy dance-move attempts, she kissed her grandma on the cheek.

"You be a good girl for Aunt Daphne," Vera told Mabel.

"I will." Mabel nodded somberly. "I promise, Grandma."

"I know you will."

And then Daphne and Mabel gathered up Mabel's things and were off.

Feeling very much like a stuffed and wrinkly sausage, Daphne took her place in the bridal party and when her turn came, she slowly walked down the aisle. It was odd seeing her father standing up in front. Almost as if something about this was all wrong. Shouldn't he be by her side, escorting her up to the pulpit where her intended would be waiting for her?

As she lined herself up with the rather elderly bridesmaids, she tried to refocus. This was her dad's wedding. Karen's big day. And she was happy for them. She spotted Sabrina and Mabel in the third row. Mabel's eyes were big and round, taking it all in. Before long the wedding was over—without a hitch the couple was hitched, and now Ricardo was escorting Daphne down the aisle and to the back of the church.

"Thank you very much," she said.

"The pleasure was mine." He smiled. "You look very pretty."

Daphne giggled. "Really? You don't think these dresses look like giant sausage casings?"

He chuckled. "Well, on you . . . sausage has never looked so lovely."

She laughed. "Thanks. And for that, I should insist that you save a dance for me at the reception."

"Consider it done."

Daphne found Sabrina and Mabel and before long, they were making their way into the hotel where the reception was being held. Already the music was playing and the champagne was being poured. It wasn't long before Dad and Karen went out for the first dance, with "It Had to Be You" playing. After that dance, just as planned, Dad came over to ask Daphne out onto the floor. Meanwhile Karen asked her older son to join her.

"Well, you did it, Dad," Daphne said as they glided to the music. "Congratulations."

"And just in case you're wondering, the water is fine. You should think about trying this out for yourself." His eyes twinkled.

"Thanks, Dad. I'll keep that in mind."

"I know you and Karen aren't that close yet," he said. "But when you get to know her better, you'll see that you actually have a lot in common. You're both strong, intelligent women."

"Yes, it takes strong, intelligent women to keep a guy like you in line." She grinned.

"When we get back from Maui, two weeks from now, I plan to move into Karen's place."

"Oh? What about your condo? You seemed so happy there."

"I might rent it. Her place is bigger. We'll stay there until we find something we both like. We decided that was best—to have a home that belongs to both of us. Don't you think that makes sense?"

Daphne nodded. For some reason her eyes were filling with tears. "Yes, Dad," she said in a choked-up voice. "And I'm really happy for you."

He stopped dancing to give her a big hug. "And I'm very proud of you, Daphne." He looked into her eyes. "Someday you and I are going to be dancing at your wedding, darling. I just know it."

Her mouth eased into a smile, her eyes watering, as the song ended. "And I promised to ask Ricardo to dance."

His eyes lit up. "Yes! Hurry and do that before someone else nabs him."

She winked. "Think I should sprint across the room?"

"Why not?"

She made a face, then turned and walked over to where Ricardo was standing with the other groomsmen. "I wonder if I might have this dance?"

"You got it." He laughed at the other groomsmen. "See you guys later."

After dancing with Ricardo, she explained about her young date. "I promised to get Mabel out to the dance floor. And I can tell she's eager."

"Well, if she needs a partner, I'm the man."

"Thanks, Ricardo."

Before the reception was over, Mabel had danced with both Ricardo and Dad a couple of times. She also danced with Daphne and Sabrina. And Daphne danced with a variety of fellows, including

Jake. She was a bit surprised to see him there but then remembered he had done some legal work for her dad.

Jake was a fine dancer and she would've enjoyed dancing with him more, but Karen's nephew Calvin seemed intent on monopolizing her time. For the last dance, she and Sabrina and Mabel did a little jig on the dance floor together.

"It's time to throw the bridal bouquet," Diane called out. "Come on, bridesmaids and single women. This is your big chance."

Of course, thanks to the bridesmaids, Daphne was pushed to the forefront. "I should've brought my catcher's mitt," Daphne teased as Karen turned her back to them and gave a big toss. The bouquet sailed up high, but thanks to Daphne's height advantage, she could reach it. For a split second she hesitated, then her hand shot up and she snagged the flowers right out of the air. Everyone burst into laughter.

"Looks like you're next." Karen came over to join the fun.

Daphne hugged her new stepmom. "You guys have fun in Maui," she whispered. "Make sure Dad wears his sunscreen or he'll end up looking like a boiled lobster."

Karen grinned. "You can count on that. We'll both be taking real good care of each other from now on."

As Daphne carried her prize bouquet over to show to Mabel and Sabrina, she thought about Karen's words. How sweet it must be to have someone to take care of like that. Even to have someone like Mabel to watch over . . . it would be lovely.

Chapter 25

O n Sunday after church, Daphne took Mabel home. And since she had so much stuff to carry, Daphne grabbed the backpack and went into the house with her. Once inside, she went to check on Vera. The house, as usual, was quiet and still. And the drapes, which Vera had recently been opening, were pulled shut.

As Mabel carried an armload of things into her room, Daphne tapped on Vera's door. When Vera didn't answer, Daphne quietly peeked inside. But as soon as the door opened, a chill ran through her. Something was wrong.

She went over to Vera's bed and instantly knew—something was terribly wrong. "Vera?" She reached to touch Vera's pale hand. It was cold. She touched her colorless cheek. Cold and lifeless. Vera was not breathing. And it appeared she'd been dead for hours.

"Grandma?" Mabel called as she came into the room. "I brought you some wedding cake from the—"

"Let's go back out." Daphne guided Mabel toward the door. "This isn't a good time right now."

"Is Grandma sleeping?" Mabel whispered.

"Come on," Daphne said in a trembling voice. "You're going to stay at my house again. Let's get some of your things, okay?"

"Is Grandma sick?"

Feeling confused and overwhelmed with sadness, Daphne sat on Mabel's little bed and, leaning forward, she put her hands over her face, trying to hold back the tears already streaming down her cheeks.

"What's the matter, Aunt Daphne?"

Daphne looked up at Mabel. "Oh, Mabel."

"What happened?" Her little chin was quivering now. "Why are you crying?"

"It's your grandma." Daphne reached out and gathered Mabel into her arms. "She's gone."

"But I saw her. She's in her bed."

"I mean she's gone . . . to be with God. She's in heaven now."

"You mean Grandma died?" Mabel looked at Daphne with big brown eyes, full of fear.

"Yes." Daphne pulled Mabel close again while both of them cried. "But your grandma is with God, Mabel. I know it."

"But she's still in her bed," Mabel said stubbornly. "I *saw* her."

"You're right. You did see her. Except you only saw her body. Because your grandma's not in her body anymore." Daphne pointed to Mabel's pajamas still on the floor from yesterday, from when Mabel had excitedly put on her dress for the wedding. "See how your pajamas are right where you left them? When you had them on, they were running around the house, but now they can't really do anything—because you're not inside of them. Do you understand?"

"Uh-huh."

"That's kind of like a person's body when they die. The real part of the person leaves the body behind—kind of like those pajamas."

"Why?"

"Because people don't need their earthly bodies in heaven, Mabel. You didn't need those pajamas at the wedding, did you?"

"No."

"So you left them behind. They stayed here while you were gone having a great time. It's like that with your grandma's body. It stays here because she doesn't need it in heaven. Does that make sense?"

Mabel nodded. "I guess so."

"Her earthly body was all worn out. That's why she was sick. But because your grandma believes in God, she's with him right now. In fact, she's probably laughing and dancing—kind of like we were doing at the wedding reception yesterday."

"Grandma is dancing?" Mabel's eyes were full of wonder.

"Dancing or running or walking or flying or whatever they do in heaven. Can you imagine what fun she's having?"

"Is she with Mama?"

"I think so." Daphne ran her hand over Mabel's head. "Your grandma's in a much better place now . . . because she's not sick anymore."

Mabel used her hands to wipe her damp cheeks. "You think she's happy?"

"I do." Daphne stood. "And now you will be staying with me."

"You mean all the time? Before school and after school and everything?"

"That's right." Daphne nodded. "You will live with me until your Uncle Daniel comes home at Christmastime, okay?"

"Okay." She nodded.

"Let's get some of your things . . . and let's go . . . home."

Daphne still felt slightly in shock as they gathered what Mabel would need for overnight and school tomorrow. She should call someone about Vera. But she could do that from home. Most of all, she just wanted to get Mabel out of here. Two deaths within months of each other . . . it seemed more than any child should have to bear.

At home, she sent Mabel up to the spare room to get settled and then called Sabrina. She quickly relayed the sad news. "Can you call someone for me—I'm not even sure *who* you call. The police? Not an ambulance? Anyway, I don't want to have that conversation in front of Mabel. You know?"

"Oh my, yes. Of course. I'll get right to it. Poor Mabel."

"And I left the house key under the frog. If you wouldn't mind letting them in for me."

"Not at all."

Daphne thanked her, then hung up, and went to see if Mabel wanted some lunch. Mabel nodded without enthusiasm, so they both went to the kitchen and fixed grilled-cheese sandwiches together. However, after they sat at the table, neither of them seemed to have much of an appetite.

"Aren't you hungry?" Daphne asked.

"I guess not."

"Want some hot cocoa?"

"Okay."

"I'll make us both some," Daphne told her as she took out the milk. "I think we might need it just now."

After Mabel was tucked in bed and soundly sleeping, Daphne called Sabrina to find out how it went. "They asked about Vera's next of kin," Sabrina explained. "I mentioned Mabel and the uncle in the army."

"The Marines. Daniel is a Marine."

"Yeah. Well, I didn't know his name." Sabrina told Daphne the number of the contact person at the mortuary. "I told her you'd call tomorrow. Okay?"

"Yes. Thanks. After Mabel goes to school, I'll go down to Vera's house and see if I can find Daniel's address and phone information. I'll handle it from here on out."

"How is Mabel taking it?"

"Oh, she was very sad, of course. We talked about it a lot. She seems to be accepting that her grandma is gone . . . not coming back. When she prayed before bed, she asked God to take care of her grandma and mom. She told God she missed them. But she didn't cry anymore."

"She's a tough little girl."

"Yeah, I think so."

"What do you think Vera's son will do when he hears?"

"I don't know."

"Do you think the Marines will let him come home?"

"His mom just died . . . his sister died . . . his niece needs him." Daphne sighed. "I can't imagine they'd say no."

"Probably not," Sabrina said. "Are you worried he's going to take her away?"

Daphne sighed. "I'm trying not to think about that right now."

The next day after dropping Mabel at school, Daphne went back to Vera's and began sleuthing around for information about Daniel. It didn't take long before she found what she was looking for. And although she knew someone else would probably contact him, she wanted him to hear the sad news from someone who personally knew his mother. She wasn't even sure where Daniel was stationed or what time of day or night it might be there, but she called him anyway.

"Sergeant Myers," a deep voice answered.

Daphne quickly introduced herself as Vera's neighbor and friend, explaining how she'd been helping with Mabel. "And I'm very sorry to be the one to give you this sad news, Sergeant Myers, but your mother . . . Vera . . . she passed away this weekend." The truth was, Daphne didn't even know exactly when Vera had died. Was it on Saturday or Sunday? Maybe it didn't matter.

"My mom . . . is dead?"

"Yes, I'm so sorry." Daphne told him how Vera had seemed to rally the previous week. "She was up and doing things. She seemed happier. I honestly believed she was getting better."

"But then she died . . . ?"

"Yes."

"I planned to come home for Christmas. Just for a week. I was working on getting discharged early. I know Mom needed my help—" His voice cracked.

"I'm just so sorry. I know it must be a shock."

"How is Mabel doing?"

"All things considered, I think she's doing okay. She's a tough little girl."

"After what my sister did, I guess so." His voice was tinged with anger now. "All that didn't help my mom much. That's for sure."

"Well, I know your mom loved Mabel. I'm sure she enjoyed having her with her . . . these last few months."

"Yeah, you're probably right."

"Anyway . . ." She tried to gather her thoughts. "I assume someone will call you in regard to the, uh, the other details about what's to be done and all that."

"Who's taking care of Mabel right now?"

"I am. Mabel and I have spent some time together lately. I was trying to help out your mom—lighten her load a little. I live just a few houses down from her. And I work from my home so Mabel is no trouble at all. In fact, we get along rather well. She's a dear little girl."

"I feel like I barely know Mabel. The last time I saw her, she was in diapers."

"She doesn't remember you either."

"But Mom expected me to take care of her . . . to raise her. And I can do that. I plan on doing that. She's all I have left."

"Well, don't you worry about Mabel for the time being. I'll take good care of her until you can get home." Daphne gave him her phone number and address and e-mail and everything she could think of to reassure him that Mabel was in good hands. "I know I must seem like a stranger to you, but believe me, I really care about Mabel."

"I appreciate that."

"And now that I have your address and your e-mail, maybe I can have Mabel write to you. We can send you photos. To help you get acquainted with her."

"That would be great. Thanks."

"And again, I'm so sorry for your loss, Sergeant Myers."

"Thank you, ma'am. And please, since you feel almost like family . . . why don't you call me Daniel."

"Okay . . . Daniel."

He gave her a little more information about where he was stationed and the time difference. He sounded like a nice young man— but it was obvious he was hurting. And when Daphne hung up, she had fresh tears flowing down her cheeks. It was as if she could feel his pain coming right through her phone. To be so far from home, to feel as if he had no control over these situations . . . how hard it must be on him.

For some reason she had the impulse to call her dad, to tell him what had happened and to ask for his advice. But, of course, he was on his honeymoon. One didn't call one's parent when he was honeymooning. Still, she was longing for some fatherly advice, some wise counsel. And she probably needed to speak to someone about the legalities of this situation. After all, she had just taken custody of a child—but she hadn't done it legally. What if something happened to Mabel? What if she got hurt at school? Who would they call? Or what if she needed medical treatment? Who would authorize it? Or pay for it?

As she walked back home, she called Jake. But since he was in court, she could only leave him a message. "Tell him it's very urgent," she told his assistant.

"Is it an emergency?"

"Sort of," Daphne told her. "It could be."

"I'll let him know as soon as he gets back."

Daphne thanked her as she went onto her porch.

"Hey, Daph!" Sabrina came jogging over. "How's it going?"

Daphne gave her the latest update about Daniel. "He sounds like a nice guy. I feel so sorry for him though. Being so far from home . . . and having all this happen."

"That's got to be hard."

She told Sabrina about calling Jake. "I think I need some legal advice. I don't want to get in trouble with any social workers or the court or anything. I have no idea how these things are handled."

"You're wise to call Jake." Sabrina gave her a sly look. "And while we're on the subject, I saw him looking at you on Saturday. At the wedding. When you were dancing with Mabel, Jake was just staring at you—almost as if he was under a spell."

"Oh, don't be silly."

"I'm serious. I get the feeling that man is a more interested in you than he has let on."

"No way." Daphne firmly shook her head. "I've already been over that bridge. And it's been burned and knocked down. Believe me."

"I wouldn't be too sure. I'm pretty certain I saw stars in Jake's eyes when he watched you and Mabel dancing. It was real sweet." She chuckled. "Come to think of it, Jake wasn't the only one with his eyes on you. Ricardo seemed to be watching you pretty closely too. And Karen's nephew Calvin as well. In fact, if it came right down to it, I'd have to say you were the belle of the bridesmaids' ball, Miss Daphne."

Daphne gave her neighbor a tolerant smile. "When it comes to imagining romance, Sabrina, you win first prize."

"I'm not imagining this, Daphne. I happen to be a very observant sort of girl."

"All those men falling for me at the reception—swooning for a woman dressed in a wrinkly sausage casing. Very likely indeed."

Sabrina laughed. "Oh, you know men. They're usually totally clueless when it comes to fashion. Besides, that sausage casing, as you call it, showed off your curves real nice, Daphne. But I guess you didn't notice that."

Daphne waved at her. "Thanks for trying to cheer me up, Sabrina. But I've got a million things to do today. I need to call Mabel's school. Then I want to get Mabel's stuff all moved over here before she comes home and—"

"Let me know if I can help."

"Thanks. I'll gladly take you up on that. I figure I should do what I can in Vera's house. At least get the food and stuff out of the kitchen before it goes bad. Maybe clean up some."

"Let me know when you're heading back there and I'll come with you."

Daphne promised to be in touch, then just as she went into the house, her phone started ringing. "Daphne, are you okay?" Jake asked anxiously.

"Yes, I'm fine."

"Oh, I thought you had an emergency."

"It's sort of an emergency." Daphne explained about Vera.

"Sorry to hear that."

"Yes . . . so anyway I have Mabel staying with me. But, of course, I don't have legal custody." She sighed. "I wish I'd asked Vera about it . . . like you suggested. I just wanted to get past Dad's wedding first. But now it's too late."

"That does complicate things. But how about if I start asking around for you? I'll see if we can get you temporary guardianship of Mabel. At least until the uncle comes home. I'll do some investigating to see if Vera had a lawyer or a will of any kind."

"Thank you, Jake. This means so much to me."

He chuckled. "It just figures that you'd get yourself a child before you found yourself a husband."

She let out a groan. "Thanks for reminding me about that too."

"Yeah. Sorry."

Neither of them said anything now. "You know what I thought," Jake said quietly, "when I first saw the message to call you, saying it was an emergency?"

"What?"

"Well, I—uh—I thought maybe you'd found your Mr. Right and that you were getting married and wanted to let me know so I could settle your inheritance. But then I realized that wouldn't necessitate an emergency—at least not on your part. That's when I got really worried. I thought maybe you'd been in a car wreck or something. I'm sorry about Mabel's grandmother, but I'm glad you're okay. And, to be honest, I'm glad you're not getting married . . . just yet."

She couldn't help but feel somewhat amused. Maybe Jake cared more about her than she realized. Perhaps Sabrina hadn't been entirely wrong about him at the reception after all.

Still, as she hung up she knew she didn't have time to think about such things. For the time being she needed to remain focused on Mabel and doing all she could to smooth out the rocky road life seemed to have handed out to this sweet little girl.

Chapter 26

Thanks to Jake's legal savvy and help, Daphne was awarded temporary custody of Mabel a few days later. Jake also helped to handle Vera's affairs by reading through a handwritten will. Because Vera owned so little, there was no estate to speak of, and she'd already made the arrangements to be cremated, requesting that her son handle the "memorial service upon his arrival." And since Daniel had been in communication with Pastor Andrew, Daphne felt assured that these plans were in good hands. Daniel was expected to arrive before Thanksgiving.

In the meantime, Daphne and Sabrina worked to clear out Vera's house. They moved all of Mabel's things into the spare bedroom that had been renamed "Mabel's Room." And then because Vera's house had been a rental, the two of them, aided by some friends from their church, boxed up all of Vera's possessions and stacked them in a large storage unit for Daniel to go through at his leisure.

By the following week, the house was completely emptied. Jake worked together with Daniel to tie up a few loose legal ends, but he assured Daphne that there really was very little to attend to. Just the same, she was grateful.

"I don't know how to thank you for all you've done these past couple of weeks," Daphne told Jake as they met for coffee the week before Thanksgiving. This time the meeting wasn't accidental. Daphne had invited him—and she'd bought his coffee.

"I've been happy to help. So much of my legal work seems to lack the humanity factor. It's a pleasure helping Mabel. And I've enjoyed getting to know Daniel. He seems like a nice guy."

"Yes." Daphne nodded. "He and Mabel have been exchanging regular e-mails. And we printed out some of his photos and hung them in her room. She even took a picture of him to school for show and tell. He's a good-looking Marine—and Mabel is very proud that he's her uncle." Daphne sighed. "Hopefully these connections will make the transition easier for her when he gets here."

"You mean when he takes her?" Jake seemed to be searching her face.

"Yes. It would be difficult for her to go off with a perfect stranger. I want her to feel comfortable. She's been through so much. She doesn't need to be hurt anymore."

"What about you?"

She shrugged. "I'll be fine."

"It's obvious you've formed a real attachment to Mabel."

"Mabel needed someone to be attached to her." Daphne forced a smile. "And Daniel seems like a kind and caring uncle. I feel confident he will be a fine guardian for Mabel."

"It was good to hear that he's being discharged."

"I think your letters helped." Daphne gave him a genuine smile. "Daniel will be flying home on Wednesday."

"Just in time for Thanksgiving."

"Yes." She nodded. "Mabel wants to have a real Thanksgiving feast for him. She's already invited some of the neighbors. I hope I can remember how to cook a turkey."

"Need any help?"

"Cooking a turkey?" She tipped her head to one side. "Really?"

"I've cooked a few turkeys in my day." He grinned.

"Seriously?"

"Just ask Jenna. Last year I even soaked our turkey overnight in a brine solution." He smacked his lips. "Very tender."

"So are you saying you don't have plans for Thanksgiving?"

He sadly shook his head. "Just Jenna and me . . . all alone."

"What about Gwen?"

"What about her?"

"Well, I just remember how you guys vacationed together in August . . . I thought perhaps you would spend Thanksgiving with her too." Okay, Daphne was fully aware that she was fishing here. But didn't she deserve to know the truth?

Jake's brow creased. "You actually thought that Gwen was on vacation *with me?*"

"Well, wasn't she? Mattie told me she'd gone to the lake and—"

"Gwen invited herself to stay at my sister's cabin at the lake. She said it was to spend time with Jenna. But that was all it was. I hardly saw Gwen during the whole time I was there." He frowned. "Did you honestly think that Gwen and I . . . well, you know?"

She shrugged. "I don't know."

"Daphne?"

"Well, you and I . . . we'd been doing some things together," she said lamely. "And then you were suddenly off on vacation. You never even told me you were going. I learned it from Mattie and—"

"Wait a minute." He held up a hand. "Let's rewind a bit further. Do you not remember the day when you very clearly told me to stop intruding into your life?"

She frowned. "Well . . . maybe I said that. But it was only because you had told me that you didn't want to pre-read the column anymore. You said I didn't need you."

"That's right. You didn't need me looking over your shoulder for the column. I knew I was going to be gone a couple of weeks. I wanted to assure you that you could stand on your own two feet."

"But I thought you were pushing me away. So I pushed you away even harder."

"So I noticed." He looked slightly confused. "I just thought maybe we both had needed some space. But when I got back from vacation, I was looking forward to reconnecting with you." He scowled. "But by then you already had your Aussie boyfriend by your side. I felt like you were sending me a message loud and clear. And in fact, you even told me to butt out of your life. Remember?"

Daphne felt slightly sick. "First of all, Collin was not my boyfriend. And besides that I was hurt. I thought you had dumped me. And, of course, there was Sabrina suddenly turning herself into my matchmaker and—"

"Daphne. Let's not go back and rehash everything. Not right now anyway."

"Thank you." She sighed. "I would rather not."

"It seems like we both made some mistakes."

"That's for sure."

He reached across the table, placing his hand over hers. "Do you think you could give me a second chance?"

She nodded gratefully. "But I do have a question."

"Yes?"

"What about the blind dates you set me up on?"

He pressed his lips tightly together. "Uh . . . yes?"

"Did you honestly think I'd like those guys? Tony and Spencer?"

He gave a sheepish grin. "I sure hoped not."

Daphne laughed. "Well, you got that right."

"Although Spencer is a nice guy. You could do worse."

"He's nice enough. And we've committed to be in a writers' critique group together. But that's as far as that goes." She studied him. "But you still didn't answer me. Why did you send me on those dates?"

"A friend helping a friend?" he said tentatively.

"Really?"

He chuckled. "Or maybe I was just helping myself."

"How so?"

"You want the truth?"

"Of course." She tilted her head to one side.

"I suppose I secretly suspected that you wouldn't go for either of those guys."

"Then why would you set me up with them?"

"Maybe I wanted to help you see that you were looking for someone else. Kind of like a selection by elimination. Not so different than speed dating."

She frowned. "I hated speed dating."

"What about your architect friend—didn't you meet him speed dating?"

"Harrison?"

"Yeah. You guys seemed pretty cozy that night I saw you together."

She shrugged. "He still calls sometimes. But we've been kind of like ships in the night."

Jake looked slightly concerned.

"But just so you know, I'm not seriously involved with *anyone* right now. My focus has been solely on Mabel." She sighed. "But I suppose that's about to change."

"Do you want me to talk to Daniel?"

"About what?"

"I could suggest the idea of you sharing guardianship of Mabel."

"Is that even possible?"

"Anything is possible. If people agree."

"Do you think he would?" She felt a flicker of hope.

"I think it's worth discussing." Jake made a note on his iPad. "I know Daniel was struggling with leaving the service before retirement. He's got seventeen years with them. Three more and he could have a nice retirement package."

"Meaning I could have Mabel for three more years?"

"Maybe."

As promised, Jake came over on the night before Thanksgiving to show Daphne how to soak a turkey in a brine solution. He lined a five-gallon bucket with a clean trash bag and filled it with water and sea salt and sugar. Then he dropped in the turkey.

"The turkey's taking a bath," Mabel proclaimed.

"And he'll stay in the tub all night long too." Jake carried the strange-looking concoction out to the laundry room so the cats wouldn't get to it.

"I finished the name cards for the table," Mabel told them. "Want to see?"

They followed her to the dining room where she already had the little paper turkeys all set up. "There's Wally and Maria there. Mrs. Terwilliger here. Ricardo and Mick and Sabrina are over there. Jake and Jenna can sit there." She pointed to the other end of the table, looking up at Daphne. "And you and me and Uncle Daniel can sit here. Okay?"

"Speaking of Uncle Daniel." Daphne saw headlights in the driveway. "I wonder if that might be him. He was supposed to get here around now."

"I'll go see!" Mabel ran through the house and threw open the front door.

"You're ready for this?" Jake asked her.

She nodded.

"And just because Daniel hasn't made up his mind about sharing guardianship, doesn't mean the conversation is over," Jake said quietly. "I think it's only that he wants to see you face-to-face. He wants to be sure you really have Mabel's best interests at heart."

"Can't fault him for that," she said stiffly as she watched Mabel running across the yard. "I'd do the same." She turned to Jake. "And thanks for making the effort to contact him before he got here. That will make it so much easier to have this conversation. I really appreciate it."

He smiled at her. "Don't worry, it's going to turn out okay. I'm sure of it."

"Uncle Daniel is here!" Mabel guided a man in uniform into the house. "Look, everyone. It's my uncle. He's a *Marine!*"

"Looks like the Marines have landed," Jake said jovially.

Daphne went into the living room to greet Daniel, smiling as he firmly shook her hand. "It's a pleasure to finally meet you," she said a bit shyly. She wasn't sure if it was his height or his uniform. But this guy was even more handsome than his photos. "I hope you had a good trip. I know it was a long one."

"Thank you. I'm relieved it's over." He looked directly into her eyes, seeming to study her carefully. "Thank you for everything, Daphne. And thank you for welcoming me into your home."

"And this is Jake." She turned toward Jake who was standing behind her. "Of course, you've met on the phone already."

"Yes." Daniel nodded as he shook Jake's hand. "Pleased to meet you too. And thank you for all the help you've given me with my mom's estate and with Mabel."

"Want to see my room, Uncle Daniel?" Mabel said eagerly. "I have pictures of you in it."

"You bet," he said happily as she grasped his hand. "Lead me to it."

"All right! It's upstairs. And your room is gonna be right next to mine," Mabel announced as she led him through the living room. "It used to be Aunt Daphne's room. But she moved her room downstairs to Aunt Dee's room. I never met Aunt Dee before, because she's with my mama and grandma—up in heaven I mean. But this used to be Aunt Dee's house. Now it's Aunt Daphne's and mine." Mabel continued rambling on and on as they went upstairs.

"Wow." Jake chuckled. "Sounds like Mabel's got it all worked out."

"Daniel seems nice." Daphne went back into the kitchen to check on the pumpkin pies, which had been baking for more than thirty minutes.

"Good-looking too." Jake cocked his head to one side.

"Uh-huh." She slid the knife into the pumpkin filling, but seeing it was still gooey, closed the oven door and added a few minutes to the timer.

"Well, the turkey is all set to go for tomorrow. Looks like my work here is done." Jake glanced around the kitchen.

"Thanks for your help. I've told everyone dinner will be at two, but feel free to come earlier if you like." She grinned. "I'd be happy to put you on KP."

As Jake was leaving, Mabel and Daniel came back down. "I'm going to help Uncle Daniel carry his bags to his room," Mabel said proudly.

"Why don't I lend a hand too?" Jake offered. "I'm sure your uncle is worn out from all his flights."

"Yes," Daphne said. "Feel free to turn in whenever you like, Daniel. You must be exhausted by now. Not to mention jet lag. And sleep in if you want tomorrow. I've already warned Mabel she should be quiet in the morning."

Mabel put her forefinger to her lips. "I'll be quiet as a mouse."

"I'm a pretty sound sleeper," he told her. "So don't worry." He thanked Daphne again and before long, Jake and Mabel had helped him to get settled up in his room.

"Daniel asked me to tell you good night," Jake told Daphne when he came back down. "Poor guy is totally exhausted. He said he nearly fell asleep driving here."

"I can imagine." She smiled. "Thanks for helping, Jake."

"My pleasure." He reached over to touch her cheek. "And thanks for giving me a second chance, Daphne." He glanced up the stairs. "I just hope that handsome Marine doesn't try to turn your head." He chuckled. "I hate to admit it, but I'm already feeling jealous."

"Oh, Jake." She shook her head. "Really."

"The good news is that you've already made a great impression on him. That will certainly help your case. I mean in regard to shared guardianship of Mabel. If he feels confident in you, he might want to return to finish out his stint in the Marines."

She felt her spirits rise. "You really think so?"

He nodded but his smile faded. "The bad news is that you could've made such a great impression on him that he might want to stick around . . . if you know what I mean."

She laughed. "Oh, Jake. You're too funny."

He didn't look very amused.

"Go home and get some rest." She walked him to the front door. "You'll need it because I plan to put you to work tomorrow." She watched as he went outside and down the porch steps. It was sweet that he felt that protective of her . . . and even confessed to feeling jealous. But really it was ridiculous. She barely even knew Daniel. And as hard as she tried, she'd never really gotten over Jake. Not that he needed to be fully aware of this. But what would Jake possibly have to worry about?

As Daphne turned out the lights and went into Aunt Dee's old bedroom, she felt a sweet sense of contentment. And as she prepared for bed, it was almost as if she could feel her aunt looking down on her—perhaps with Vera and Mabel's mother standing next to her, assuring her that all would be well.

Dear Reader Friend,

Due to some big changes at B&H Publishing, the third and fourth installments of the Dear Daphne series will release in the form of ebooks only (at least initially). For more information on these books, go to my website at www.melodycarlson.com and sign up for my monthly newsletter, and I promise to keep you posted.

Book three *Home, Hearth, and Holidays* should be available right on the heels of *Dating, Dining, and Desperation*. And the fourth and final book (which will include a wedding) will follow shortly thereafter. The good news is, there will be very little waiting for the reader who has access to an ebook reader. And hopefully we'll figure out a way to get some paperback books out as well. My apologies for any inconvenience and thank you for your continued interest in the *Dear Daphne* books!

Blessings!

Melody Carlson

Discussion Questions

1. Despite Daphne's determination to fully enjoy herself in Aunt Dee's lovely home, she's troubled by the fact that her dream life could come to an abrupt end once her year is up. How would you advise her?

2. Daphne's new neighbor Sabrina is almost a complete opposite of Daphne—and yet they get along. Describe a relationship you have with someone who's your opposite. Why do you think it works?

3. Sabrina initiates Daphne's makeover in the hopes of making her more attractive to potential suitors. Explain why or why not you think this is this a good plan.

4. Daphne gets to know her neighbors by placing her "free produce" box in the front yard. Describe what you might do to get better acquainted with your neighbors.

5. Why does Olivia seem so concerned over Daphne's double-date with Sabrina and the Aussie guys? Do you think her concerns were valid? Why or why not?

6. Even though Daphne writes the advice column, she often seems slightly clueless when it comes to her own life. Why do you think that is?

7. Daphne appears to have written off Jake early in this story. Why do you think she was so quick to give up on him when it's obvious that she feels an attraction? What advice would you give to her?

8. Why do you think Daphne struggles with her dad's engagement? What helps her to resolve herself to his nuptials?

9. Daphne seems to have plenty of available bachelors to choose from. Which guy would you pick for her? Explain why.

10. Young Mabel's need for Daphne's friendship is obvious and visible. But why does Daphne need Mabel in her life?

11. Were you curious as to why Jake seemed overly eager to send Daphne on dates with his "friends"? Did you guess his real motive?

12. Project what you think Daphne's future might look like. What is the worst that might happen? What is the best?